I0653091

THE SILK NOOSE

other stories & essays

MARCUS MCGEE

PEGASUS BOOKS

Copyright © 2005, 2009 Marcus McGee
All Rights Reserved

Copyright © 2005, 2009 Marcus McGee. Printed and bound in the United States of America. All rights Reserved. No part of this book may be reproduced or transmitted in any form or by any means, electronic or mechanical, including photocopying, recording, or by an information storage and retrieval system—except by a reviewer who may quote brief passages in a review to be printed in a magazine or newspaper—without permission in writing from the publisher. For information, please contact Pegasus Books c/o Ms. McGhee, P.O. Box 235, Neptune, New Jersey, 07754.

ISBN 978-0-9673123-6-1

Comments about *The Silk Noose* and requests for additional copies, book club rates and author speaking appearances may be addressed to Marcus McGee or Pegasus Books c/o Ms. McGhee, P.O. Box 235, Neptune, New Jersey, 07754, or you can send your comments and requests via e-mail to marcus.media@yahoo.com

This is a work of fiction. The events described are imaginary, and the characters are fictitious and are not intended to represent specific living persons. Even when the settings are referred to by their true names, the incidents taking place there are entirely fictitious; the reader should not infer that the events set there ever happened.

For Richard McGee, Sr.

In memory of my father

I am incapable of expressing in words the love, honor and respect I will always feel for that great man

THE SILK NOOSE

other stories & essays

Cover Art: Marcus McGee

DÉNOUEMENT

I've never been one to believe in ghosts or *Devil's Triangles* or luck or spells—basically anything supernatural. I've always been a practical guy, though most people (and notice I didn't say friends; I have no friends and don't need any), most people who know me would call me cynical. I guess that's because I've never been able to temper my scathing commentaries and outbursts when I've heard morons talk about things like UFOs, alien abductions, out of body experiences and things like that.

Basically, stupid people offend me, though I've never understood why. And by stupid, I mean the idiot who's sat near me for eight years in the next cubicle at work. This guy watched Sunday night paranormal crime shows and spent Monday and Tuesday describing, pouring over and analyzing the damn story to everyone in earshot. Unfortunately, I was *always* in earshot. And by stupid, I also mean my ex-sister-in-law, Odette, who consulted an astrology book before getting out of bed in the morning. If the book suggested anything negative, she stayed in bed all day. And my Bible-thumping grandmother—she spent her life preaching about everlasting life and promptly dropped dead on the day of my high school graduation. You guessed it. I'm also agnostic.

I never believed any of it: God, the Devil, Heaven, Hell, sin, redemption, the afterlife, eternal damnation, miracles or curses. I long ago concluded that all this supernatural crap was a continual crock cooked up and served by successive classes of social predators from the beginning of civilization until now. It's predicated on humankind's greatest flaw: the urge or need to believe.

For everything there is a rational, logical explanation; everything is the result of a causal relationship, implicit or explicit. But don't get me confused with one of those philosophers. They're quacks, all of them, scourges from society's extremes. No, I simply live in a world of reality, a world where faith, spirit and symbolism have no meaning.

But today, I'm forced to admit I'm a little confused. It's nothing that happened today specifically; rather it's happened over the last seven days.

One week ago as I sat at my breakfast table for morning tea, I happened to glance out the window. And just so you know, I've never given a damn about John Audubon, but as I looked out onto the balcony of my seventh floor apartment, I noticed a little bird out there. It was perched on the rail with its head cocked to one side, like it was peering through my window at me. I wasn't being paranoid. I'd seen many birds perched on the rail in the course of morning tea, but this one was different. It unnerved me and I couldn't understand why.

I discovered later that it was a tit, which is short for titmouse. They're supposed to be active, perky little birds, but this one just sat there, staring at me. I left the table to get dressed, forgetting about the tiny bird, so I was a little uneasy when I came back to find it still sitting in the same spot. Now that in itself didn't alarm me, but when I got to work, which is exactly thirty-three miles from my apartment, and when I looked out my window, there was either that same tit or another tit that looked just like it sitting on a branch outside my office window, staring in at me in that same peculiar way.

Naturally, I rationalized that they were different birds of the same species and they were probably common to the area. And the reason why I hadn't noticed them before is that I'd never been one to fixate on stupid little birds. Why I had noticed the bird *that* particular morning—I had been scanning through the newspaper as I drank my tea. There was a small article on the second page about local birds. I hadn't read it, but the title must have stuck in my mind and made me notice the bird.

I live alone, so I never have dinner at home. On Mondays after work I always go to a restaurant called The Canard downtown on Seventh Street for the *Roasted Pheasant Under Glass* special. I have a regular table there next to a window, and when I looked out, there was that same tit or another tit perched atop a hedge, staring in at me. The Canard was at least ten miles away from my job. That little bird couldn't have flown that far! I hurried through dinner, sped home, rushed to my dining area and flung open the drapes to my great relief. The bird I saw that morning was still sitting there. There was no way the bird from outside the restaurant could have beat me home. The species was just very common in the area, I concluded.

I didn't sleep well that first night. I felt disturbed, though I didn't understand why. My life seemed to be going all right. I hated my job, but doesn't everybody? I had no friends to bug me with the troubles and dilemmas of their pathetic lives. I lived far enough away from my family to avoid visits, invitations and all that other domestic crap. So I was okay, but I still couldn't sleep.

Somewhere in the middle of the night my thoughts kept returning to a single incident from my youth. I was thirteen years old and in the eighth grade. I had a classmate named James Finch who was a natural born troublemaker. He wasn't a friend of mine—I had no friends. In fact, I had a couple of run-ins with James before he was banned from the school bus. He had to walk home every day. Anyway, one day I missed the bus and having to walk from school, I found myself trailing James by about twenty feet as he made his way to our shared neighborhood. We lived on the other side of the highway, so we had to cross by means of a pedestrian overpass.

I was just starting up the incline when I saw James at the top, staring over the railing at the cars that were passing under. In his suspended hands he held a bread loaf-sized boulder. I stopped, watching him as he tried to gauge the timing of the release, and then I watched him let the rock fall. It crashed into the windshield of a station wagon, which screeched its tires, spun and careened into the highway's retaining wall, exploding into flames. James fled to the other side of the overpass and I retreated back toward the school, where I called my parents to pick me up.

I didn't find out until the next day that the car James victimized contained one of our classmates, Amy Winger.

Fortunately, no one in the car was killed, but Amy's back and neck were broken. In fact, she spent the rest of eighth grade in the hospital and all of high school confined to a wheelchair as a paraplegic.

The school and the local district attorney launched an intensive investigation to find the person responsible, but nothing ever came of it. The school asked me directly if I had any information or idea about who may have dropped the boulder, but I said nothing. I didn't want to get involved.

James Finch was stabbed to death during a knife fight when we were in the eleventh grade, so I was the only person who knew what really happened. Amy lived with her parents until they died, and she died a year after that, when she was twenty-three. I suppose it was a good thing. Who'd want to live to old age as a paraplegic?

When I finally fell asleep that first night, it must have been about three-thirty. So I tossed and turned for three hours before I rolled out of bed to begin the morning ritual: sit, shower and shave.

It was seven o'clock when I sat at the table with my Earl Grey tea. I was curious, so I paused a moment before I drew the drapes. The tit was still there, and next to it was a much larger bird, about eleven inches long. This new bird was brown with a white chin and breast; its beak was black and curved slightly downward. I found out later it was a black-billed cuckoo. It sat close to the tit, its head cocked in the same fashion, staring in at me.

When I got to work at eight, I checked the branch outside my office window and sighed to myself. The branch was empty. I ridiculed myself for even letting the presence or non-presence of a little bird outside my window bother me. And yet, I couldn't stop my eyes from cutting toward the branch every few minutes. I was having a hard time concentrating on work. And then at nine when I glanced over, there they were: a tit and a cuckoo, on the branch, heads cocked, peering in.

Coincidence, I concluded. Somewhere in their evolutionary histories, the two species must have developed a sort of symbiotic relationship. It was nothing I hadn't seen or come across before. In Africa, there's a bird, a honeyguide, which is something of a cuckoo I think, that leads honey badgers to beehives to benefit from the plunder. And many other bird species benefit from a sort of cooperative predator lookout and warning system. I had read about such things. So there was a rational explanation for the birds sitting together outside my window, even if it remained unknown to me.

The birds stayed on the branch for the rest of the day while I did my best to ignore them. By lunch I had lowered and closed the blinds, though I still checked the scene outside at irregular intervals. At the end of the day I was angry with myself for letting something so stupid distract me for much of the day. They were just damn birds.

I had dinner at my regular Tuesday night spot, The Oyster Catcher, but I opted for a seat in the middle of the dining room rather than at my regular window table. As I ate, I resolved that I would not check the window when I got home. In my real world, what did it matter whether or not there were birds sitting on a rail outside? I figured I'd put an end to the disquiet about the birds by simply ignoring them.

I thought I would sleep better that second night, but I didn't because I couldn't. It wasn't the birds. No, it was something I hadn't thought about for years. When I was a much younger man, I had a girlfriend named Robyn. She was a pretty girl and she was a very sweet person, so sweet in fact that I never trusted her. She was nice to everyone—old geezers, bums, obnoxious friends of hers, family and stupid people. She seemed genuine, but that was the problem the cynic in me had with her. No one is nice for the sake of being nice.

I asked her to marry me only so she would sleep with me, and everything was working out fine until she and the rest of the world started pressing me for a wedding date. I put it off for three years, thinking we wouldn't last that long, but we did. So when we got six months out, I began to worry.

Here I had this incredibly beautiful woman who was intelligent, witty, kind, optimistic and always happy. She told me every day she loved me and dreamed of the day when she would be my wife and the mother of my children. She brought handmade gifts, gave sentimental cards and wrote poetry for me. She clipped my toenails, pulled my nose hairs, cleaned my ears and refashioned my wardrobe. She was just too good to believe, and so I didn't.

It took some doing, but I found the most eligible bachelor in town. His name was Stephen Crane, a rich, good-looking up-and-comer with an affable, infectious personality. Unfortunately, he also had scruples, so it took some doing and $1,000 to persuade him to put the moves on Robyn.

On a weekend I planned on going out of town, he was supposed to casually introduce himself to her at the senior center where she volunteered and accomplish a no-holds-barred seduction. Then I would come home, and she, riddled with guilt, would confess her transgression, giving me an excuse to call off the engagement.

It didn't work. She turned him down cold. Ego bruised, this handsome guy said he never stood a chance with her. She told him she was totally in love with her fiancé. And while some men would have taken the result as an indication of Robyn's veracity, I was all the more convinced it was only a matter of time before she would betray me. Women are false, all of them.

I couldn't go through with it. As the day neared, I felt like the world was closing in on me. When I looked at Robyn I saw Guinevere, I saw Cressida, I saw Pandora. I should have come clean with her, but I didn't. Instead, on the morning of the scheduled wedding, I packed my things and left town. Just like that. I didn't tell anyone I was leaving; I didn't leave any clues; I just disappeared.

I found out later Robyn never really got over the shock and disappointment of being jilted at the altar. People said she never found anyone else. She withdrew and just eked out a quiet life. They said her once shapely, supple body withered over time like a cut leaf. I felt bad about it, but if I hadn't done it to her, she would have done it to me. I know it.

I think I drifted off to sleep for about fifteen minutes before the alarm went off. I guess I was so caught up reliving the relationship with Robyn that I completely forgot about the birds as I went about my morning routine. That is until I opened the drapes. A tit was there, and beside it was a cuckoo. But there was another bird on the rail, a large black bird, a corvid, clearly a crow or a young raven.

So by that morning I had three birds staring in at me, and for some odd reason just then, it struck me as funny. Not so much that I laughed, but those three birds sitting there looking in like that, they just looked funny to me. I even thought about getting out my camera and taking a picture. I laughed to myself as I sped to work, almost hoping three birds would coincidentally appear outside my window there.

A tit and a cuckoo showed up at nine and ten respectively, followed by a crow at eleven. It seemed the crow was just curious, as I understand crows are. I've read they're the most intelligent of all birds. The crow probably flew by and noticed the tit and cuckoo staring in the window. So it landed on the branch because it wanted to explore what had the other birds so captivated. They were all looking at me, as if they were waiting for me to do something. I made a face at them once and rushed the window another time, but they did not react. They just sat there for the entire day.

That was Wednesday, and it was Greg Teal's birthday. Greg is the idiot I mentioned earlier, the one who's sat in the cubicle next to me for the last eight years. I call him Gullible Greg because he's a guy who will believe just about anything: Area 51, X-Files, the World Wrestling Federation, the Bible and probably even the Easter Bunny. He's a fat, annoying man who talks too much, a man with a constant need to be overheard. For example, when he's on the phone, he intentionally talks loud enough for people twenty feet away to hear. And when he's having a private meeting in the cubicle, it sounds like an office broadcast. He has no concept of intimacy. Sitting in the next space, I've heard disgusting chronicles from his dim-witted life in slow, agonizing and exaggeratedly loud detail over the years.

On his birthday the entire office sans me pitched in and bought him a cake. Right after lunch, they all converged on his desk and congratulated him for reaching his fiftieth birthday. The big boss compelled me to go over, though I didn't sing when the rest of them were singing. After snatching plates of cake and cups of punch, all those phony, backstabbing idiots dispersed, leaving Gullible and me in the cubicle. On a whim, I asked him if he wanted to see something funny and took him over to the window next to my desk. The birds were gone.

Fifteen minutes later, after Gullible had left and he had settled his big butt in his seat, they were back. I thought to go over and get him, but it was way too much trouble. I had it all figured out anyway. As we walked over earlier, the birds saw this big, fat eating machine coming at them through the window and fluttered away in fright. Birds are smart in that way: they have an innate fear of fat people. It's why they've been around for so long.

My sister had a planned rebuttal for every excuse I could make, so I was practically forced to go to her house for dinner that night. She lives in the suburbs, forty miles from me. Because I hate driving, I was irritated by the time I got there. She had invited my parents and all our siblings to celebrate the silver anniversary of her marriage to Bob White, the goofy husband she eloped with twenty-five years earlier.

The family was resistant to Bob early on, but most of them had warmed to him over the years. Not the case with me. I've always seen him for what he is. Bob's an ass. I accept the fact that my sister apparently loves him, but he's an ass, end of story. I figured I'd go to their house and make a brief appearance, though I wasn't about to congratulate the couple. Their marriage, like every other marriage I had seen, was a big lie. I wasn't going to perpetuate the lie by pretending they had done something wonderful by putting up with each other for twenty-five years.

My sister wouldn't let me smoke in the house. I was forced out to the backyard where her smelly and mangy old mutt, starved for attention, tried to elope with my leg. I was sitting there, cigarette in my right hand and left hand fending off the dog's amorous advances, when I saw a suspect crow tiptoeing along the fence top. When it stopped and sat, it was nestled next to a cuckoo. The cuckoo, in turn, was rubbing shoulders with a tit. I remember the moment. For a fleeting instant just then, I wondered if maybe the birds were following me.

I realized soon after that such a notion was impossible. Once again, it had to be a coincidence, just a routine coincidence. And then it still could have been the result of some sort of a symbiotic relationship of avian nature, one that logically could involve three active participants, and maybe even more in some cases. It wasn't for me to figure out. Anyway, my thinking was interrupted when my sister stuck her head out the patio door to ask me if I wanted wine with dinner. When I turned again to the fence, the birds were gone.

When I got home that night, I still had three birds on my patio rail. I wasn't surprised or bothered by it. It was just three birds on a rail, something that happens all the time. And still, I wondered what the odds were. A triplet of birds of three different species huddled together at my house, at my job and at my sister's house, and all in the same day? Certainly it could all be reduced to some abstract statistical number with a decimal point and lots of zeros. If I wanted to do it, I'm sure I could have, but I had someone right under my nose who would probably get his jollies calculating the odds. Old Gullible over in the next cubicle loved challenges like that.

About six years ago, two years after I met and determined I didn't like Gullible Greg, I played a prank on him that I regret until this day, though not from a sense of guilt or anything like that. I hated the guy from the start.

He put me on the spot at our initial introduction by asking if I was a Christian. Then he asked if I believed in extraterrestrials and if I thought California was going to break off and sink in the Pacific. Unlike me, the man believed in God and evolution, in Heaven and reincarnation, in stigmata and Taoism, in space aliens, time travel, Internet hoaxes, magic crystals, numerology and love, you name it. He was pathetic.

Anyway, six years ago I decided to teach Gullible a lesson, for his own good. With some people you wonder if they're married or single. Not so with Greg. Anyone looking at his unkempt ugly mug would have known he was single— no self-respecting wife would have let nose hairs grow that long. So to teach Gullible not to believe everything, I wrote him a letter from a secret admirer. I invented a twenty-one year old, hard-bodied, redhead working somewhere in the building with a crush on him. The first letter ended with the words, "You make me totally hot!"

Naïve though he was, I still thought Gullible would see right through the prank. It was ridiculous. What would a good-looking, sexy, single young woman see in a walrus? He should have known it was too good to be true, but he didn't. He perked up after he read the letter. Suddenly he was all over the office, trying to be helpful and charming. And the day after, he wore a new, color-coordinated outfit from Macy's to work. He actually looked better. One letter from a secret admirer and Greg was falling all over himself to be less offensive. That gave me an idea.

In the next letter I told him to trim those gross nose hairs and get a haircut, and by the next morning it was done. He had even dyed his hair to remove the gray. As he visited my cubicle that morning, I noticed he was wearing cologne. And the music on his desk radio changed from elevator to hip-hop. My cynical nature would not let me believe mere flattery could provoke such profound change in a person. So in the next letter I told him to lose some weight, and lo and behold, I overheard him on the phone with a nutritionist the next morning.

Ironically, I wasn't the only one to notice those changes in Greg. Georgia Kite, the CEO over at Kite

Enterprises, our closest competitor, had always respected Greg for his work product. But after his complete makeover and his manifest level of new confidence, she determined to lure him over to her company. She actually offered to double his salary if he'd come over.

Greg was in love. He didn't know who his secret admirer was, but he didn't want leave her, not even for double the money. Not if there was a chance they could get together. It was confirmation of his idiocy. I wanted to rid myself of the cretin, so I told him he should definitely accept Kite's offer, but he wouldn't listen. All he could to is talk about Procne, the name I had given to his made-up secret admirer.

Frustrated, I sent another letter to Greg from Procne saying she had found someone else, a younger, better looking guy, and that she would not be writing again. I thought the letter would do the trick, but Greg maintained faith that Procne would eventually come to her senses and realize his worth. He turned down Kite's offer the next day.

Beyond that, he began to obsess with Procne. He subscribed to *Cosmopolitan*, *Glamour*, *Essence* and other women's magazines in the hope of understanding what dysfunction she might be experiencing. He even contacted the *Oprah Show*, seeking her assistance in making an appeal to the love of his life.

Notwithstanding, his productivity at work suffered. He was written up twice in the first month after Procne's last letter. I overheard the supervisor tell Greg that until that month, the company had him first in line for a big promotion that would have sent him to New York and paid him thousands more per month. He said the sudden drop in productivity nixed Greg hopes of any promotion, and he predicted that Greg could expect to be in that cubicle until he left the company.

So at the least, my deceitful letters had ruined Greg's professional career, but worse than that, they condemned him to that cubicle for all this time and doomed me to the obnoxious questions and conversations, the disgusting body sounds and odors and the faith and gullibility I've had to endure for all these years. *That* is why I've lived to regret the prank I played on him.

When I awoke on Thursday morning, I wasn't surprised to see a tit, a cuckoo and a crow on the rail outside my dining room window. But there was a big, sinister gray bird, a gull of some kind, lined up next to the crow. Four birds, a new one each day! But I had seen people do the same thing. One person gets in a line, and other people just line up behind him. It's a sheep mentality, but apparently humans and birds are similarly afflicted.

My natural curiosity was piqued as I settled into the chair at my desk, though I wasn't surprised when a tit, a cuckoo and a crow showed up in successive hours beginning at nine. I just didn't expect any gull-like bird to show. I was going to put the supposition before Greg that morning so that he could assess the odds of single birds of three different species showing up in three remote places on the same day, but if there was a fourth bird, the odds would be longer. I decided to wait to see if the gull showed. And then at five minutes after noon it happened. A big ugly bird squawked as it settled on the branch next to the other three. Then it tilted its head in roughly the same angle as the other birds, and like them, began to peer through that window at me.

I laughed to myself. They were just birds, after all, and just four of them. It wasn't like the Hitchcock thriller where the entire town was besieged and threatened by thousands of them. Just four birds on a branch! I could go out there with a stick and shoo them away if I wanted to, but that would be giving in to the notion that a few birds on a branch had any significance in my life.

Instead I went to Greg's desk and put the question before him. I projected it out a little, adjusting for the possibility of birds showing up outside the Old Eagle Tavern, the place I usually ate on Thursday nights. Greg seemed delighted to get such an interesting problem, but he told me it would take a while—maybe until the end of the day or the next morning.

As I looked out Greg's window, I realized I could see the branch from there. I tipped around to the back of his desk until the branch was in full view. To my surprise, the birds weren't there. So I rushed back to my desk and window, and there they were, sitting still, not a feather stirring. Then I went back to his desk. From his window, the branch was empty. Back at my desk, the birds hadn't moved.

It wasn't until after I got off work that I realized the mistake I had probably made. I was most likely looking at two different branches. I was probably in a slight state of paranoia, brought on by my acute insomnia of late. In my confused condition, it would be easy to mistake two different branches for a single branch.

I didn't eat at the Old Eagle that night. Instead, I went to a newly opened Chinese restaurant called Peacock Palace. The Peking duck was good. I remember sitting there, not wanting to leave the table. When I started getting dirty looks from the waiter and the manager, I ordered another bottle of expensive wine, the meritage. I figured two bottles of wine would help me sleep. Anyway, after one half-glass from the new bottle, I paid the check and left.

It was late, so I didn't expect to have any delays as I drove home. However, the intersection right before the highway entrance ramp was backed up. When an ambulance with lights flashing rushed by, I realized there had been an accident perhaps a half mile ahead. I didn't care. It gave me the chance to have a smoke. After the cigarette, I rolled down the window to air out the car like I always do, but it wasn't until I rolled the window up that I saw the birds. In a tree directly next to my car, a tree whose disfigured, nude branches were illuminated by a tall flickering streetlamp, I saw a gull, a crow, a cuckoo and a tit.

Rain had begun to fall by the time I arrived home. Shielding my head with my jacket, I rushed upstairs and promptly got in bed. Once again, I could not sleep. I was exhausted, but I could not sleep. Frustrated, I uncorked the wine and poured myself a huge glass.

I met Odette at the engagement party. She was Gail's younger sister and she was going to be the maid of honor in our wedding. I don't remember how it happened, but we kissed that same night. It was her eyes. They were dark and mysterious, full of a bold, almost magical energy. And the way she cut them this way and then that way—I was enchanted from that first moment.

Gail never knew. She had no idea that Odette and I had planned a rendezvous for the very next night. Odette was direct. She wanted sex and money, and I was helpless to deny her either. We met regularly throughout the eight-month engagement under the pretense of planning and friendship. On the very day of the wedding, she visited my dressing room at the church just before I went out and vowed fidelity to her sister.

After I was married, I slept with both sisters on a daily basis. When Odette asked if she could stay with us to save money for a house, Gail practically begged her to move in right away. Gail was such a moral person that she couldn't conceive of what was going on whenever she left us alone. If Gail was ever suspicious or jealous, she never showed it.

Odette was another story. She told me she didn't mind me sleeping with her sister, but she would not put up with me having a child by Gail. And during those times she thought her sister might be fertile, Odette would instigate an argument between Gail and me.

Unfortunately, Gail really wanted children and urged me to get her pregnant. During the first year, I complained that it was too early. During the second and third years, I suggested we should wait until we were better off financially. By the fourth year, she was tired of my excuses. She demanded performance. I was forced to fake orgasms to make her think I was trying. Two more years went by and she still wasn't pregnant. The resentment grew to the point where she began to hate me.

Gail reached her breaking point when Odette became pregnant. Initially, she was happy for Odette, but that excitement slowly turned to envy and resentment. Seeing the maternal evolution of Odette's body over time didn't help things either. When Gail asked who the father was, Odette just blushed sheepishly. Odette had never moved out in seven years. She was pregnant with my child.

During the sixth month of her pregnancy, Odette bought a house and moved to the other side of town. Two weeks later, I got a letter from her demanding that I pay her $3,500 per month in child support. If I refused, she would tell Gail and the district attorney who the father was. I began paying that very month and continue to pay until today. Odette works part-time jobs when her astrology books suggest the auspices are right, and that's only rarely.

I thought things would be better between Gail and me when Odette left, but Gail's heart was poisoned against me. The sad part about it: I was just beginning to realize how wonderful she was. Over the seven years we had been married, she had gone out of her way to cater to me: she encouraged me when I was insecure; she cheered me up when I was down; she was always there when I needed her for anything. And all she had ever asked is to have a child with me.

I tried to make it up to her. I stopped seeing Odette and tried to rekindle things with Gail, but it was too late. On the day she left me, Gail complained that by neglecting her, I had stolen her youth, her fertility and any joy she could have hoped for in years to come. Her love for me had turned into hate. She went to live with Odette, "the only person in the world who ever really cared about" her, and she's still there now.

By seven o'clock on Friday morning, the rain was really coming down. My apartment was freezing because I had forgotten to turn up the thermostat when I got home the night before. I had also left the window in the bathroom open. The sill was spattered with cold, miserable raindrops.

Shivering in a woolen blanket, I sat at the table sipping my tea. I was cold, tired and cranky. I didn't feel like going to work that day. I didn't want to go out in that bitter, wretched clime. And just then it came to me. Every cloud has a silver lining, I thought. No creature would be without shelter on such a day. The birds would surely be gone!

When I yanked open the drapes, my surprise was so sudden and violent that I knocked over the table behind me as I recoiled. I screamed, but the sound stuck in my tight throat. There at my window was the biggest, blackest, most dreadful sight I had ever seen in my life. It was huge and hideous, its outstretched wings reaching beyond the window frame on both sides. It sat there looking at me like a balding old man in a black robe, like a dark angel, a grave judge or a grim minister. I think it was its eye! Yes, that was it! One of his eyes resembled that of an old man—a pale blue eye with a film over it. When it fell upon me, my blood ran cold.

Scrambling to upright the table and retrieve the shards of my shattered tea set, I stopped and took a breath to calm myself. When I looked back out the window, I realized what I had seen. It was a large turkey vulture, sitting on the rail, stretching out its wings to let the rain drain from its feathers. And under the aegis of its right wing, shielded from the weather, were a gull, a crow, a cuckoo and a tit.

The situation was getting ridiculous. There *had* to be a reasonable explanation. There had to be a perfectly logical rationale. I read somewhere that birds are acutely sensitive to the Earth's magnetic field. Maybe the iron railing outside my seventh floor window was generating some sort of magnetic anomaly that attracted birds. And the ions from the falling rain must have served to amplify the signal or distortion. That certainly would explain a turkey vulture roosting in the center of a crowded city.

I was ashamed of myself for considering any less logical an alternative. Debilitated by fatigue, I was letting an insignificant little group of birds drive me to stupidity. Yet for the first time, I felt an antagonism for the birds out there. I was tired of looking at them. I wanted them gone.

They were on a rail outside a decorative window that was fixed in its frame. I couldn't open it to shoo them away, so I banged on the glass, lightly at first and then so forcefully that I feared the glass would break. No bird even ruffled a feather. None deserted its rank in the fixed, unblinking gaze of the collective.

I grabbed a baseball on the way out, thinking to throw it up at the birds when I got downstairs. But after I got outside my building and looked up toward my window, they were gone. It made me wonder if the birds in fact knew the way to my office. The tit would have to fly pretty fast or get a head start in order to show up on the branch outside my window at nine. Same birds, different birds—I was getting annoyed.

I watched the clock all morning at work, waiting for one o'clock. I was actually *hoping* a turkey vulture would show up to roost beside the other birds that showed up an hour apart, beginning at nine. The tit, cuckoo, crow and gull were ordinary birds that people saw every day. But let a turkey vulture soar down and station itself in a tree in the middle of town. Certainly it would be noticed. Repulsed by its odious appearance and the implied omen and augury associated with vultures, nervous, superstitious people would drive it away. In the process, they would probably frighten away the other birds on the branch and that would be the end of the story.

The turkey vulture seemed even more hideous and its face more human-like in the oblique winter sunlight. By one forty-five, it had been sitting there for over a half hour and no one seemed to have noticed it. I called one of the mousy office assistants to my desk on three separate occasions that afternoon, hoping she would see the vulture outside the window and make a commotion. She wasn't terribly bright, because she either didn't notice the ugly bird sitting there or she wasn't smart enough to realize the oddity of a vulture sitting on a branch outside an office window in a crowded city.

Just before the workday was over, I called Gullible to my cubicle and asked him if he noticed anything irregular outside the window. He went up to the glass and studied the scene for at least three minutes before he turned back to me, announcing he saw nothing unusual. It was an ironic twist. There I was, urging the gullible buffoon to attribute meaning and to interpret the symbolism of the presence of five stupid birds perched outside my window!

To this day, I don't know whether or not he saw the turkey vulture or the other birds, because he never reacted in any way. I wanted to ask if he saw the vulture in particular, but my sensible, logical nature precluded such an irrational inquiry.

True to form, Gullible didn't pass up the opportunity to elucidate on the symbolism of the window itself. He said that windows allegorically, like eyes, could be gateways to the soul. And more literally, the purpose of a window was to shed light or illuminate.

When I asked if he had ever solved the probability in the hypothetical I presented Thursday morning, he had concluded the odds of the four birds being in all those places together at all those times in that range was less than one in forty-four million. And his odds didn't include the vulture.

It had to be the chronic sleep deprivation I was experiencing, I thought. Maybe I was hallucinating. Maybe there were never any birds outside my window in the first place. It would explain everything. A hasty Internet search supported the conclusion.

Without adequate rest, the brain's ability to function quickly deteriorates.
Its ability to problem-solve and distinguish illusion from reality is greatly impaired: decision-making abilities are compromised, and the brain falls into rigid thought patterns that make it difficult to generate new problem-solving ideas. Insufficient rest can also cause people to have hallucinations!

The reason why no one else noticed the birds—maybe they weren't there. I had to get some sleep! So on the way home I bought a bottle of sleeping pills and a pint of cognac. One way or another, I would get rest. When I got home, I took four pills and two shots of cognac. Yet I lay there in bed for a long time, unasleep.

I wasn't sure whether or not it was a dream or a

memory, because sometimes the lines get blurred over time. But I remember driving home on a dark road after a late dinner at an extravagant lakeside restaurant called Cygnet. To get to the place, I had to take an exit on the highway that led away from the city. The long, narrow winding road meandered over and between hills before it plunged into a thickly wooded area. Three times I crossed wooden bridges that forded a swiftly moving stream, no doubt one of many watercourses that fed the huge lake.

Sitting at the restaurant bar, I met an angry old man who was drinking dark chartreuse. I liked the mean old man and imagined myself one day being as old and cantankerous as he was. He said he had a *right* to be angry. Without trepidation, he said he hated God, characterizing him as a "crusty old troll in the sky who takes and takes and takes, but gives nothing back."

When I told him I didn't believe in God, he laughed, mocking me. He said God found most people boring, but that he loved making fools of people like me. That was God's saving grace, he said, God's cruel sense of irony. The old man said he was going to have a showdown with God "pretty damn soon."

An attractive middle-aged woman interrupted us, scolding the old man for drinking and admonishing me for engaging him in his foolish dispute with God. I thought her passion was sexy, so I apologized right away and helped her get her father to a dinner table. We exchanged introductions and she gave me her business card.

As advertised, the food at Cygnet was exquisite. I had three pan-fried quail with wild forest mushrooms in a truffle sauce. The first bottle of wine was a smoky chardonnay from Carneros. Then I drank a silky Cab from Alexander Valley as I sampled sun-ripened blackberries, currants and boysenberries for dessert. And as always, I had two fine brandies before paying my tab, tipping the maître d' and leaving.

A ghostly mist had descended on the lake, woodlands and surrounding hills. The fog along the narrow road was so thick that I could scarce see two or three feet beyond my headlights in the lower elevation. For the first five minutes, I carefully proceeded at a snail's pace, creeping along. But with time and experience grew confidence. By focusing on the reflectors on the left side of the road, I was actually able to move along at twenty-five, thirty miles per hour.

The impact was sudden and definitely carnal. I was certain it was a deer or fawn, but I stopped anyway. Whatever it was, it was in the road in front of the car. Wading through the fog, I edged toward the amorphous form that lay perhaps ten feet ahead, just out of the range of the headlights.

When I stumbled upon the cracked dentures, stained with blood, I hesitated, realizing the victim in the haze was human, and groaning aloud. Looking back at my car, I could see a huge dent in the hood and the spider-webbed epicenter of the impact in the shattered windshield. It wasn't my fault. This person had just bolted from nowhere into the path of the car. I had no time to react.

Leaning over the body, I grasped a shoulder and turned the poor victim toward me to my profound horror: it was the old man from the restaurant. His toothless mouth was trailing bright red blood down his chin as his eyes tried to focus on my face. Though his body was cracked, he managed to force a sarcastic smile before saying, "So we finally meet. Take it. Take what's left, you greedy old bastard! You've already taken everything else!"

His eyes were still open, but he seemed dead to me: they were glazed; the anger was gone; his body had fallen limp. I didn't know what to do, but I didn't want to be involved in anything so serious. He was already dead. I couldn't help him. So I dragged his body to the side of the road and left it there. Then I got back in my car and drove home. The next day, I rented a storage unit, parked the car in there, bought a new car and tried to put the whole event out of my mind.

Two days later, I watched a news story about the man. Apparently, he was a multi-millionaire who had lost much of his money to bad investments and pretty young wives. It turned out the attractive woman he had dinner with wasn't his daughter at all. She was the lucky wife who happened to be married to him when he finally cashed out. He was a confused eighty-nine-year-old man who had stumbled in front of a car, so the police investigation was half-hearted at best. I wasn't about to say anything about my part in it. The man was going to die anyway.

I met his grieving widow, Phoebe, at the funeral and managed to sleep with her three times before probate was concluded. After that, she was a rich woman and I quickly became too old and too undistinguished for her new, wealth-infected tastes. As soon as she got that money, she dropped me, calling me "a nobody who would never amount to anything." My mortality before me, it was a huge blow to my ego.

The old man said God loved irony. And what could be more ironic than Phoebe ditching the man who, albeit unwittingly, killed her husband and brought on her great fortune? I put the whole episode behind me, and I have told no one the story of how I actually killed a man until this very moment.

I awoke on Saturday morning musing about the nature of birds. At work on Friday afternoon, I had done a little bird research on the computer. It's no wonder they were the most popular animals used in ancient mythologies.

To ignorant people, these creatures flew into the heavens, disappeared and returned with omens and augurs from the gods. The Greeks and Romans believed that if a bird flew through your house or pecked on your window, you would die. It could be a life-long illness or a murder, but you would die. They also believed that witches transformed themselves into owls and sucked the blood of babies at night. Of course there were birds, like eagles and doves, which boded good fortune. But for the most part, the presence of birds outside a person's home heralded some impending misfortune.

I wasn't worried. I'm not superstitious in the least, but I did wonder how the birds could sit so long outside my window without going away to eat. And as I understood from the research, because of their high metabolisms, birds require large amounts of food at regular intervals. This peculiarity further supported my most recent theory: that I had been hallucinating as a result of sleep deprivation.

I rolled over in bed and looked at the clock. I had slept past noon, a good eleven hours! Finally I would have some peace. I felt refreshed and re-energized as I rose from the bed. In fact, I hadn't slept so well in years. As I donned my robe, I debated about whether or not I wanted to draw the drapes and look out that window, and I didn't do it for the first two hours. But then my curiosity got the better of me.

My heart sank in my chest as I sank into the chair, staring out. When I drew the drapes, there they were: a tit, a cuckoo, a crow, a gull and a turkey vulture. And there was a new bird beside the vulture. Ironically, it was a bird whose image I had viewed on the computer a day earlier. It was relatively small, with a white breast and a sharply pointed beak, a mockingbird.

Yet I remained unconvinced that I wasn't still hallucinating. Sure, I had rested well the night before, but I read somewhere the effects of chronic fatigue can endure for days or weeks. The good night's sleep however, had restored my rational faculties. I realized nothing supernatural was going on. Either I was hallucinating or I wasn't. I believed I was.

To test my theory, I found my camera, loaded new batteries and took a few pictures of the birds that seemed to be perched on the rail outside my window. Later in the day, I would take the film to be developed at the mall photo shop. If the birds showed up in the pictures, I could logically determine I was not hallucinating. Then I would have to develop a theory that would explain why they were out there.

But if the birds did *not* show up in the pictures, I could then put the remarkable though explainable peculiarities of the past six days into a sensible perspective. It would mean the birds I was seeing were not real birds. And I understand such a conclusion would seem odd coming from a realist like me, but it would be the only conclusion I could draw. Hallucinations are real in the mind, though they are actually not real.

The sun was out on Saturday, so the drive to the mall was pleasant. I remember scanning the denuded trees as I drove, wondering when or if I'd see them. Anyway, I got to the mall. On the way to the photo shop, I visited a garden shop, two stores down. As I approached the counter, I overheard an older man telling a young couple how to keep pigeons and other birds from making nests on the roof. He recommended an owl decoy and a CD containing aggressive raptor sounds and distressed cries of birds being attacked. I bought both.

The foul-mouthed girl at the busy photo counter complained that the shop was understaffed and orders were backlogged. She said it didn't matter that the store was advertised as a one-hour photo shop, because my prints would not be ready until noon on Sunday at best. If I hadn't already dropped the film in the collection slot, I would have gone elsewhere.

I had dinner at a hole-in-the-wall Mexican restaurant not far from the mall called *El Ganso Grosso*, where I really liked the Chicken Colorado. I had practically forgotten about the birds by the time I finished dinner. I was enamored with Anhinga, the cute little waitress who was flirting with me to earn the generous tip I always left. I knew the owner, so he let her join me for sangria on the kerosene heater-warmed patio.

I had just slipped my tongue in her ear when, looking over her bare shoulder, I saw a mockingbird flit from my sight. Then on a table in the patio corner I saw the motley crew, all just sitting there, their heads tilted at roughly the same angles, watching me. It was enough of a shock to make me drop the wineglass. Tracing my gaze to the corner table, Anhinga looked over, but she didn't react to the birds at all.

It was two in the morning when she got up from my bed and got dressed. I heard her call her husband from the bathroom, explaining how a late rush at the restaurant had delayed her return home. She had exhausted me, but I still couldn't sleep. Instead, my thoughts again returned to the past.

A few years ago, we had a senior vice president at work by the name of Dennis Woodcock. Dennis was one of those upper management people who pretended to be everyone's best friend. But when the big boss came around, he cracked the cruel whip like he was Simon Legree. And always, after the boss was gone, Dennis would come back around, sucking up and apologizing. Then he'd explain why his scathing, mean-spirited abuse was actually making our jobs more secure. Most people licked their wounds and eventually forgave him, but I never did.

One day while Dennis was on one of his tirades in front of the boss, reaming Gullible for dressing like a slob and screaming at another guy for excessive phone use, on a day he told the secretaries outright they'd have to *gain* a few IQ points just to be *ditzy*—one of the "useless" girls made the mistake of disagreeing with him in front of the boss. Erupting in rage, he fired them all on the spot.

It just so happens I was just on the verge of sleeping with one of them. She was young, nineteen at best, and I had been pressuring her for weeks to come over to my apartment after work. I promised her that if she slept with me, she would never lose her job.

When she got to work that morning, she told me I could expect to have the night of my life. She showed me an overnight bag stuffed with sexy lingerie, silk stockings, body flavors and a pair of stiletto heels. She wore a low-cut top and short skirt to work that day, deliberately advertising the sweets she was ready to surrender. And then in one idiotic Dennis moment, she was gone.

It was beyond excusing. Over the next few sexually frustrated days, I decided to strike back. On a day Dennis was up in Seattle for a meeting, I let myself into his office, careful so no one saw me. Armed with his login codes supplied by a ditzy, disaffected former secretary, I sat at his computer and composed a company-wide memo. It was a coming out, really. In the memo Dennis was coming out of the closet, confessing to the company and the world that he was gay. I closed the computer without sending it, supplying the instruction that the message should be sent out at the next login.

On the next morning, the response was immediate. The whispering and gossiping were rampant as Dennis was uncharacteristically reserved about my wicked lie. The memo had caught the whole company by surprise. And yet as its true author, no one was more surprised than me when Dennis called the office together and announced that the memo was accurate.

A day later, we were stunned again to find out that, moved by Dennis' brave confession, the big boss, who was a married family man, confessed to being gay. The company reacted by transferring Dennis to a lesser assignment in Killdeer, North Dakota.

The big boss' wife was the personification of a woman scorned, as she ruined him in the divorce. Six months later, the stresses in his life brought on a stroke, unemployment and dementia. When I saw him two months ago, he was a bum—dirty, stinking, being refused service in the very restaurants he used to frequent. He asked me for a handout, but I refused. I never give money to itinerants.

When I awoke on Sunday morning, my first thought was head down to the mall to find out if my prints were ready, but I hung around the apartment for the first few hours. I had gone past the window a few times before I felt brave enough to draw the drapes. I had slept maybe seven hours, so I wasn't sure what I would see out there.

They were all there, the six birds I saw on the patio the night before. All six of my little friends. And as expected, at the far right there was a new bird. It was an odd little bird with what seemed like black lapels on its breast. There were black crescent stripes that went from each side of its black beak, over each of its eyes and tapered to points on each side of its neck. Its breast under the lapels was white, while its wings and back were light brown. It had a demi-tiara with a tiny black tuft of feathers sticking out either side of its head. From a side view, they looked like little horns. All the other birds I was able to identify, but this one I couldn't.

Just for the sake of curiosity, I set up my portable CD player next to the window and put on the disc with the aggressive raptor sounds. I turned the volume up so loud that the window shook in its frame, but the birds didn't move. All seven still stared, unblinkingly. And for the sake of curiosity, I placed the owl decoy on the windowsill. Again no reaction, not even from the smaller birds.

I made it back to the mall at two, stopping first at the garden shop to get my money back for the ineffective CD and the dummy owl. Then I went to the photo shop and picked up the prints. I could have opened them there, but I didn't. By that time, I realized what was at stake.

If I looked at the prints and the birds were there, I'd realize I was dealing with a profoundly strange, though rational phenomenon. *That* I could handle. But if I looked at the pictures of the rail outside my window and the birds *weren't* there, then I might be forced to consider the possibility that the arrival and ominous presence of the birds, birds that only *I* could see, stressed the boundaries of conventional reality. The supernatural I had denied my entire life, the spirituality I had rejected from the very core of my being, may have been staring me in the face.

It was a disturbing thought, and worse than that, for some reason the old man's words began to play in my head. Stupid old man! He laughed at me. He had mocked me when, sneering derisively, he said God loved making *fools* of people like me. He said God's saving grace was his cruel sense of irony.

Truly, what bothered me was the strange sense of irony I could feel encroaching on me just then, the impression of some force working behind the scenes to make a fool of me. I could hear the fingers tapping at the keyboard. It was as if I had been singled out and placed on a stage to be mocked.

Here was a rational man, too intelligent to believe in God. Here was a true realist, a man who had transcended the frailty and infirmity of the physical mind. Here was a logical man, unaffected by the utterly weak and flawed mortal urge or need to believe. Here I was, a man who believed none of it!

And yet, if the birds were not in the pictures, for the first time in my life, I would be confronted with a singular unexplainable phenomenon. I would not deceive myself any further. I was not hallucinating. I saw seven birds, the same seven that roosted in a bare parking lot tree and stared down at me as I sat in my car.

I went home and closed the drapes. I didn't want to see what would definitely appear on the rail outside my window. I didn't understand why, but they were following me, reminding me. I finished the rest of the cognac and took four more sleeping pills. In the stupor, I remembered.

I was seventeen years old, almost eighteen. So I had practically finished high school. Truth be told, it was the day of my graduation. I really didn't care whether or not anyone in my family attended the ceremony. It was just high school. But it just so happened that my grandmother was ill. She had been diagnosed with a malignant, inoperable brain tumor seven months earlier. It was just a matter of time, and it was obvious that time had run out.

The living room at our house had been transformed into an infirmary. My grandmother lay dying in a borrowed hospital bed. There was a rack behind her with bags of fluids, tubes going this way and that, an IV in her forearm and pure oxygen blowing into her nose. She was in bad shape.

Anyway, on the morning of my graduation I went in to look at her. I was standing there, when to my sudden surprise she grabbed my balls. I recoiled naturally, but I wasn't sure how to react, as her hands seemed to be playing with them. Her face was blank, though her eyes were open. "Next to the tool shed," she whispered, and at once she clutched my balls firmly and let go. "It's next to the tool shed."

To this day, I have no idea why on her deathbed, my Bible-thumping, eighty-year-old grandmother fondled my genitals on the morning of my graduation. Maybe her hand, detached from any process of thought, had gravitated toward the warmest part of my body. Or maybe in tumor-induced delirium, she thought I was my grandfather. But when she whispered those last words, the last words she would ever whisper to anyone, I instantly knew what she meant.

For years, I had heard the story. Everyone in the family knew it. My grandfather had served in the military when he was a young man. And it just so happened that, during a three-day winter blizzard in the 1940s, he had been separated from his unit somewhere in the Kentucky hills of Meade County. Near death, he had scraped his way along the edge of a boulder and crawled into a crevice. Inside, he found a box full of gold and silver coins and bundles of five hundred dollar bills.

He lost all but three fingers to the cold, but when the sun came up, he managed to clamber to a place where he could be spotted by one of the search teams. The military discharged him honorably due to the injury to his hands. But he had marked the entrance to the crevice, and he returned weeks later to claim his treasure. In that way, he came out to California with a small fortune.

For the rest of his years he lived in fear that the government would one day come and take the money from him. He imagined they had spies all around, that they were constantly watching him, waiting for him to lead them to the cache. In fact, he was so paranoid that he never spent a cent of the money. Instead, he hid it in the ground, lived a modest life and died a relatively poor man.

My religious grandmother called the money a curse and insisted it should remain hidden, though we all suspected she alone knew where it was buried. When she was diagnosed with the brain tumor on Thanksgiving Eve, most family members lost faith that the money would ever be recovered. So when she whispered the words, "next to the tool shed," to me on the morning of my graduation as she held my genitals, I knew she was telling me where to find it.

I went to my grandparents' property and dug up the treasure box on that very night because I knew that, upon hearing my grandmother was dead, other family members would come looking for it. Behind the country home, I had noticed a slight depression in the ground about six feet to the right of the tool shed and found the heavy framed wooden box five feet down.

After more than six hours of digging, raising and dragging the mud-encrusted box, I struggled to lift it and drop it in the trunk of the car I borrowed from my parents for grad night. Then I refilled the hole with dirt, covered the tire tracks and drove to an abandoned home in the neighborhood. The home was abandoned because no one would buy it.

Thirteen years earlier, a man named Jim Shrike had murdered his four stepchildren and his wife in the huge house. When police arrived, they found the children impaled on wooden stakes downstairs and their mother stabbed to death in her bed upstairs. Sprawled next to her, Shrike had placed a shotgun barrel in his mouth and had pulled the trigger with his toe.

The house had been boarded up since a week after the murders, but I had found a way in through a rear door. I considered it my private getaway because everyone in the neighborhood believed the house was haunted. The bloodstains were still on the wall. Anyway, I dragged the cumbersome box into the home and broke the lock with a pickaxe, causing the chains that held the box to fall immediately to the floor.

I was up all night. I counted the paper money three times. I could not believe how much was there. On the obverse was a portrait of President William McKinley, an "L," denoting Federal Reserve Bank of San Francisco and the date of printing, 1934. The reverse featured a Trumbull painting. There were four bundles of five hundred dollar bills, each containing one hundred individual bills, and fifty loose five hundred dollar bills, adding to a total of two hundred twenty-five thousand dollars.

The luster and detail of the uncirculated,

unblemished, double eagle, twenty-dollar gold coins was unreal. There were fifty of them, minted in 1933, shining in a wooden case lined with black velvet. Next to them was a line of shining silver perfect coins; I later identified them as 1836 Capped Liberty Bust silver half-dollars, sixty-eight in all. I hid the box in the bedroom where Mrs. Shrike had been stabbed, certain that fear and superstition about the house would keep the ignorant world away.

The family did converge on my grandparents' property as I expected. After an extensive search of the house, they came outside and found the place next to the tool shed where something had been removed from the ground. Suspicion and animosity swirled, though no one was sure who had recovered the box. So they all waited and watched to see which one of us would suddenly start spending large amounts of unaccounted for cash.

It was the ultimate irony. It was enough to make me disparage God, if only I believed in him. Here I had wealth beyond my imagining, but I wasn't able to enjoy it. Six months went by, and I hadn't spent a cent. So just when I started thinking I would have been better off surrendering the money so it could be evenly divided by my family, the unthinkable occurred.

Stupid, idiotic people. I've always hated them. Rumors circulated through the neighborhood about a phantom that moved in and out of that house on random nights. Neighborhood kids feared it was the angry ghost of Mrs. Shrike seeking out kids to kill to atone for her own murdered children.

When I knew anything, it was too late. Four or five frightened kids had taken a gasoline can up to the house and had lit the place on fire. Horrified beyond belief, I ran down the street toward the house.

Upon arriving, I saw a group of children and adults standing there, just watching as the old house burned. No one had called the fire department. When I looked back, I could see the crowd growing larger and more excited by the moment. They didn't want anyone to put the fire out. The Shrikes were still in there. That entire frightened neighborhood *wanted* to watch the house and the memory of the Shrikes burn down to the ground!

I screamed at them, denigrating their utter irrationality. I ran wildly toward the house, clawing at the walls to get in to save my fortune, but the heat was too great. I swooned and fell back, only to be restrained by a group of men who thought I had lost my mind, and it was true. If God or the universe loved make fools of people like me, it was a day of glory.

Because of its age, the great old house, groaning aloud as it collapsed, really did burn down to the ground, and with it my future. Days later, when the smoldering ceased, I picked through the coal and ashes, hoping to find the gold and silver, but I never found anything, not even with the metal detector I employed. It was as if the molten metals had somehow found their way into a manmade drain or an earthly chasm. It was all just gone. It was all a lark. It was... a lark.

And then it hit me. I checked the clock, which indicated nearly midnight, but I bolted up from the bed, threw on my robe and went directly to my dining table by the window. When I yanked the drapes apart, it was exactly as I suspected. At the far left was the tit, then the cuckoo, then the crow, then the gull, then the turkey vulture, then the mockingbird, and at the far right was the small bird, which had arrived just that morning—the bird I hadn't recognized at first. It *was* a lark.

I grinned sardonically. I could hear laughter that seemed darkly divine. Was it the old man's or was it mine? I withdrew the sealed package of prints from the pocket of my robe and opened it. Wagging my head, I flipped through the pictures, one by one, acknowledging, after each turn, the truth before me. They were pictures of a rail, but there were no birds.

So why were there seven birds sitting on the rail outside my window? Why had the tit appeared on Monday, the cuckoo on Tuesday and so forth? And why were the birds following me? Why were they all different? Why were they things I could see, but no one else saw? And why were they real on the rail and absent in the pictures? There had to be a rational answer.

I let the pictures drop to the floor, one by one. And then my eyes fell upon the softball sized glass sphere on a stand that rested on the table just under the window. Gullible had given it to me years ago and I never liked it. I just hadn't gotten around to throwing it away. As I leaned toward it, I thought I could see the birds reflected in it. That asshole Greg had given me a god-damned crystal ball! Impulsive, I grabbed it, and before I thought better, I hurled it toward the window and the birds.

The sound of the shattering glass seemed to go on for minutes, just as it seemed it took forever for the pane to explode and the shards to fall. When it was all over, the birds were still there, only the rail seemed closer. I screamed aloud, rushing the window, but the birds did not stir. Blood trailed from gashes in my cheek, on my forehead and from my hands. I continued to scream, shouting profanities toward that anathema, that disgusting, mocking abomination before me. I could no longer stand their cold, collective glare. This was not real.

The door was unlocked. I have never been up here before, on the roof of the building, exposed to the wind and rain. Looking over the edge made me weak in the knees, but it didn't stop me from kicking off my slippers and climbing onto the ledge, my feet oozing blood onto the concrete. My apartment window is right down there, three floors below the spot where I'm standing. Craning my neck slightly forward and fixing my eyes downward, I can barely see the rail, and yet I see no birds.

When day breaks and the sun peeks over the eastern line, they appear. Sometimes they are faint and indistinct while at others they are stark and intense. Today I had watched them. I examined the way they crept westward from dark corners and crevices of the early morning, sneaking out, extending, growing bolder with every minute, mocking things above, nearly disappearing at midday. And then they stretched eastward, fleeting, ephemeral and ethereal as the light in the skies began to fade.

The transition was subtle—the way the essence of an event, a figure or a deed gently slips from the tangible to the intangible. I tried to ignore the growing suspicion that the margins between the real and the unreal are feather thin if they even exist at all, and yet there is a certain continuity that begs faith, that begs belief.

At some times those phantoms are slight, but they are always there, reflecting choice, chance, will and fate. They are cast even in the darkened places, where the light cannot etch their outlines.

A certain epiphany came as I gazed eastward earlier this evening, that mocking, burning celestial eye slipping halfway past the horizon behind me. Along the edge of earth in the fading light of day I fancied I saw those shadows take wings and fly into the heavens.

Only then I knew. Only then I understood the reason the birds had arrived, as heralds, to remind me of things hidden or forgotten. They weren't birds, they weren't birds at all. They were the transformed shadows of my life, and they had tracked me down, they had found me, they had reacquainted themselves with me. They were the hidden sins of my life, and they had come home to roost.

In order to accept that, I would be forced to believe. I would have to believe that the events of my life had cast shadows on the Earth, shadows that had become birds, birds that had returned to me to mock me, to persecute me, to test my resolve.

And still, I've never been one to believe in ghosts or *Devil's Triangles* or luck or spells—basically anything supernatural. I never believed any of it: God, the Devil, Heaven, Hell, sin, redemption, the afterlife, eternal damnation, miracles or curses. For everything there is a rational, logical explanation; everything is the result of a causal relationship, implicit or explicit. I have lived in a world of reality, a world where faith, spirit and symbolism have absolutely no meaning.

That is why I jumped from the ledge, and that is why it is at this precise moment as I stretch out, suspended in the sky, falling, I chose to share this story with you. None of this is valid, and thus by jumping I pierce the veil of reality. Sooner or later, you'll be forced to do the same. I'll see you in the real world.

DORK

My fellow Americans: perhaps once in every generation, a leader comes before the people and delivers a speech that, for its timing and place in history, is destined to become part and parcel of the fabric that makes America.

On April 19, 1951, it was the fading General Douglas MacArthur, speaking before a joint session of congress. In September 1952, it was Richard Nixon in his living room with his little dog, Checkers. In 1992, it was Bill and Hillary on Superbowl Sunday, explaining on *60 Minutes* that their marriage was far from perfect, but that having a perfect marriage was not a prerequisite for the U.S. presidency.

It's different with me. The fact that I'm here has nothing to do with something I've done or any crisis I've created for myself. I've spent my life working diligently to bring about meaningful changes in this country. I am dedicated to the ideals of America, evidenced by my long and decorated military career.

But I am a fellow damned in a misunderstood name, and tonight I'm here to honor that name. Five decades ago, a distinguished American vice president reminded us that *in real life, unlike in Shakespeare, the sweetness of the rose depends upon the name it bears. Things are not only what they are. They are, in very important respects, what they seem to be.*

For those of you who don't know me, I might as well get it over with. My name is Winston Princeton Dork. Now most people don't have rhyming first and middle names, that's rare enough. But my last name—and you can check your phone book white pages—I'm one of the last Dorks left. The Internet directory lists less than 50 Dorks nationwide, and a lot of those Dorks are way up in age, eighties and older. The sad truth is most of the authentic Dorks have caved in and legally changed their names. They're sell-outs.

Well folks, I have no intention of changing my name. I come from a proud legacy of Dorks. One of my great grandfathers, Leland Parnassus Dork, was almost a general in the War of 1812. And my grandfather, Titus Clitus Dork, was an unsung hero from the Normandy invasion. He died on Omaha Beach on June 6, 1944, but only after parachuting behind enemy lines and single-handedly taking out one of the key German positions. He was a true American.

My father, on the other hand, always seemed somewhat ashamed of the name. He was a successful stock trader who went by the name of Stanley Morgan rather than Stanley Morgan Dork. My two brothers followed his lead. They won legal petitions to become Morgans, leaving me alone to carry on the Dork name.

I come before the American people to make my petition for the U.S. presidency. In reality, it should not be an issue that my name is Dork. But unfortunately, to many Americans it is. And that's why I'm here tonight. I'm here to share my story and give you a chance to know me.

Hopefully, after you've heard me, many of you can transcend your preconceptions and prejudices enough to listen to me. So tonight I'm *not* asking for your vote. I'm only asking for you to look past my name.

I was born on August 8th, 1960. I realize that makes me a young candidate, but unlike Dan Quayle, I am worthy of the Kennedy comparison. I am a graduate of the West Point Academy, a Rhodes Scholar, a decorated Iraqi war veteran, an interim law professor at Yale and I own a Fortune 400 company.

And yet, had my name been Smith or Jones or Taylor, I would have no doubt been eminently more successful. Shakespeare briefly mused, "What's in a name?" Well, when your name is Dork, you realize that even the most open-minded people are far more affected by a name, or in my case a surname, than they would ever care to admit.

My name is actually a derivative of the Eastern European name Turk, and it is related to a slew of other names, including De Turck, Dark, Deorc, Dirk, Dorge and Dorick. When my ancestors came to Ellis Island in the early 1800s, the Americanized name they innocently settled on was Dork.

I say "innocently settled on" because there was no way my ancestors could have known that the name or word would take on such a pejorative meaning. I'm not sure when it happened, but over the years the name took on a negative context. It's not very different from the way the names Fink and Mudd have suffered as a result of American history. But once again, I must point out that the negatives associated with my name had nothing to do with any transgression or deficiency on the part of my forefathers. On the contrary, the Dorks have always been exemplary Americans.

Unfortunately, and I've done the research on this, at some point in the early 1900s, the word "dork," specifically as a noun, came into usage. And as a noun it was used to describe a stupid, inept, or foolish person. Now this new noun had absolutely no association with the family name. That can be proven. In fact, the Dorks of America have always been a highly educated family. Dating back to the time we arrived, our family has always placed a high premium on advanced learning. You'd be hard pressed to find a single Dork who didn't have a college degree.

At this time, I must address another unfortunate misassociation with my family name. You've probably heard it. I know I have, and it's wrong, wrong, wrong. It's misinformation of huge proportions. So I'll say it for once and for all. A dork, (and once again, the word is being used as a noun), a dork is *not* a whale's penis. I don't know exactly how the association began, but I see it as highly offensive when insensitive people, in their garish ignorance, make that misapplication.

Etymologists will tell you, there was never any association between dork and a whale's penis until these kids on the Internet began with it. It's an Internet hoax, an outright lie. The Internet, for all the good it has done, has been a huge factor in trivializing the word and degrading my family name, and I'm not exaggerating. If you type "dork" on a search engine, you'll get no less than five pages of websites dedicated to reinforcing the misinformation associated with the word.

I must admit that circa 1916 there began an association between the word and a *penis*, though it was never a *whale's* penis. But that isn't any different than the same association with the name Dick. And I know a lot of Dicks: Dick Gephart, Dick Armey, Dick Lugar, Dick Shelby, Dick Hastert, Dick Nixon, Dick Cheney—we've had at least two vice presidents who were Dicks—and the list goes on. Yet they've all succeeded in spite of the association. The penis association hasn't made the name an issue with voters in all those cases.

So now that we have that behind us, let me take this time to share a little information about myself. I was born in Hoboken, New Jersey, during the Eisenhower era. As I alluded to earlier, my father, Stanley Morgan Dork, or Stanley Morgan to the world, was the owner of a large stock brokerage company in New York City. I spent my early life completely immersed in the world of finance, learning the logic, precedent and politics of Wall Street and the Federal Reserve. My father insisted that it is finance, not money, that makes the world go around, and he trained each of us boys in the business from the time we could read, write, add and subtract.

My mother was the Mary Seacole of Hoboken. In the early 1960s, she started out with a dilapidated old building on Willow Avenue that she inherited from her parents. Shrewder than my father (and he admits it), she somehow wrangled a group of local itinerants into going in and fixing up the place. Six months later, she opened the first of seventeen soup kitchens she operated on both sides of the Holland Tunnel. She taught us the virtue of compassion.

When I was eighteen, I entered the United States Military Academy at West Point, where I received the most comprehensive undergrad education offered in the world. Upon graduation, I was sent to work at the U.S. Embassy in Beirut. A month later, an Iranian national drove a truck into the Marine barracks and detonated the largest non-nuclear explosion ever on the face of the Earth, killing 248 Americans and effectively driving the U.S. from Lebanon. A month later, I was wounded in a separate incident when several Hezbollah agents attacked the embassy with machine guns and RPGs.

After recovering from three gunshot wounds, I was selected to receive a Rhodes scholarship to Oxford University, where I studied global economics and politics. When I returned to New York, I started up a small investment firm, and pioneering the use of computers to predict market trends in commodities, my company stunned Wall Street with unprecedented profits for five straight years. I sold the company for a small fortune and opened a financial consulting business, handling major stock portfolios for learning institutions.

I'm not sharing any of this information to brag about myself. I'm simply attempting to illustrate that, had my name been Lincoln, Roosevelt or Kennedy, this whole competency issue would be non-existent.

But because my name is Dork, I have been unfairly subjected to ridicule, criticism and illogical rancor from late night talk show hosts, comedians, and the public at large. Even the news commentators, news agencies and newspapers, entities that have traditionally avoided personal smear campaigns and heckling, have played word games and made puns about my name.

Notwithstanding America, beware. American voters, beware. I'm not so worried about the late night talk show hosts and the comedians. When your name is Dork, you tend to develop a thick skin, or foreskin according to Leno. But beware of the twisted idiosyncrasies of American politics. Beware of the illogic. Beware of the double-standard.

We live in a country where a man is supposedly judged, not by the color of his skin, but by the content of his character. And yet, if you're a black man, you won't in your wildest dreams get elected president. Not today; not for at least another 20 years. Race matters.

We live in a time and society in which women and men are considered equals. And yet, if you're a woman, you'd sooner raise the dead or walk on water than become president. Sex matters.

If you're fat, bald or ugly—forget it. Single or too good-looking—it won't happen. Jewish American, Mexican American, Asian American, Iraqi American—they tell you it's an open election; they tell you the possibility to become president is open to every American citizen, but it's never worked that way.

What is presidential in America? Someone who is male, tall, Caucasian features, average-to-good-looking, educated, married, well-connected and egotistical? Will America ever get past the superficial? I'm the perfect candidate, except for one thing. My name is Dork.

I like to think I'm a fairly intelligent man, but my advisers will tell you that I bucked conventional wisdom when I entered this election. After careful polling and research, they told me I had to change my name, that I could never get elected as a Dork, that Americans would never choose a Dork as their leader.

My advisors, a whole panel of highly-skilled professional consultants, pollsters, pundits, experts— whatever you want to call them—they advised against using my name. The essence of what they said: American voters are shallow and not very bright. They said that in their business, the only thing they can really count on is the idiocy of the American people. Sounds harsh, but they actually made some valid points.

To American voters, it's irrelevant who the best candidate is. According to the U.S. Constitution, the only real qualifications for becoming president are being a natural born citizen 35 years old or more and being a resident for 14 years. So aside from those requirements, how *do* Americans decide who would make the best president?

My experts summed it up this way: it all boils down to three groups, but only one, the worst of the three, chooses our president. The first group is immaterial. They are the eligible voters who, for whatever reason, do not vote. So if the ballot represents power, then this group of about 19 million expresses its power by choosing not to use it. You can't hate them for that. They're voting in their own way—they just don't realize it.

The second group is a little more esoteric and enigmatic. Strangely enough, this is the group of American voters who take the time to know the candidates and the issues. They are the educated voters who are actually passionate about politics and about their role in the entire process, a political elite of sorts. Unfortunately though, there aren't many in this second group—probably two or three million in a registered population of 130 million, a candle in the wind.

And that leaves us with 110 million American voters without a clue. According to my experts, they are the mindless mainstream, the ignorant electorate, the gullible majority that elects our presidents and representatives.

It's a fickle group, completely at the mercy of ruthless political operatives and spinmeisters who pander to the baser instincts of fear, ignorance, jingoism and prejudice. Of the three, this group is the most predictable, especially during times of crisis. Tap this group's vulnerabilities and you win elections.

In the end, party affiliation is irrelevant because loyalties don't run deep for group three voters. According to the pundits, group three suffers from ADD and chronic short term memory. A catchy four second sound bite, an emotionally stirring image, a scare tactic, a promised rebate, and you've got yourself a movement.

So saying as much, my advisors told me that as Winston Princeton Dork, I could never be elected president. Some suggested changing the name to Dark, while others argued the country still isn't ready for a Dark president, even if in name only. The consensus choice was Dirk, though it held its own liabilities because it looks so much like Dick. Winston Dirk, President Dirk. I thought about it, but I just couldn't get used to the name.

Well, I didn't buy my advisors' routine about it all boiling down to three groups. I didn't buy the bit about the primary electorate being shallow and clueless. And so putting my faith in the prudence and intelligence the American people, I proudly stood before you as a Dork, ready to serve.

More than that, I determined I would be the best president America ever had. How would I do that? By cutting through all the conservative and liberal rhetoric and reaching the heart of Americans. Because what is really in our hearts? What do we need? What do we want?

White, black, brown, rich, poor, native, immigrant— we basically want the same things. We want security for ourselves and our loved ones. We want to live in a reasonably clean environment where we don't have to fear our friends and families will be attacked by terrorists, victimized by criminals or exploited by powerful interests. We want a government we can trust, led by an executive and chief-of-state who is decisive, wise and above all, honest with us.

And that's how I present myself to you. I'm an honest candidate. I won't lie to the American people and the world about weapons of mass destruction in order to justify a war that has killed tens of thousands, among those many of your children, siblings and parents. And I won't question or mischaracterize the patriotism of any man, woman or child who demands answers for the actions of his or her president or government.

My name is Dork. I accept that I'm not above misapprehending a situation or making an error in judgment. And knowing this, I vow to always follow founding father Thomas Jefferson's advice when it comes to making crucial decisions that have potentially far reaching consequences.

Prudence indeed, will dictate my actions. So rather than engaging in posturing, threatening and issuing ultimatums—when presented with a challenge involving the security of America and Americans, when the issues involve global human rights and social justice, I won't play cowboy and just shoot from the hip. I won't insist that the most loyal Americans should mindlessly accept party line propaganda and disregard facts they can ascertain with their own eyes and ears.

Instead, I'll make a careful examination of the facts as they are presented to me. I'll acknowledge the essential hunger of the hawk, and yet I'll appreciate the sensible caution of the dove. For this reason, mine will be the most politically, philosophically and racially diverse cabinet in the history of America. Diversity makes America strong; polarization makes her blind. From many we truly are one.

Presented with the facts, I'll begin by relying on the wise men and women of my cabinet to put those facts into some meaningful perspective. Only then will I begin to form my opinions and consider what actions or decisions would be appropriate and whether or not an exigency exists.

Then I'll come before you, the people, to discuss the situation, supported by those facts our national security will allow me to present. I will never ask for your blind faith. I will never ask you to sacrifice your children, spouses or siblings to war unless my objectives are clear and my motives are unimpeachable.

I'll come before you with situations, but I will also come before you with assiduously proposed plans. Ultimately, I will carefully consider the concerns, the opinions and the will of the American people before deciding on any action. Beyond that, I have a decent respect for history and for the opinions of all humans.

The election of the president of the United States of America is a world changing event. Arguably, it is an event that will likely change to course of world history. So as Americans, you must not underestimate the awesome power you wield in the process; you must not undervalue the responsibility you have to the world and to history.

America needs a leader who can pull the country together and create unity based on pride and responsibility. America needs a captain who can pilot a nation that is the flagship to world peace and prosperity. America needs a Dork.

So I challenge you tonight, my fellow Americans, to truly look at the choices before you. I challenge you to look past the superficial. Whether or not you are able to get beyond my name says much more about you than it does about me. I take great pride in being a Dork, and as a Dork I am confident that I can help build a greater America.

One of my fondest hopes is that by my coming before you, Dorks all over America can begin to accept the fact that being a Dork *doesn't* have to be a negative. Dorks are capable of great things, and that includes becoming the leader of the greatest nation in world history.

My fellow Americans, earlier I said I came before you tonight not to ask for your vote. Instead, in the course of these few minutes I wanted to give you the chance to see me for who I am. Hopefully, when the election is over and all is said and done, the world will gain a new respect for America as a place where even a Dork can get elected president. And that my fellow Americans, speaks volumes more about our nation than it does about me. God bless America.

I wrote "Dork" in autumn of 2004, at a time many months before Barack Hussein Obama announced his candidacy for President of the United States, and when he did, I was cynical about his chances for success, not for any lack of perceived experience or qualifications, but for a lack of belief in the United States electorate to look beyond race, gender, appearances and yes, even a name to elect a president. I am proud to say, "I was wrong."

THE SILK NOOSE
(COMMENCE)

As hard as it might be to believe from where *you're* sitting, I went to college. I believed the bullshit myth about higher education. I bought into the noble lie, the one that promises a college degree somehow equates to success in life. So I sold my financial soul to attend a pedigreed university. I took the classes, I catered to the self-absorbed professors, I kissed every ass that was put in my face and I graduated. And where did it get me? Here, trapped in a small Kansas town where tomorrow I'll be hanged until I die. Hanged by the neck. You see, my friend, the sad truth is that in the end, my institutionalized education failed me. Yes, they graduated a fool into the world, with honors mind you, but they meant well.

I read *King Lear* during my sophomore year. My instructor was a stiff and severe 80-year-old woman who had apparently slipped on a bar of soap and fell ass-first onto a stick years earlier. She insisted we call her Prof Noble. A few of us figured out why she was considered one of the world's foremost authorities on English literature, and more specifically, on Shakespeare's work. She was *doin* him way back when. She knew every word of his every play, or at least it seemed she did. I suppose I was impressed then, but now I realize she was an idiot of "Byronic" proportions.

Prof Noble completely missed the point. She forced us to analyze Shakespeare's clever use of meter, made us examine his gift for language and wordplay, compelled us to marvel at his unparalleled literary genius, but never once did she encourage us to think, to consider the message. She was in effect chained to the cave wall, content to engage in the hollow, pompous, high-browed debate and dialogue that defined her and other institutionalized persons like her.

Under the threat of failure, we scrutinized *King Lear*, we dissected it and stood it on its ear, we searched for hidden meanings, but we all missed the point. We missed the simple truth of what Melpomene, through Shakespeare, was trying to say. Had I understood it then, had Prof Noble done her job as a teacher, had I gotten my money's worth for my indentured soul, I would have never have been old till I hadst been wise.

You wag your head. You think I'm bitter, don't you? It's not bitter, really. Like Lear, I've come to that single moment in life where reality bites. If you seek truth, if you're headed in the right direction, you'll eventually come to this same place, regardless of the path you've chosen along the way.

You see, I was not always so cynical. I was just like you. I was married even; I see your ring. Yes, I was married to a woman who was plain, though not plain in the sense you're probably thinking. She was plain in the way Prof Noble defined plainness. It derived from the Latin word *planus*, which meant level; it meant outspoken, frank and straightforward. In my wife's case, it meant *leveling* nonstop complaints and criticism at me. I loved her, but I decided in the end I didn't like her plainness. At the same time, she decided she did could no longer tolerate my acquiescent nature. Naturally, I understood and let her move on.

During our brief courtship and marriage, I resented the fact that she knew me so well. She pegged it on the first day we met: She said my accommodating nature was my tragic flaw, and she was right. She said it was rooted in my profound vanity. I detested when she said that, but now I understand what she meant. And like all tragic flaws, this vanity was my undoing.

Stop tapping your fingers. I hate that. I know I've been rambling. You came here to hear my story. Well, it begins like every other tragedy I have ever known—with a single event. Here it is for you and the world to hear:

Earlier this month, I got a call from my ex-wife at 3 a.m. She said she was stranded in Kansas City of all places. I offered her money for a return flight, but she refused. She said an attempted hijacking in New Jersey two days earlier had traumatized her about flying. She wanted me to physically come get her and drive her home.

Drive her home? I thought. By car, it would take me at least four days to get to Kansas from my apartment in San Francisco and five days to return, since I would have to drop her off in Los Angeles. So I offered train fare and then bus fare, but she said her anxiety extended to all forms of public transportation. When I asked why she hadn't called her boyfriend, she said he wouldn't understand. She told me I was the only person on Earth who really understood her. She was crying and begging, and so with some reluctance I promised her I would start driving to Kansas City later that morning.

My certifiably dim-witted manager at Acme Advertising flatly told me I could not take time off for my "personal emergency." When I reminded him that I hadn't taken a single vacation day in seven years, he argued it was only six years. The company needed me, he insisted. He warned that if I left, I might as well clean out my desk. My job would not be waiting for me when I returned.

So what do you think I did? I did what you would have done. I cleared out my desk. I wasn't crazy about that life sentence anyway. You know what my job was? I wrote advertising copy. All the money I had spent on my education, all the labor and analysis I had spent on the world's great literature, and I wrote magazine ads for pantyhose lines and television commercials for tampon brands! The job had gotten me by for 18 years, but then on that day it was done, just like that. It was liberating, really.

My flat on California Street was only two blocks away from my job on Clement, so I had little need for a car. But because all successful people had cars, somewhere along the line I thought I should have one. I had bought a Dodge Reliant fifteen years earlier but had hardly ever driven it. It had traveled no more than 3,000 miles, if that. It was due for a long trip, so I filled it up, checked the fluid levels, bought a map and hit the road.

I headed east on Interstate 80. What's wrong? You don't know the major highways? Interstate 80 is the highway that goes east and west from San Francisco to New York. In my case, I had to go east. The highway doesn't go through Kansas, so I figured I would head south at Cheyenne on Interstate 25 and continue south through Colorado until I got to Denver. Then I'd pick up Interstate 70 and drive east into Kansas.

The first day was the most ambitious. I had driven across California and entered Nevada by about one o'clock in the afternoon. I stopped to eat a Cobb salad in Winnemucca. Later that afternoon, a spectacular thunderstorm raged over the desert-like landscape. I had never seen the sky so large. Dark, towering cumulonimbus clouds reached higher than piety and the roof of the car would allow me to raise my eyes. Lightning streaks flicked continuously, illuminating the column-like sides of the clouds.

As the sun kissed the horizon, it seemed for a moment I was driving through a city full of skyscrapers. I think I arrived at Salt Lake City at ten o'clock that first night. I pulled off the highway and stayed at a dilapidated motel. There were crickets in the rust-stained shower. I was beat, so I drank a suspiciously weak beer and passed out.

As I drove the second day, I imagined I was on an adventure aboard the USS Reliant. I fancied the high desert of western Wyoming was an alien scene. I could see the highway ahead of me for a hundred miles, reaching right to the edge of the planet. It seemed more digital than real. Hypnotized by the sheer regularity of the geography, I nearly fell asleep a few times before I reached Cheyenne. The Dinosaur Inn—I think that's where I stayed that second night, but for some reason, I keep remembering penguins.

On the third day, I headed south toward Denver. Yet by noon, I was beginning to lose faith in my trusty Reliant. The hills and inclines really taxed the poor car. I had to pull to the far right lane to let the line of cars behind me pass while ascending and then to cool my break pads while descending. That's when I began to have second thoughts about my rescue mission. Nevertheless, I forged ahead bravely and reached Kansas State Line by 7 p.m. Another night, another dirty motel.

Why are you writing? I thought you were taping this. Anyway, I had driven maybe a hundred miles into Kansas when—waitaminute, they call this the Sunflower State and I haven't seen a single sunflower since I've been here. Don't you think that's odd? They also say the geographical center of the country is here. I'm thinking they made that one up too. Excuse me.

Ah, this *is* good brandy. I don't know how you got it in here, but I appreciate it. I'm going to *die* tomorrow, after all.

So I was telling you, I had driven maybe a hundred miles when my car started running hot. The needle was way in the red, lying flat, but I was in the middle of nowhere. So I kept on driving until I saw a sign. No, it wasn't a sign from God; it was just a sign that said, "Polite, 5 miles." I thought about pulling over and walking to spare my car any further agony, but the Reliant made the decision for me. The car died two miles outside the small town.

Fortunately, a couple of teenagers on bicycles stopped for me as I walked up the road. They were a boy and girl, both probably 17. The girl offered me her bike, insisting that she and her boyfriend would be plenty comfortable sharing his bike on the way into town. They were so friendly.

As we got to town, I saw a huge banner that read, "Welcome to Polite, The Friendliest Small Town in the World." The boy led me to the town's only automotive repair shop, called Friendly Automotive. He took great care to introduce me to the owner/manager, thanked me for deciding to visit the small community and hugged me hard before leaving. His pretty young girlfriend kissed me... on the lips!

Clyde Kissup, the owner of Friendly Automotive, was ready to have his lunch when I walked into the empty shop. He was a large, hairy, bear-like man with a booming voice, minty fresh breath and a clean, citrus body odor. He stood, spread his arms and hugged me. Then he invited me to have lunch with him. I was hungry, so I ate, and then I told him about my car. He laughed.

"Sounds like a water-pump problem ta me. Easiest thing in the world to fix on GM cars. I can do it in 45 minutes at most, and I won't even charge ya for it."

He smiled.

"One problem though. I don't have that part. I'll have ta send for one from my distributor in Kansas City."

I was beginning to worry about my stranded ex-wife.

"And how long will that take?"

"Two days, max. But don't worry. It's a blessin in disguise. Serendipadoo! Consider yourself lucky to be stranded in the friendliest small town in the world!"

When I asked Clyde if he could arrange to have my car towed to the garage, he explained that tow trucks were unnecessary in the friendliest small town in the world. He said he and a buddy would take his pickup out and drag the car over in the morning, free of charge. In the meantime I asked about where I might find a hotel to stay the night. He laughed again before pointing to a sign in the distance.

It was obvious that the people of Polite had spared no expense in furnishing their hotel. There was a wonderfully manicured garden in the front, sculpted and tiered in various hues of green, with pastel floral accents. The path to the front door of the cottage-style office was of polished cobblestone.

The office itself was elegant, adorned with rich, handcrafted furniture and exquisite art. The walls were paneled with dark wood, guiding eyes toward two prominently displayed authentic Jackson Pollock paintings. Tea roses; I remember the spicy scent of freshly cut tea roses. The smooth marble counter was a burnt sienna color, with chocolate brown veins running throughout. The office seemed completely deserted, so I reached over and rang the bell.

"Thank you so much for visiting us here in Polite. Do you like our hotel?"

She was a stunning young creature with soft, brown doe-like eyes. At once, I sensed a pristine innocence and passion in her that I had never encountered outside the leather confines that bound the Bronte heroines. She could have been a young Jane or Catherine. I reflected longingly: Serendipadoo?

She told me her name was Fawn and that she was single, but looking. It was unnerving, actually. She was holding my hand, stroking my palm with her index finger. I glanced over my shoulder after gazing into her yearning eyes, certain she was coming on to someone behind me, but we were alone. A single phrase kept going through my head: *If it seems too good to be true, then it probably is.*

Freud supplied the lubrication.

"We need to get a room."

I was mortified.

"I mean I need to get a room. I need to get a room here, for the night."

She giggled.

"Don't be silly. This is the Polite Hotel all right, but no visitor to town has ever actually *stayed* here, not for the last 75 years at least, not since the New York Times published an article calling us 'the friendliest small town in the world.'"

She reached out and gently caressed my face.

"Now what would that look like? A stranger having to stay all by himself in a big, lonely hotel? That has *never* happened in the friendliest small town in the world until now, and it won't happen tonight. We'd risk losing our title. It's settled. You're coming home with me. I'll make you a delicious dinner and then I'll draw you a nice hot bath."

Several of the townsfolk stopped Fawn and me and congratulated her as we walked down Main Street toward her quaint little cottage. Others thanked her for keeping the town's reputation intact. The mayor winked at me impishly, whispering that I was in for the night of my life.

You seem to be drooling a little there. *You* want to know what happened when we got to her house, don't you? All in good time. I was a little anxious myself, but then I remembered my ex-wife. She was expecting me in Kansas

City that day or that night. I could not in good conscience enjoy an evening and night with this intriguing young goddess creature knowing that my very plain ex-wife was languishing in some strange, daunting hovel in Kansas City, crying the blues.

"Can I use your phone?"

A minute later, I was livid.

"What do you mean she's gone? I was coming to get her. I came all the way from San Francisco!"

The hotel clerk in Kansas City told me my ex got tired of waiting. He said she found courage at the bottom of a scotch bottle and had flown home to Los Angeles two days earlier.

I sat on the porch with my face in my hands, struggling to deal with equal feelings of outrage, hurt, disappointment and self-loathing. What had I been thinking? I should have known better. Once a sucker, always a sucker! So now, what the hell was I doing in Kansas?

"Dinner's ready."

It wasn't all bad. My inner turmoil dissipated instantly when I watched Fawn's firm rump wiggle as she slipped back into the house. She had changed into short shorts and a tiny top. Her narrow, sculptured waist was bare and sexy. Her legs were shapely and incredibly smooth. I followed, entranced.

Candles flickered on the dining table. On a lacy white tablecloth, there were a wine bottle, wineglasses, plates, silver and linen napkins. Smiling, Fawn poured the libation.

"It's a marvelous White Zinfandel from California. You ever try this one? The clerk at the A&P said it's probably the finest in the world."

White Zinfandel? And for a fleeting moment I thought she was pouring wine. I sat in silence for a while, weighing my response. In the basic compendium of Wine Law, it was one of the principal commandments: *Thou shalt not partake of the White Zin, not even to curry favor with crude though beautiful young women.*

Otherwise, White Zin was an insider's joke, an opportunity to discreetly lampoon the buffoon uncivilized enough to order it on any given occasion. I was glad no one but Fawn could see me as I raised the glass to my lips and sipped the toxic liquid. My mouth was literally numb.

"Yeth, White Zinfanthel. Delithious."

And that was the beginning of the end for me. Under the influence of that vulgar brew, I fell victim to her charms, completely unaware that her tender trap was set, aroused and ready.

Okay, so even before we could finish dinner, she stood and slinked over to me. When she put her mouth on mine, I was still chewing my steak, so she used her tongue deftly to extract the tasty morsel and eat it right out of my mouth. No one had ever done that to me before.

Her hand in my lap expertly measured and gauged distance, angles and girth, though the landscape down there was changing rapidly. Fawn had proven her unique ability when eating the meat from my mouth, but her lingual prowess was not limited to steak. It may have been a reaction to the White Zin, but what she did next with her mouth to my neck and ear lobe was nothing short of remarkable. Abruptly, she stopped.

"Your bath! I said I'd draw you a nice hot bath. Come on."

No one had ever washed me the way she did that night, not at least for free. No, it's not what you're thinking. It happened in a hospital. My insurance paid for the stay. Anyway, as she washed my back, my shoulders and my hair, I could feel the stress slipping away. She supplied more of the White Zin, which I drank, though it was as awful as ever.

As I swallowed I distinctly remember thinking of Adam and Eve and the original sin. Fawn was Eve, I was Adam and the White Zin—the White Zin was the forbidden fruit. She was causing me to sin! Eve was deceived, but Adam was seduced. I stood, putting it all together in my mind.

"Frailty, thy name is Woman!"

"Don't be silly. It's *Fawn Oliver*."

The serpentine A&P clerk had deceived the woman, and using all the feminine guile she could muster, Fawn had seduced me into sinning along with her. My eyes had become open, and suddenly I realized I was naked.

Not that I didn't realize I was naked before. I was taking a bath, after all. But when a man has clothes on and a woman applies the feminine muster, his pants have a tendency of hiding and suppressing his... his uh, interest and intent. You know what I mean. But naked men are honest men. So seizing upon my interest, she unabashedly poured more of the White Zin down my throat.

The very thought traumatizes me even now. I can still see it. I drank the White Zin right from that bottle. No decent human being would ever drink wine from a bottle. And though White Zin is technically not really wine, I drank from a wine bottle nonetheless. Little did I know that Fawn was getting me drunk in order to take advantage of me.

Still seizing on my intent, she, like one of Lot's daughters, dragged me to her bedroom where I'm sure she continued to seduce me to the natural conclusion. I don't completely remember the night because I, uh, I passed out. All I know is when I awoke in the morning, she was nude as she snuggled up next to me. She held me tight when I tried to stir, and she whispered the three words.

"I love you."

I was shocked. I mean, she was so young and I had only met her the day before. And after only one night she was telling me she loved me? Though my head was pounding, I managed to tell her it was impossible for her to love me. I told her she knew nothing about me. I even brought up our age difference.

With great passion, she told me age didn't matter. She told me knowing me didn't matter. She said it was like she had known me forever. She told me I was simply the best lover she had had, that I had taken her to Heaven and Hell and everywhere in between the night before.

She told me my sexy body and my *je ne sais quoi* or whatever inspired love and demanded jealousy. She told me my ex-wife was a fool to let me get away (which I already knew). Then she held me tight, kissed me gently and told me again how much she loved me. Now I didn't remember what I did the night before, but I am a pretty good lover you know, so I wasn't surprised. I might not look like much, but I *am* a pretty incredible lover in bed.

After I showered, I went to see Clyde at Friendly Automotive. He made me breakfast and asked if I wanted to go fishing with him. When I asked about my car, he said he had ordered the part, but he had bad news. As it turns out, when he and his friend went out to drag my car to town, it was missing.

"Either the Highway Patrol got it, or some kids from a town up the road called Plain got it and went joyridin. It'll turn up. They *always* do."

"Waitaminute," I said, "How could they go joyriding in my car? It doesn't work."

Kissup laughed again.

"Ya don't know them Plain kids. Born mechanics! When we find it, it might be fixed, might even be tuned up an washed. I swear them kids got cars in their blood. Let's go fishin."

I should have known by the name, Throwback Lake, that Clyde was one of those confused guys who spent thousands of dollars on a boat and equipment and countless hours on lakes only to catch fish and then just let them go back in the water.

But these were the biggest bass I had ever seen in my life. They were monsters, and they were practically jumping into the boat. I didn't have a rod and reel, so Clyde loaned me one of his. You should have seen me. Within five minutes, I had hooked into a gigantic lunker that had to be at least ten pounds or more. I must have fought with the fish for over 15 minutes before I finally got it in the boat. Then began the resentment that was so evident from the townsfolk at the trial!

"Serendipadoo! Hold it up. I'll take a picture of you with it so you can get it back in the water."

It was the biggest bass I had ever seen, let alone caught.

"No Kissup, I'm not throwing *this* one back. I'm taking this fish home."

He politely argued with me for about five minutes until I, in moment of sheer frustration, took a small pair of cutting pliers, raised the leviathan's gill covers and snipped one of its gills. Deep red blood spurted wildly, spraying my shirt, my face and my hands. Jerking, the monstrous fish arched its huge body and gently relinquished its life.

"It's dead now, Clyde. Now I *have* to keep it."

Clyde was civil, though I could tell he was perturbed with me for keeping the fish. In fact, I knew it when he uncorked a nearly full bottle of White Zin, pulled two glasses from his satchel and filled only one. Not that I *wanted* a glass of that dreadful keg bottom brew, but I resented the fact that he didn't at least *offer* me a glass. I mean he was from the "Friendliest Small Town in the World," after all. There was no water in the boat, and my throat was getting dry.

"Uh, Clyde? Would you mind too terribly much if I had a glass of your, you know that pink stuff in the bottle?"

He wouldn't even glance at me.

"What you done ta that fish was just plain mean. Far as I'm concerned, it's nothin shorta murder. Now I'd love ta pour ya a glass of this godly nectar, but I can't bring myself ta drink with your type. We'll be home in an hour. You can wait till then."

That's when I realized at least one person in Polite wasn't everything the town was chalked up to be. Clyde was polite as ever, yeah, but he was fine letting me thirst to death in the hot sun. I was forced to sit and watch him sipping that ice-cold White Zin. I remember even lusting after that pitiful concoction. I must have been delirious.

I had forgotten that the fish had sprayed blood all over me, so as I walked through town back to Fawn's house, gore oozing from the bass's gills, I got stares and double takes from Polite people that ranged from mild surprise to terror. I didn't care that people crossed the street to avoid walking by me, I didn't mind that parents were shielding their children's eyes as they passed, and it didn't even bother me when the geeky reporter took the picture. I was parched.

Suffering from extreme thirst, I had lost all shame. I was given to turpitude as my thoughts became vile and immoral. I craved it, I imagined it, I lusted after it. I knew Fawn would be waiting for me, probably wearing something very sexy. I knew she would give it to me anywhere I wanted it: in the kitchen, in the bathroom, in the bedroom, and any *way* I wanted it: from a glass, from a bottle, or from a shoe if I asked. And I knew she had it, plenty of it. She had run out and bought a case at the A&P just that morning.

Yeah, I had no shame. I'll admit it: I craved that White Zin like nothing I've ever craved in my life. It didn't matter that it was a rock gut wine substitute or that the residual sugar in it masked the fact that it was made from the lowest quality grapes with absolutely no winemaking skill or technique. I *wanted* it.

She stopped me at the front door.

"You can come on in and clean up, but you can't bring that bloody fish in here."

"But I caught it for you."

"Don't matter. You can't bring that dead thing in here, period, exclamation point. Throw it away. The garbage can's right there."

Well, as you can probably imagine, I was at a bit of a quandary. She was telling me to throw the biggest bass I had ever seen in my life in the garbage. It was a perfectly good fish—a trophy.

"Throw it away, and I'll pour you a nice cold glass of White Zin."

With great shame, I'm sad to admit, I sinned against nature by tossing that magnificent work of God into the trashcan. It was a despicable sin that would come back to damn me.

I had finished the bottle before my senses began to return, but then my senses re-blurred as I began to suffer from the effects of the alcohol. By this time, Fawn was sitting in my lap, pouring the poison as fast as I could drink it. My mind was lost in Kansas, but my stomach retained its Californian sense of propriety. It rumbled in angry protest for being force-fed the sully, rose-colored wine imitation.

"I'm hungry. What's for dinner?"

She kissed my forehead, topped off my glass and answered.

"Fish, soon as I can fry it."

I awoke three hours later with a pounding headache and a roiling stomach. Fawn was naked in the bed next to me, smiling with great satisfaction. Her young body was so soft and voluptuous. I wanted her, but my head seemed ready to split open for the throbbing pain. Then I heaved, nearly throwing up in the spicy-scented bed. Fawn's forearm across my chest prevented me from sitting up.

"Where're you going? Don't leave me."

She began kissing my neck.

"I mean, you were so incredible earlier. No one's ever pleasured me like that in all my life."

I was thoroughly confused.

"Did we do it?"

"Oh, over and over! You were awesome."

Her feelings seemed hurt.

"You mean you don't *remember*?"

"Of course I do. You were, you were really good too."

It bothered me that I didn't remember. No, it made me angry. After all, I was doing this incredibly hot young woman. I was rocking her world, apparently, and I wasn't remembering it. I knew I was quite talented, but I wanted to know what I was *doing* to her. My intestines spasmed.

"And we had dinner, right?"

"Fish may have been bad. Smelled a little funny when I was cookin it. I don't think it was especially fresh. It was a carp. I didn't eat any."

Yeah, the woman fed me a rotten goldfish when there was a perfectly fresh bass in the trashcan.

"How much did I eat?"

"Three good helpins."

I heaved again. I had to get up.

"Why are you putting on your clothes? Where're you goin?"

"I need to get some fresh air. I need to go for a walk."

In truth, my bowels felt ready to explode, but I'm a very modest man. The bathroom was right next to her bedroom, but earlier in the day she had taken the door off the hinges to paint it. It hadn't been replaced, so the toilet was in full view from the bed. Straining, I lurched to stave off the abdominal contractions, determined not to use the bathroom in her presence.

"Are you okay? What's wrong with your face? You're actin strange."

I walked the walk. You know the walk, when you gotta go. My shoulders were scrunched, left shoulder slightly dipped, my back was arched; my butt muscles were in a state of contraction as I limped down her walkway to the sidewalk. I was in pain. I saw dark spots swimming before my eyes, like bass. No, like damn carp!

The one gas station in town was closed. The one coffee shop—closed. The drug store—closed. The entire place was dark. There wasn't a toilet in sight. I remember, at that precise moment, I realized that historians had probably taken for granted how profoundly the irritated bowel had probably shaped world events.

Thuclydides focused on the genius of Themistocles, on the Greek strategy of employing Triremes in the water battle and the lavish sacrifices to the gods before the battle of Salamis. But he may not have mentioned, or perchance he didn't *know* the crews of the Persian ships may have been suffering from the scourge of diarrhea or gas, intestinal complications that could literally take the wind out of an army. *My kingdom for a toilet!* I was miserable, as *you* would have been in my situation.

I wandered around the small town for about 30 minutes, knocked over three trashcans and set off several choruses of dog barking before I realized I would have to venture to the outskirts of town to relieve myself.

I had never done it outdoors before, but I had heard stories and I had seen dogs and cats do it hundreds of times. Fingers fumbling along the rock wall at the edge of town, I pried out a wide, flat piece of limestone I figured I'd fashion as a digging instrument.

Crawling through the low hanging boughs of a huge black oak tree, I found a small clearing and in it I scraped out a depression in the humus. Needless to say, I exited those branches greatly relieved, though I felt a little unclean.

Walking sprightly, I felt like a new man, and then I thought of Fawn. I had spent two nights with her. I remember thinking it was a little unfair: during those nights, she had had all the fun. The way she described it, I had ruined her for any other man—no man would ever come close to pleasing her as well as I had. But for me, I was foggy about those nights. I don't completely remember what I did, though I know I'm a natural. I figured I was probably better on automatic pilot than most men were at their best. It wasn't fair. I wanted something I could savor too.

All my previous malaise had passed from me to the oak tree, so I felt better than ever. I felt like jumping in the air and clicking my heels, and yet I was thinking of a much more pleasurable physical activity. If Fawn thought I was incredible before, she was in for the ride of her life. I planned it out in my head: I was going to go in, take a shower, refuse all offers of White Zin and take Fawn to a level of ecstasy no woman of Earth has known before.

"Come to daddy!"

Apparently he had come in when I was in the shower. All I know is I had left Fawn on the bed, in a sexy negligee and heels, eagerly awaiting my return. But when I, completely naked, wiped the water from my face with the bath towel, the sheriff was standing in the room and Fawn had put on a robe. His affected smile was an uncomfortable mask, sitting askew on a face that held deep concern. Quickly, I covered myself, speaking to Fawn.

"It's, it's one in the morning. What's he doing here?"

The man transferred his hat to his left hand so that he could extend his right.

"Sir, my name is Ben Kissup. Clyde is, or Clyde *was* my cousin. Would ya mind too much if I asked ya a few questions?"

Tucking the wrapped towel at my waist, I shook his hand. We all sat.

"Not at all. Is, is Clyde okay?"

He and Fawn exchanged an uncomfortable glance before he answered.

"No one's seen Clyde. Not since he went out fishin with *you*."

I wasn't sure if he was accusing me or if he was fishing himself.

"What? Do you think something *bad* happened to him?"

"Wife said he just never come home. That ain't like Clyde. Only way he wouldn't go home is if he *couldn't* go home."

He pointed to my shirt on the dresser.

"I couldn't help but notice all the blood on your shirt there. Mattera fact, few folks in town said they noticed you was real bloody comin back from the lake this afternoon. I'm sure you have a good explanation for that."

It sounded like an accusation to me, albeit polite.

"It was bass blood. Waitaminute, are you trying to suggest that maybe I *killed* Clyde or something?"

He raised his hands.

"No, not at all. I'm very, very sorry if I made it sound like that. No one's accusin ya here."

He bowed his head, humbly.

"It's just that, well, you was the last person that saw im. An we was jus hopin that maybe ya'd help us out a little. Maybe ya could come down ta the station an talk ta us.

Maybe give us a clue or two about what mighta happened ta him."

"Are you arresting me?"

He laughed.

"No Sir. You're jus comin ta the station with me. No handcuffs. Ya can ride right in the front of the car with me. And it ain't no police car. It's the car I take ma family ta church in every Sunday mornin."

Fawn sat down beside me, took my face in her hands and kissed me.

"Can't do no harm goin down to the station. He's just worried about his cousin is all. I'll be here all dressed up an waitin for you when you come back."

I sighed aloud. I could *feel* it. How many times in my life had I defied my better judgment? I should have refused. I should have called a lawyer, but Kissup and Fawn were so nice that I just sorta went along with things.

Ben gave me the unofficial tour of Polite on the way down for questioning. He took me by the old train station, by the cemetery, by old man Kent's mansion and over to his grandmother's house where his relatives were keeping a vigil, waiting for news about Clyde. Ben was the Sheriff, so the building he occupied doubled as the county jail, only the jail didn't seem like a jail at all.

"Why don't you have cells or bars?"

"Cuz bars, they're kinda confinin. Doors an bedrooms are just fine. Sides that, we haven't arrested no one in this county in over 60 years, but we got the rooms fixed up real nice case we do."

The inside of the jail looked like an upscale three bedroom penthouse, with the bedrooms serving as holding cells. The lush carpet in the living area was cream-colored. A chocolate brown Italian leather sofa and a matching love seat dominated the main living area where they sat before an 80-inch television screen. The stereo could be set for surround sound and was programmed to play separate channels in the individual bedrooms. There was a beautiful palm by the southern-exposed bay window and a luxuriant ficus along a wall by the kitchen. The refrigerator was stocked with fresh fruit, deli meats, breads and a whole shelf of White Zin.

Ben answered the ringing phone, glancing over his shoulder while whispering something, and he excused himself into the bathroom. When he came out, he was tucking his shirt in his pants. Looking up, he narrowed his deeply set brown eyes and crossed his arms.

"Would ya care ta comment about the 'plethora' of blood they found in Clyde's boat? An that's what the forensic detective called it—'a plethora of blood,' in the boat."

How many times did I have to tell him it was bass blood? Fish blood!

"It's like I told you earlier. Of course there was blood. I clipped the gills. I did the gill thing. The blood spurted all over the place."

He looked at me like I was some sadistic serial murderer.

"Did ya realize what would happen if ya cut im?"

"Of course I did."

I was beginning to get the sense that ol Ben was a little obtuse.

"Did you realize that'ld kill im?"

"Of *course* I did. I meant to kill him! I've done it plenty of times before."

Once again he narrowed his eyes, nodding his head.

"Ah ha! So ya meant ta kill him an that's exactly what ya did."

He was a moron, an idiot!

"Yeah, I was tired of Clyde arguing with me about it, so I got mad and just did it. He was dead in a few seconds."

"An what did ya do with the body?"

"I threw it in the garbage."

"Uh-huh."

He walked to the door and locked it. He shrugged, smiling.

"I'm sorry I hafta do this. But sir, ya have the right ta remain silent. Anythang ya say or do can be used against ya in the courta law."

"So you're *arrestin* me?"

"Ya have the right ta an attorney."

Yeah, he arrested me. He arrested me for killing a bass, though at the time, I didn't realize he had been *taping* our conversation. And so he went about explaining all the house rules to me. I couldn't have company unless it was approved, I couldn't talk on the phone without permission, I could watch television only two hours a day unless it was sports, though I couldn't watch R-rated movies at any time. I could go out for 90 minutes each day, but I had to tell him where I was going, and I had to be back on time. I had to be in bed by 11:00 with the lights off and oh, I had to do chores—clean my bathroom, wash and fold my laundry on Mondays, vacuum on Wednesdays, stuff like that. Ben said he always washed the dishes and took out the garbage.

I remember scanning the seeming bachelor pad and thinking the people of Polite, Kansas were a big joke. *"Friendliest Small Town in the World,"* my ass! And so that's how I was arrested, in a manner unlike an arrest in any other place in the world, except Polite of course. I could barely tell it even happened.

As it turns out, no one in Polite could remember anyone ever being arrested before in the history of the town. Old man Kent said he thought he had a grandmother who thought she remembered a man being arrested in 1921 for bootlegging, though she wasn't sure if it had happened in Polite or in nearby Plain.

I know this because the local newspaper, *The Polite Whisper*, ran a front-page story about me and about the arrest in the paper the next morning. The caption read, "Under Arrest." A reporter and a photographer had come over less than an hour after Ben Kissup arrested me. They brought cognac, croissants and warm cashews. The photo session lasted two hours and the interview went on for six. Never before in my life had anyone been so interested in me.

By the next morning, a great crowd of curious Polite residents had assembled outside the building. Initially, I worried that it was the beginning of a lynch campaign. I imagined being burned at the stake or being dragged behind a pickup truck or something, but my fears were quickly allayed when visiting hours began.

My first caller was Ben's daughter, Dido. She brought breakfast fixings: eggs, bacon, avocados, smoked salmon, sour cream, potatoes, English muffins, orange juice and coffee. She also brought a suitcase. She said her father had assigned her to stay with me full-time because he had to attend to job duties elsewhere. I nearly melted when she smiled.

"Looks like we'll be roomies. I'll be right next to you. There will only be a wall between us."

Dido was 25, attractive and educated. Dressed in a deep violet business skirt suit, she could easily have stepped right from the pages of *Vogue* or *Woman's Day*. We hit it off instantly. In fact, she had graduated from San Francisco State. We had visited a few of the same places and had crossed some of the same bridges even.

After she had cleaned the table and washed dishes, she asked if I had time to talk to a few people on the visitor's list. I agreed to the visits, but I asked her to hold off until I could finish reading the story about me in the paper.

It was an enormously flattering article, really. The writer described my parents and what they did, he talked about my birth and about my siblings, he detailed my educational history and he even told about my connections with Hollywood and the show business industry. The tampon commercials I wrote at Acme had gone nationwide, after all.

Toward the end of the story, there was a bit about Clyde Kissup and his disappearance. One of Ben's detectives said he had found a large amount of blood in the abandoned boat. He and divers would be exploring the bottom of Throwback Lake in an attempt to locate Clyde's butchered body. One of Fawn's neighbors recalled a stranger roaming the town on the night of Clyde's demise. Other townsfolk recalled dogs barking and a sinister figure that walked past the rock wall at the edge of the city, only to return after about 30 minutes.

My second visitor was a 12-year-old boy called Sonny. He had brought a camera and asked if he could have his picture taken with me, something Dido was kind enough to do. He asked if I knew Capone, Dillinger and Don Corleone, and then he asked if I knew Bonnie and Clyde. He said I was the first gangster he had ever met and insisted he wanted to grow up to be just like me. I didn't know what to say. I'm not a ganster, but I didn't want to hurt his feelings, and so I gave him my autograph anyway. I called myself "The Gill."

The next person who came in was supposedly "the prettiest girl in the friendliest small town in the world." Maybe her parents saw it coming, because her name was Vanity. She really was pretty, though she had an agenda. It wasn't my imagination, I assure you, but she suggested right away that we go into my bedroom so that I could do to her whatever I wanted in exchange for an introduction to Spielberg. And yet, before I could even respond to the invitation, Dido threw the young woman out.

I had time for one more visit before my scheduled massage with Dido, who had taken classes in San Francisco. Sly Placido was the owner of Sly Motors, the only auto dealer in town. He came with a lawyer and an offer: he was prepared to pay me $15,000 and give me a slightly used car in exchange for a television commercial endorsement.

It seemed like a pretty good deal, so I looked over the contract and signed. However, when the television ad aired two days later, my name did not appear in text on the screen like Sly's did. On the screen beneath my image was the bold title "The Gill, Famous Gangster." They dressed me in a dark, pinstripe zoot suit, slapped a hat on my head and stuck a violin case in my hand even.

In the meantime, a steady stream of gawking, fawning visitors arrived daily to look at me, to offer words of encouragement and to add their comments to the next morning's newspaper story about me. I was the main daily feature. According to one anonymous insider, I got the name "The Gill" from the way I slashed the necks of my victims.

And I would kill anyone audacious enough to call me by my real name.

"Poor Clyde!" the man commented, "but he had a temper. I always told him ta mind his temper. Probably called The Gill by his real name. I'm sure The Gill didn't really wanna *kill* im. But it's some kinda gangster honor thing. The Gill had ta send him ta sleep with the fishees once he said it."

And this was a guy who had never visited me at the condo. Oh, and there was another one: I was the government's number two choice when they were trying to hire a hit man to take out Saddam Hussein. The woman who offered that one, in the most complimentary of terms, extolled me for being "a very loyal American who is obviously respected by the government."

The one this morning was totally ridiculous. I can't believe they printed it: someone said they heard I was the actual shooter in the Kennedy assassination—as if I could be that old. And yet, everything they wrote and said about me was done in a spirit of kindness. It was as if they all admired me. I was a bona fide celebrity in Polite.

What? Who? Oh, *you* want to know about Dido Kissup? Funny that you should mention her! How did you know? Did I give it away? Okay, yes. All that time we were spending together, all the hot oil massages, all that White Zinfandel in the refrigerator—I should have known from the beginning that something was going to happen.

You see, I'm not exactly *slow* on the uptake. I knew what was going on. I knew the White Zin was the reason for all my problems since I had been in Polite. That is, I thought then, if you could *really* call them problems.

You see, there I was, in the nicest condo I could ever imagine, living with a totally hot, younger woman who had incredible... hands. My picture was in the newspaper every day, people brought me wonderful gifts and kids dressed themselves to look like me. Nubile, beautiful women came on to me, and within one week, I had earned over $35,000 for product endorsements. I was a star. I was at the top of my game. I was the king of the world!

Oh, I'm sorry. I got a little carried away. Back to the story. It all started one night as Dido sat at the dining room table. Since the very first night, she had sat in that same place at the same time. She always lit two candles, put on a jazz CD, poured two glasses of White Zin and sat staring at the flickering flames. I wondered if one of the glasses was for me, but I wasn't sure.

So one night, about seven days after the arrest, my curiosity got the better of me. I stood by the table, clearing my throat, but she wouldn't look up. I couldn't tell whether or not she was crying, so I quietly slid into the chair across from her.

"Does this seat belong to the person you're thinking about?"

She laughed.

"I *was*, I was remembering an old flame. Is it that obvious?"

Nearly mistaking it for wine, I almost grabbed the glass for a sip. After recoiling, I began seriously.

"I think it's glaringly obvious that you don't belong here."

"Where? In here, with you? Or in Polite?"

"In Polite, of course. You're not like the rest of the people here."

She smiled, sipping from her glass.

"That's because I've lived in San Francisco. Gotta few Kissups there too."

In the flickering light of the darkened room, I realized for the first time how truly lovely Dido was. Her eyes were dark and intense; her complexion was smooth and clear; her shapely body seemed firm; and she exuded unmistakable sensuality. Because I had spent the past week at close quarters with her, I was becoming attracted to her.

But then, I thought of Fawn and that tragically forlorn look on her face when Ben took me away. She said she'd wait for me... in the negligee and high heels. I imagined her still sitting there, still wanting me, still needing me, crying her little doe-like eyes out.

That's why I reacted so ambiguously when Dido leaned over and kissed me on the mouth. I objected angrily. Dido was beautiful, but I didn't want to kiss her, though my lips did. I didn't want to do anything with her, though parts of my body did. But I had to be loyal to Fawn. Backing, Dido seemed surprised and disappointed.

"I'm, I'm sorry. I just thought that... What? Is there someone else?"

"Yes there is. I'm sorry."

"Do you love her?"

I stood, flattening the front of my shirt with my hands. I suppose I sounded a little defensive.

"Well yes, I think I do. I mean, of *course* I do?"

Tears in her eyes, she shrugged.

"Just my luck. I know this is going to sound incredibly sophomoric of me, but I've actually fallen for you over this past week. I had thought I would never love again, that I'd come here to Polite to waste away as a spinster in the friendliest small town in the world. I never imagined someone like you would come along. I fell in *love* with you."

I was taken aback by her honesty. In my experience, honesty and ovaries just don't go together.

"Really?"

"Yes."

She smiled.

"This is going to sound even sillier, but I had planned on seducing you tonight. I was going to try to make it the most sensual night of your life, the first of many, I hoped. I've spent years studying and perfecting a range of Kama-sutra techniques. You know, I haven't been with a man in three years, so I'm extremely horny, and I wanted you so bad. I even bought sexy lingerie, perfume, whipped cream and hot tea, the works."

Her voice broke as the tears began.

"And then, just as I was about to give you my heart, my soul and my burning, aching, starving body, you tell me you're in love with someone else. So once again, my heart is crushed."

I reached for the White Zin and took a huge swig to cool a sudden warm feeling that was coming on. She really did have a wonderful body. Her gown fell open as she walked over to the couch and sat. She looked exactly like one of those airbrushed photos from Playboy magazine. Not that I've ever *read* that magazine, but I saw a picture once, or twice. Okay, maybe more. Anyway, she was crying.

"What is it? Am I *that* undesirable?"

For some reason, unbeknownst to my brain, my shivering right hand was pouring me a second glass of the pink stuff. She was so hot! Why hadn't I noticed it before! And she wanted *me*? I pulled out my shirttail to hide my... elevated interest as I walked over to the couch.

"That's not it at all. I think you are *very* desirable."

"But you don't want me. You love someone else."

Me and my big mouth! Somehow, Fawn didn't mean as much to me in that moment. You should have seen Dido sprawled on that couch! Her legs, her waist her... hands! She had incredible hands!

"I'm not married. I'm not even close."

"Yeah, but I know how you are. When *you* love someone, you're extremely loyal. You're an honorable man who wouldn't *think* about cheating. That's what I totally love about you."

She stood.

"And now I feel silly. I feel really stupid. Here I poured out my heart to you. I told you how much I wanted to have sex with you, I told you about the chocolate sauce raspberry fantasy and you already have someone. I should have known!"

Chocolate sauce raspberry fantasy? Somehow I hadn't remembered her mentioning that.

"I better go. I'm so embarrassed."

Tears in her eyes, she went about collecting up her belongings. She moved quickly as I stood in one place. I was still pondering the chocolate sauce raspberry fantasy. So before I knew it, she had her suitcase and she was at the door.

"Where, where are you going?"

She pursed her pouting lips and took a deep breath to build resolve.

"I'm smitten and I can't stay here. It would be torture to me."

"No, no! Don't go! I'm sorry. We can work this *out!*"

She walked out the open doorway, wagging her head.

"No, *I'm* sorry. This coulda been the start of a beautiful friendship. I'm goin over to Plain to waste the rest of my life away."

And that was it. She left just like that. She must have called her father to inform him of her decision, because he was there the next morning.

"Ya know Gill, the way Dido went on an on bout cha, I thought for sure I was gonna have ya for a son-in-law."

"You know my name. Why do you call me Gill?"

He laughed.

"Well, ya know Gill, after what happened ta Clyde after he called ya by yer name, I don't think anyone in this town wants ta take any chances."

I didn't get it. Did *everyone* in Polite really think I was some kinda gangster murderer?

"Look Ben, I realize Clyde was your cousin and all, but I didn't *kill* him. I don't know what happened to him, but it had nothing to do with me."

"Ya already admitted it on tape, Gill. Sappose ya were just doin what underworld people like you do when someone crosses the line an says their name. I'll admit, I was really sore at you at first for 'clippin Clyde's gills,' as ya call it, but then I realized folks like you live by a code. Clyde shoulda known better. He probably egged ya on, and then he made the fatal mistake of callin ya by yer real name."

I literally looked around for the cameras. I thought for sure that I'd stepped into an episode from the *Twilight Zone* series.

"For the hundredth time, Ben, and I'll say it slowly so even you can comprehend: I-did-not-have-*anything*-to-do-with-Clyde-Kissup's-disappearance!"

Ben seemed a little confused by the slowness of my speech and my exaggerated enunciation.

"Well, I guess that's what y'all folks are supposed ta do when yer accused by the law. You'll get yer chance to make up a defense and threaten jurors and whatever else yer used ta doin when the murder trial begins on Monday. The court already appointed ya an attorney. He'll be here tomorra. They say he's the best defense lawya in the county. We got cha the best, but what else would ya expect ta happen in the friendliest small town in the world?"

"A trial?"

That's when I realized that the visit by an overly friendly judge a day earlier had somehow amounted to an arraignment. He looked like an older version of Danny Glover, I thought, and he brought brandy, so I figured it was just another visit by one of my fans.

But I started thinking about it later. The pretty girl who came in with him and sat in the corner with the dictaphone must have been the court recorder... and the middle-aged woman who came in with papers, the triple quarter-pounder, the super-sized order of fries, the super-sized diet coke and the super-sized butt must have been the clerk. Ben came that day, probably as the bailiff.

The judge had asked a few general questions about the day Clyde and I went fishing on Throwback Lake. In passing he had asked if "clipping gills" was something I had done much of, and I answered, "not much." I said I did it only when I needed to settle one down in a hurry.

The judge, and I found out later that his name was Knott, Judge Knott seemed like a normal guy, so I was sure he was talking about fishing. But no wonder he seemed so appalled when I said laughing, "you should have seen the look on Clyde's face when I actually did it!"

Now you're looking at me like *I'm* obtuse, but I'm not really, and I wasn't back then. It's just that up until that moment, and that is the moment Ben told me about the upcoming murder trial, I hadn't taken the whole situation seriously. I mean, I knew I hadn't *killed* anyone. I was sure it was just some crazy misunderstanding fueled by the paranoia of the bizarre people of the world's friendliest small town.

But a murder trial and its potential consequences? Reality had just taken a super-sized bite outa my ass. In that moment I realized that even though we try to duck, dodge and escape to places like Polite, the flaws of our characters will always find us, test us and ultimately undo us unless we somehow learn to conquer them.

Nervously, I spoke to Ben.

"You were saying something about a lawyer?"

He seemed distracted, definitely irritated.

"Ya know, ya really hurt my, my little girl by rejectin her the way ya did. She's been through so much, California an all. Hell, I was ready ta forgive all and be your father-in-law."

I could hardly believe my eyes. Ben Kissup was actually crying.

"Now I don't know what your girl back home in San Francisco's got goin for her, but I'll bet you can't find a prettier, nicer and more decent person than my, my Dido."

Girl in San Francisco? There was no girl in San Francisco! I never said that. I just figured Ben and the whole town knew that I was involved with Fawn, that she and I were an item.

After all, she was wearing that sexy negligee and those pumps when Ben arrested me from her bedroom. And Fawn, I figured she was pining away for me, telling the whole community how much she loved me and wanted to marry me. I figured she was making women envious with stories about how incredible I was in bed. I just thought everyone in Polite would know Fawn was my *girl*!

But just then it hit me. I had had maybe 30 or 40 visitors since my arrest. I had taken perhaps 200 phone calls. But just then I realized that Fawn had never come by. She

had never even called. Not that it hadn't crossed my mind
before. I just figured she was so in love that it just would have
been too painful to come out and see me in detention. And I
figured she hadn't called because she had sunken into a
miserable grotto of depression. It couldn't have been any
other way.

Maybe it was the way Ben alluded to some girl in San
Francisco, but right then I was struck with the most profound
thought: what if I was wrong about Fawn?

With new doubts beginning to germinate, I didn't
dare tell Ben that the girl I rejected his daughter for was
Fawn, but I wanted to *know* about Fawn. Was I only
imagining that she was in love with me? That she was pining
away for me?

"Hey Ben? You remember that first night you
arrested me? I was staying at this woman's house. What was
her name?"

As Ben grinned, chewing his wad of gum, he seemed
to be reveling in a very specific and sensual memory.

"Who, Fawn? Oh yeah, nice little woman there, that
Fawn."

At least he had memories; I clinched my teeth,
jealous for my lack thereof.

"Yeah, she's a very nice person. I stayed with her the
first night I came to town."

He winked and nodded his head, grinning even
bigger.

"Then *you* know what I'm talking bout!"

I felt duped, but maybe Fawn had changed since Ben
knew her in the way he was suggesting he did. I had to know.

"Yeah. Hey, do you think you could do me a favor,
Ben?"

He sighed, sat on the couch and crossed his leg.

"Oh sure. Anythang for the man I thought was gonna
be my son-in-law."

"I didn't get to say goodbye to Fawn when I left, and she seemed a little sad. Would you mind too much going by to check on her to see how she's doing?"

Now he was picking his teeth with an unfolded paper clip.

"Don't have to."

I was confused.

"Why's that?"

"Cuz I already know."

He cocked his head, lowering his tone.

"Day after I arrested ya at her place, nother fella come ta town lookin for a room at the hotel. Think he might be a professional basketball player or somethin, cuz he had these really big hands and really big feet, the biggest hands and the biggest feet I ever seen. I think Fawn liked that. He's been at her place ever since."

I was instantly jealous. I felt betrayed; I felt deceived. And what was it with the really big hands and really big feet thing? So *what* if he had really big hands and really big feet. So what! Was that supposed to imply that he had a really big... brain or something?

"Not that it means anything, Ben, but how, how big *were* his feet?"

Ben began with his palms together and spread them to indicate size—it looked like 14 or 15 inches. My heart dropped.

"You're exaggerating. They don't grow that big."

He nodded.

"I think I was actually underestimatin. Fawn told ma wife that after he took off his clothes, she measured. Had ta be at least 15 inches. That's standin up, of course, cuz naturally they're bigger that way."

So there you have it. Once again, I had leveraged my morality, some of my close-held values and my natural common sense for a woman who valued the size of a man's extremities over the content of his character. And at what price? Dido. For the first time in my miserable life I had met a woman who was more a sucker than I was, a woman who seemed to actually like me for me. And what had I done? Like the base Indian, I threw away a pearl richer than all the tribe.

Ben had put on an apron and was standing at the sink, doing the dishes.

"So what about your girl back home in San Francisco? Is she comin out for the murder trial an all?"

I just sank into the couch, wondering whether it would be Thalia or Melpomene who would write the ending to the ridiculous drama that had somehow snagged me. I felt sorry for the sick, demented audience out there that perhaps derived amusement or entertainment at my expense.

Why are you laughing? Don't tell me *you* think it's funny too. Hey, I'm going to be hanged tomorrow and you're sitting there smirking. It's not funny.

Just for that, this interview is over for today. If you want to hear the end of the story, you'll just have to come back tomorrow morning. Yeah, come back tomorrow morning, and I'll finish the story for you. That's the guard at the door anyway. Visiting hours are over.

Hey, you *will* come back tomorrow morning for sure, won't you? I really do want to finish the story. I want *someone* to know. I need someone to write it down. Here comes the guard. Goodbye for now.

THE LOVE TRAGEDIES

STORY TWO

HERE WRIT FOR THOSE WHO'VE TAKEN BAD ADVICE

For once upon a time within a very ancient world there lived a wise and handsome king, and in the morning of each day, this king with great discernment opened up his court to hear the problems of the world, that he, by wisdom e'er profound, might right the wrongs in his dominion.

As it was each day, his subjects traveled from remotest reaches of the earth, those from cavernous dwellings of vast mountainous retreat, and then those having intercourse with fertile earth, and then those parasites that lived on furious seas would come before the king to hear his words that their disputes might then be settled with impartial'ty.

Well now, there came before the king one day three men whose lives had been undone upon the Earth, who each had case against a hideous and wrinkled-bellied and foul-breathing vulture of a man who had not tooth within his rotting gums nor eyes within his head.

He sat on left of king with horrid face bowed low to earth. And *Woe is me!* he said, and as he reached to squash an oily bug within his hand that made a sudden snack, the many spiders and insects and worms that rode there in and on his flesh did battle for those bodily-made crevices that offered best abode. *Woe is the king! Woe is the World!*

On right side of the king there sat the three offended fellows, though less wretched than the older man, becoming sure like him.

And anger reigned in their expressions where the first could not hold up his head, that for his broken neck he carried head and face below his trembling lazy shoulders. Next the second creature there, with perm'nently-crossed eyes, sat shivering in fear while next the third sat naked on the earth and plucked off fleas and lice much like a mangy dog.

On seeing four like these before the throne so early in the day, the prudent king grew curious to hear the matter through, so to th'offended three he spoke.

"What is this matter here before the king? Who of you now professing you were wronged will be the first to set his case into mine ears?"

"I will," so spoke the first who could not see the king because he was broke-necked and thus could only see the lower reaches of the Earth.

"Speak!" so urged the king and then the first began:

"O great wise king! I was not always such a lazy broke-necked fellow as it seems I am, for I was once a happy man. And now I'll tell to you the tale of trickery and treachery as played on me by that vile fellow on your left...

"A baker I once was! Why surely you remember me! For several holy festivals you hosted in this very place I baked your royal feasts and was commended for it twice! The sweetened cakes you ate at your auspicious coronation were mine own. Enough of that!

"Well then, it happened that one day, as I was wandering alone in my deep thoughts of baking royal feasts, I stumbled on that creature there. He was upon the ledge of your great battlements, was thinking then to leap down to his death. And I, because my heart was good, I thought to teach him otherwise.

For *Woe is me!* he said, and *Woe is world!* said he.

I thought to mettle further, so (then speaking) "What is wrong?" I said. "What can this weighty matter be?"

'Tis wickedness, he said. *For I am far more wicked than a man can ever know. The world is wicked and the wicked world must die!* he spoke again as I scarce understood the speech. *And you are wicked too!* said he.

Now, knowing mine own self far better than he did, I answered him and said,

"I am no wicked man at all."

He looked so strangely with no eyes to flavour his expression while he said, *Who are you, man?* to which I did pronounce I was a baker who at times had pleased the king.

Then woe to you indeed for those poor trees! said he.

"Poor trees?" I said.

Yes trees! said he. *How is it that you fire your great ovens used to bake your bread and sweetened spicy meats?*

And for an only time I thought of it! "With wood from trees." I fin'lly said.

Yes trees! he did proclaim with anger showing on his eyeless face. *Young happy trees! Those full of life you butcher with your murderous axe. As you deserve a life, do not trees just as well deserve a life?*

"Why yes?" with some uncertainty I said while I began regretting all I'd done in selfishness.

How many trees have you thus killed? quoth he.

In truth I did not know, but then I lied to seem less guilty. "Only twenty-three," I said.

He thought a moment and pronounced a sentence there upon. *For twenty-three such murders you deserve now twenty-three odd deaths.*

And suddenly I realized how wicked I had been. With tears upon my face I sought to recompense my crimes.

"How can I right such twenty-three odd deaths with mine own life when I have only one to give? What should I do?" I said.

He thought again and spoke directly to me, saying thus, *Now you must leap headfirst from this grand battlement down to the earth one hundred feet below. Your neck will break and you will surely die.*

Somehow, his words seemed right to me, and so I leapt from that great battlement, and though I landed on my head, I broke my neck but did not die.

And now, as is so clear to see, I cannot raise my head above my shoulders here. And since that time I landed on my head and broke my neck I've found it difficult to bake! I am before the king a broke-necked knave for wicked counsel spoke by him that I accuse. I ask that he be put to death for all the evil he has put on me!"

Well then, the king sat thinking silent on his throne so that an hour passed before he spoke, and finally he cleared his throat and then began,

"I'll answer later that, but now what says this second fellow here? You there whose eyes are crossed—speak now or lose your turn!"

The second cross-eyed man rose to his feet and spoke to unseen other king beside the throne.

"Great king!" he said to empty space, "This is no ordinary man who's seated on your left. For look you closer— you will see a vile magician and a sorcerer.

"By spells and charms he lured me to demise. Hear me, and at my speech's end you have that villain torn apart from limb to limb. Thus I'll begin: I was not always cross-eyed as I am, but I was once a farmer known in all the world. Why certainly you know me well! My friend the baker bought my grain to bake your bread. And eggs, he bought mine eggs and lard and fruit and meats to make your pies!

"Well now, one day while I was walking by the sea, I came upon that man high on a lofty precipice, and he was staring o'er the craggy cliff, was ready to fall off.

"What's wrong?" I said. "If you do not draw back at once you'll surely fall into the sea!"

Then stay away and let me fall! said he, *since that is my desire.*

Well now, because my heart was good, his magic caught me quick. E'er since I was a boy I'd tarried in the field and had grew strong. It was no task for me to lift him from that perilous place to save his life.

Curse you, said he.

"Curse who?" I asked.

Curse you to save my life! For woe is me!

"Woe who?" demanded I, and he began.

I am a wicked man, more wicked than you know. It's time that I take leave of wicked world and you!

Now then, because my heart was vain, I wondered why he would take leave of me.

"Why me?" I asked, and then he smiled an evil toothless grin before he spoke.

Because you're evil!
I "evil?" said.
Yes evil too! said he. *What do you do?*
Well then I, being of proud occupation boasted of my work.

"I am a farmer of the best on earth," I said, "who grows his grain and fruit and raises tender meats for baking for the king!"

And evil too beyond compare! with bitterness he said. *Vile murderer you are! Do you not care to sell those children?*

"Children?' wondered I.

Yes they! said he, *The seeds are children of the grain and these you sell so they are crushed and ground for flour! Unmercifully!*

"And do you not eat bread?" I asked.

I never do, he said.

"But you kill vermin for your meals?" I spoke.

I do indeed, said he, *and that is why I'll jump with you to death from this high place.*

"Why should I jump?" I argued then.

For eggs and cherries too! said he. *You pluck ripe cherries from the trees! But have you ever thought how that must hurt?*

"Well no," I thought for once in life, but he said more.

To have your children plucked from you? And crushed for cherry pie! To think how that must feel! The pain! What misery!

"How terrible!" I sighed, though he would start with more.

And all those eggs, the families that you've stolen from those barren hens, and cracked or beat or boiled! To think if they were your own children cracked!

"How wicked!" then I cried. "How wicked I have been! What should I do?"

For then that fellow thought a moment there, and thus he spoke:

Because you cracked the grain and eggs and cherries too, you must jump from this cliff so that your head be cracked on rocks below, so that you die. Because I smash the insects that I eat, I'll also leap that I be smashed. Together we will fall. We'll fly at three.

And counting *three* I jumped, but he stood where he was. I fell six hundred feet, but, missing rocks, I fell into the evil sea. Incensed and angry that I missed the jagged rocks, the sea's cruel hand tossed me to them so that I cracked my skull but did not die.

And here I am cross-eyed; I now see two of everything. Thus all at once, I had two times as many weeds out in my fields, and all my problems have been doubled, and my fears! Mine enemies are twice as many as were wont! I'm far too sad and too perplexed to work and all because his magic injured me.

And so when I, head-broken on the rocks, looked up, I saw this wizard laugh aloud for witching my poor soul, and he was not alone! There then another fiend who looked like him was standing laughing too. And since that day I've been like this, wise king. Please tear him limb from limb for me, for you, for my dear friends, for all the world!

Then silent was the thoughtful king again. Another hour passed before he spoke.

"I've heard you and the first. Now I will hear the last and then decide what shall be done for all. Speak now your piece! "

The third rose quickly, for he was so badly plagued by ticks and biting fleas, and scratching itchy bloodied arms, he bowed before the king.

"O great wise king!" he said. "For surely you know me unlike you know the two who came before. You know I am your son, a prince, a sharer of your royal blood. Thus with authority of sovereign blood I say that is no man there on your left, but rather he's a wicked demon feeding on the weaknesses of man and causing pain or death or both.

"My story is not long, but true, and it began where I assisted my good friend the farmer from a blood-foamed sea, his head agape, hair parted out of place. How grieved I was!

He was mine only friend! O father, king! He told me of that demon there, of how he'd been bewitched to fall from perilous ledge.

"Well, being proud, I asked myself: 'what monstrous villain dares to devil friends of mine?'

So then I asked my friend in order to find out just where this wizard lived and found him three days later standing on the edge of Earth and sky and looking o'er the stars and other spheres out there.

And in his hand he held a bulging purse which he'd just filled. As far as I could see, that specter of a man was stealing all the brightest stars from there. And with each time he plucked a shining star from that vast sky, the world became a darker place.

"You'll steal no more!" I said, and thinking him a man, I drew my blade to end his cursed life.

Bold prince, said he. *Come tickle me with that bright blade, that I may fall from edge of Earth into the sky. For though you do not know, like you I am a prince, the brother of your father king, and as it is with those like us, in death we fall from Earth, becoming stars within the holy skies!*

Amazed because I'd never heard of such a thing, I stumbled further in.

"You say that when we die we will become the stars and planets there?" I softly whispered, then he whispered soft to me.

'Tis true. Do not you wish to be a star out there? With all the Earth residing at your feet?

Well I was haughty then and sought to know what I should do for such a lofty place within the universe.

"But how?" I begged, but he would speak no more till finally a spider crawled into his ear to wake his sudden sleep.

Stand on the edge of Earth. said he, *and taking sharpened blade, plunge deeply for your heart, and as you fall from there, you'll find a place for you with others of your kind.*

A coward who feared death, I sat the night with blade prepared to plunge into my quickly-pacing and unwilling heart, but when the morning came, I saw I stood not on the edge of Earth at all, but on a steepened hell where, far as I could see were scattered bones of fifteen million princes who had fallen from that place.

I looked again to where the demon stood, but he was gone. I, humbled of my haughtiness, set out again to find the fiend, and two days after, found him by the sea, and with a feast spread out upon a table reaching to the ends of Earth.

Bold prince, said he, and blinking eyes that were not in his head, he made a place for me.

'Tis known, because I am a prince, my judgment is above the thought of ordinary men. Where common men would strike away, I bound myself to know more of this fiend mine uncle.

Sit! said he and so I sat.

Food on this table represents the sins of man which you must eat for absolution of iniquity. There's sin and cruelty in bread and all the flesh and blood you see before you here. Eat now and you will save the world from sin.

And so I loosened up my belt and then began to eat. For days I ate, then weeks, then months, and when I finally was done, that toothless man then said to me,

You are now full of sin and other sorts of wickedness. You now must die!

"Why die?' I said, 'What have I done?"

He scowled at me, his anger growing hot before he overturned the table.

Food! he sneered, *You ate the food! You ate of bread, which is the pounded children of the grain and drank the wine which is the strangled blood of vines. You are a prince, and you well know the Law of God, that he forbidded drinking blood, and yet you drank the blood of vines!*

I thought awhile, and he was right. I'd drunk the blood of vines, and yes, I knew the Law. I knew I should be put to death, but something troubled me about the Law he spoke.

And yet before I cleared my mind to think it out, the demon deviled me again. He made me cloudy in my thoughts, and when I was at last subdued, he told me what to do.

Bold prince! said he. *Since you have eaten of the flesh of beasts and drank the crimson blood of vines, you'll be a sharer in their sufferings. Here's what you'll do: There is a field not far from here. You'll go at once and there you'll sit until the birds and beasts and worms of wilderness in turn devour you.*

I took his words as spoken law, and to that field I went to sit. So by and by beasts came to me, but did no harm, for in my sitting there, they thought I was their own. And eagles brought me figs from distant trees. I, then alone and finally at one with Nature's Law, began to heal. The magic of the demon faded then.

How terribly like a fool I felt, but coming to my senses, I proclaimed, "Well, am I not a prince? And is my father not the king?"

So here I came to find a broke-necked baker and a cross-eyed farmer that we might together come to you to tell our tales, but even as I'm here the fleas and lice of that pathetic field have followed me to bite and make me scratch and wear no clothes so that I, though a prince, a beggar looks more like.

O king! My father there! If e'er a son, a prince, did make request of e'er a father king, I ask you put the demon there to death for causing ruin in my life."

The king did look again to see it was his son, the Prince, and silent sat again. At last, and after many hours thinking there, the king's wise eyes returned to that old man whose toothless gums and eyeless head still bowed before the throne.

"It seems to me," so said the king, "that you have been accused of wrongs deserving punishment no less than death in bitter, angry eyes of these three men. How will you answer for yourself? Speak now in your behalf!"

And slowly did the so-called wicked man raise empty eyes to look upon the king.

O great, wise king! said he. *The words these men have spoke of me are true to some extent, but leave the realm of truth when wicked I am called.*

Why sure you know me well. I am your brother prince,
a sharer of your royal blood. That man who scratches fleas a
nephew is to me who shares my blood and weaknesses of flesh.

I've done no wrong to any of these three. That baker
there, who one time baked your feasts—he came to me for
mine advice, advice I freely gave, which he could heed or need
not heed. It was advice, no more, for I did wish no evil on that
man, but rather that he end the misery of life as I would like to
do. And when he flew from that great battlement, I wished I
had the heart to follow him.

As for that farmer there: when I advised him leap with
me six hundred feet t'ward treach'rous rocks and boiling sea
below, it was my full intent to fall as well, but when I counted
two, I thought six hundred feet is much too far for me to fall at
mine old age, and so I changed my mind.

He says I laughed and laughed I did—and just as you'd
have laughed if you had seen how long and far he fell, and with
that frenzied look upon his face and anger in his eyes.

Now finally, as for my nephew prince, he said he saw
me plucking stars and planets from the sky to fill my purse.
'Tis true, but represented by those stars are princely men of
Earth and this so wicked world is pictured by the sky. I pluck
these princes from the world so they will sin no more and
might shine brightly in the purse of memory.

I would not see this prince, your son, e'er doomed to
errant life like me, for me and him are more alike than you and
he. Like him, for many nights I sat with sword prepared to
plunge, but had no heart to pierce. When morning came, I'd
hate life all the more.

The feast I spread for him and his unselfish willingness
to eat the sins of man proved further that he was a foolish
prince and thus deserved to die. The eating was the sin of
disobedience when man began.

If I e'er deviled him, 'twas not by magic spell, but by his
own uncertainty of Laws of God, of what he was and what he
would believe.

The wilderness in which he sat can represent the

present world and state of man, for many men are beasts or
birds which pick us princes to the bone... while fleas and ticks
and lice are sins reducing us to seem not what we truly are.
We're better dead by our own hands than subject to these
beasts and fleas.

I sat out in that wilderness when I was young, and with
me came my fleas and worms and spiders too, which eat my
flesh unto this very day. I am no truly evil man, but though a
man who cannot do what he should do. This is mine answer to
the king and all the world.

Well now, although the king did recognize his
brother's voice, he scarce believed his ears, but like a king, he
thought a while before he spoke.

"What of the king?" he said and called his brother
forth. "What good advice have you for me?"

His brother grinned a toothless grin and stroked the
golden lion on the golden throne.

To die. he said.

"To die for what?" inquired the king.

For being king and making your good brother poor.
You sit on gold and in that purple linen clothe yourself while in
the world poor children starve. You are so cruel a king!

Then all at once the king laughed loud and long, and
to the shiv'ring man before him spoke these words,

"Dear brother, tell me how I made thee poor?"

The frightened brother of the king was speechless
while he thought to find a sin the king had sinned gainst him,
and finally, without a heart he faintly spoke.

You're older than I am, though look it not,
And to the older went the throne, to me my humble lot.

"What fault is that of mine?" said king, "To come into
this world before you did? If Earth is full of evils as you say,
you're *bettered* that I came before your stay."

But children starve! said brother of the king. *There're*
children in the world who starve, and yet you sit upon a golden
throne!

Well now, the king was not dismayed, but spoke
again.

"Would not same children starve if on a rock I sat in

midst of mud and mire?"

They might at that! proclaimed his brother prince.

"And so it does not matter where I sit," so said the king. "I cannot solve the problems of this world. I look to the Almighty God for that just as you should."

That being said, then silent was the king again. He thought awhile and then he called the broke-necked baker forth.

"Now baker," said the king. "For what good reason are you broken-necked so long when it is possible to heal or fix a broken neck?"

"I do not know my king." replied the man.

"With effort you can fix your neck, can right what's wrong so you can hold your head up high again. If you have fallen down at any cause, you need not yield to misery, but rise again. Go fix your neck."

And next he called the cross-eyed man who looked for all the while beside the throne.

"Now farmer," said the king. "It's true to say that what you see you see again besides, and yet your eyes are fixed on bad, on all your ills. It troubles you to see more pains, more woes, more weeds within your fields, but these are what you look to see. You'll be relieved if you can gain the sight of seeing good. Instead of seeing twice as many weeds, you'll see two times as many heads of grain. Instead of seeing twice as many enemies, you'll see two times as many friends, and seeing these, you'll want to work again. Go till your fields!"

And then he called the youth who scratched with fleas and lice.

"My son and prince," so said the king. "Will merely scratching rid you of those fleas and parasites which suck your blood and bring about disease?"

"O nothing will wise king, my father!" said the prince.

"I disagree," so said the king. "Immerse yourself in waters pure. Those fleas and parasites you'll wash away. Your scratching is a temporary cure, immersion is the only way.

Salvation's not from man but comes from God. Go wash away your pains!"

And when the king had finished speaking to the prince, he saw the other two offended fellows had not gone. And then, with one strong voice the three offended spoke again.

"O king! What of that fellow there who deviled us and led us three to misery?! You must pronounce that he be killed for pain and injury he put on us!"

"This man did you no wrong," thus spoke the king, "You are yourselves to blame for taking bad advice. You must not dwell on your mistakes by seeking one to blame, for you well know there is no one to blame but you because you flew to action yet you did not think. Now go your ways into the world and learn by what has passed."

So then accordingly they went their ways out from the king so that not one was left but that old fellow brother to the king.

"My brother," said the king, "Methinks what you want most in life is death, but being weak of heart, you cannot end your so-called cursed life. I'll solve that for you now.'

The king then called a guard and said, "My loyal servant and my trusted friend, since but a boy you've not refused a word I've spoke. And now please, if you will, take out your golden sword and strike of clean my brother's head. If after he seems still alive, do strike again till he no longer moves."

And then the valiant guard who knew no thing but service to the king, without a moment's hesitation drew the golden blade and meant to cleave the head from body of the brother prince for king. But all at once, the brother prince fell to his knees before the king and begged for intervention then.

My brother please, O king! thus begged the aged prince, *If he strikes off my head I'll surely die!*

The king then raised a hand and guard stood still with blade e'er posed to strike.

"I do not understand. Is that not what you want?" to

brother said the king. "You've told the court today how much you want to die. I'm granting your request and you are still unsatisfied? What is it that you want?"

Well now, the trembling prince sat thinking for a while before he spoke.

O good wise king, I do not know, but do know this: for many years I've wished to die, but when it seems I see the face of death, my heart is changed and life is valued more.

The king considered what his brother said and thought again and finally proclaimed,

"My brother prince, I hope you've learned that in this life the heart of man is treacherous: when all is done, mere wanting is a far, far better thing than having, yes, the journey much more pleasurable a place than our desired destinations where they lie. Yet since your wicked thinking brought you to this state, Go pray to God to be forgiven of your sins, and then and with my first-born son, the prince, immerse yourself in waters pure to wash away your fleas and your disease. And when you've done as I have said, the beauty of your youth and once fine health will be restored. You'll find you will gain eyes that see, so use them well. I wish you well and hope you'll act on what I've said, though that is left to you.

"Is there no end to foolishness on earth?
Those three who quickly took your bad advice
May never follow mine, however good.

And now my brother, you must leave my court and go your way. Go pray that God forgive you for your sins."

The matter being done, his brother gone, the king sat sadly on his throne again. And after thinking more with pen began,

How vain are all the varied works of man!

THE SILK NOOSE
(CONTINUER)

Oh it's you. I thought you were the guard. Sit down, sit down. When they asked me if I had any last request, I told them I wanted a bottle of good cognac. They brought me brandy. Brandy's better than nothing, but brandy's yesterday's grapes, distilled anywhere. Cognac's another story. I visited Cognac in France, before the misconstruction that led to my marriage. I had an *eaux de vie* from grapes that had ripened as the French, under Napoleon, marched from Smolensk, following the retreating Russian armies along the road to Moscow in late August of 1812. Not that I'm any kind of a snob, but I *did* ask for cognac and I *am* going to die today, after all.

I'm sorry I got so angry yesterday. I guess it was just your laughing. When I was telling you my sad story, you laughed at me. You remember, when I was telling you about how I lost Dido, probably the only girl who has ever really liked me. She's Sheriff Ben Kissup's daughter, but she's an incredibly beautiful and intelligent woman.

I just can't believe I passed up Dido for Fawn, a woman who ditched me for a supposed basketball player with really big hands and really big feet. But that was only the beginning. Did I tell you anything about the trial when we talked yesterday? No?

Anyway, so I'm standing there, in the condo that was my cell, asking Ben Kissup about Fawn, and he not only tells me that she's taken up with this basketball player with the hands and feet, but Ben also says that Fawn will be the state's chief witness against me at the upcoming trial. Then he asks me if my girl from back in San Francisco, the one I jilted his daughter for—he asks if my girlfriend from California would be coming out to testify about my character.

I wanted to tell him. I wanted to tell him that I hadn't left my heart in San Francisco. But see, I was embarrassed. I mean, how was I going to tell him that I had mistakenly fallen for Fawn right here in Polite, a girl that Ben and every stranger coming through town had apparently gotten to know in the biblical way? How was I going to admit that I had broken poor Dido's heart for a strumpet who had seduced me into drinking that disgusting White Zin concoction just so she could take advantage of me, sexually and otherwise, on the first day I met her?

Standing there, all I could do was fall back onto the couch and sink to miserable depths, my glazed eyes staring straight ahead. I was being accused of murder, a crime I did not commit.

An unsettling, ominous feeling settled on me as Ben Kissup called back a comment before he turned off the light and left the room.

"Course it's lethal injection for convicted murderers in every other county than this one. This is the only hangin county left in the state, maybe in the whole *country* fer that matter. But we're all hopin it won't come ta that."

I wasn't sure, but right then it seemed Ben was concerned that I wouldn't be hanged. Maybe it was because he thought there was still hope for his daughter and me. You probably think I'm crazy or drunk, but I think I love Dido. I realize we were only together for a week and we were never physically intimate, but for the first time in my life I felt it, a connection. I mean I felt instantly connected to her, and I think she felt the same thing.

It's ironic. I was much more physically intimate with Fawn, but the petty infatuation with her was nothing compared to the deep love that was burning in me for Dido.

You want some of this brandy? Bottle says it was made in Dusty, Oklahoma. How's that for a final request? Have some. I've got a half bottle left.

Anyway, I don't know who was telling people that the lawyer who came by to see me the next day was the best in the country. He wasn't the best dresser, he wasn't the best shaver, and as far as I could smell he wasn't the best showerer. Not in the country, not in the building for that matter.

And his name, he should have changed his name if he ever wanted to be taken seriously: Bobo Numkull, and I'm totally serious. That was his name. I thought it right away: Numkull rhymes with nuh, nuh... numbskull. I wasn't sure if it was a coincidence or omen. And then the name, Bobo— now there was one name that would have gotten more respect in a circus than in a courtroom.

Bobo claimed to have been a dashing and handsome figure in his youth, but the wrong woman had "brought him down." He was tall and lean. His hairline was at low tide, though an island of unruly, wispy gray hairs had endured on a knoll atop his forehead. The outline of his face was indistinct, owing to a straggly gray beard that flourished *au naturel*. His olive suit was stained, wrinkled and perhaps three sizes too small. He must have borrowed the shoes he wore from his brother, Bozo, because the oversized loafers he sported were orange crush velvet one of a kinds.

But these were all his strong points. Did I tell you he stuttered or did I tell you he had a lisp? Well, the truth is he had both. He stuttered *and* he had a lisp, but he made it a point to assert that he stuttered only on "n's" and "d's" and that he was in therapy to "eliminuh, nuh, nate my lithsp."

Notwithstanding, Bobo was the county's most famous criminal defense lawyer. When townsfolk and his assistants boasted that he had never lost a case, I was fairly impressed... until I found out that he had only tried one case. Technically, they were right. But just as technically, he didn't really win it. The result of the trial was a hung jury. Sad part about it, it happened when Ben's father, Topeka Kissup, was sheriff in Polite.

Ol Topeka didn't know any better. On the day he heard the jury was hung, he figured the defendant had something to do with hanging "12 innocent law-abidin citizens peformin a sacred civil duty." I'm not joking. Topeka thought that the man literally "hung" the jury in order to avoid a guilty verdict, so Topeka went to the jail, dragged the poor defendant out and hung him from the gallows that same night... with a silk noose.

"Tho why dud-did ya kill im?"

Maybe Bobo was confused. Maybe he thought he was *prosecuting* this case.

"Are you crazy? I didn't kill Clyde! I didn't kill anyone!"

"Of courth ya duh-duh-did. Tho where'd ya hide the body?"

I stood.

"I think you're all crazy in this place. I don't need this! I'm probably much better off representing myself. They're talking about hanging me an here my lawyer doesn't know which side he's on."

Bobo stood, placing a steady hand on my shoulder.

"Of courth I duh-do. Hey, will ya troth me here. I wath justh playin the duh-duh-duh-duh-Devil'th advocate. We're gonna win thith thing."

When I looked into Bobo's eyes at that moment, I felt ashamed. I mean I was pre-judging the poor man. I admitted it to myself. When I noticed the lisp and the stutter, I instantly assumed that Bobo wasn't smart. He was certainly intelligent, and I was discriminating against him solely because he had a couple of speech impediments. He must have finished law school after all.

And then I remembered the *Columbo* series on television. Here was this crack detective who stammered, acted dumb, dressed like a hobo and was generally annoying, but he had a truly brilliant mind. The brightest criminals misjudged him to their detriment and utter humiliation. Maybe I really *did* have one of the world's best lawyers working on my behalf.

"Uh Bobo?"

He was non-responsive, staring into space.

"Bobo? Bobo!"

His mind-out-of-body experience suddenly ended.

"Oh yeth! Yeth?"

"Bobo, you're drooling. Here's a tissue."

"Oh, I'm thorry. Thanth! Thanth tho much."

Before Bobo left, he suggested that I should call a friend or two from California who could testify about my character. I thought to call my manager at work, but I had walked out on my job, after all. He probably wouldn't have nice things to say about me. Then I thought of my ex-wife. I was sure she was feeling guilty about making me quit my job so I could drive halfway across the country to pick her up, only to find she went home and didn't tell me. She'd be a good character witness.

"You did what?"

"I did nothing. They're *accusing* me of a murder I had nothing to do with."

She was silent for a while before she began.

"I always knew you had it in you."

"What?"

"I saw it early on. Didn't I always say your vanity would be your undoing? You remember that time I went to visit Aunt Ethel and you purposely didn't water the house plants and they all died?"

I could feel it coming.

"Vaguely, but it wasn't on purpose. But what does that have to do with anything?"

"After that, I just got the feeling that someday you were going to do something really, really bad, like *murdering* someone. That's why I divorced you. I'm just lucky it wasn't me."

There it was: I had no one to testify about my character. I guess most people just don't consider character witnesses until they have to. So I'm warning you: think about your list right now, *before* something like this happens to you.

I had to think up a defense. Apparently, it wasn't enough to deny murdering Clyde. I had been doing that for over a week and no one believed me. I had to *think* my way through it: Clyde had obviously disappeared. *Something* had happened to him.

Maybe Friendly Motors was in debt and no one knew about it. Clyde never literally charged people for the work he did, after all. Maybe all the stress of the debt and the having to be polite all the time—all that combined with me clipping that bass's gills was too much for him. Maybe feeling great anxiety, he attached an anchor to his body and threw himself into Throwback Lake. That was logical, but would anyone believe it? The divers never found his body.

And then, maybe Clyde snapped. Maybe Clyde was a Dr. Jekyll and Mr. Hyde. Maybe Robert Louis Stevenson was right in suggesting that suppressed evil will somehow find a channel out. It had to be stressful on Clyde and all the Polite people being so nice all the time. So when I cut the bass's gills, the evil Clyde emerged and decided to frame me.

It required a mere passive malevolence. All he had to do was disappear for a while and let me get blamed for murder and then sort of lay low until they hanged me. After I was dead, he could come back, receive a hero's welcome, make up some story about being stranded and unable to contact anyone, and go back to being good ol Clyde. In the meantime, I'd be dead. Could that happen? Strong possibility, but could Bobo and I sell it to a jury? Probably not.

So then I thought: these people fear me because they think I'm a big-time gangster. So why not play the gangster role for all it was worth? I could circulate a story about a few arrogant jurors on one panel a few years ago who made the mistake of trying to convict the Gill on a murder charge. Angry and incensed, the Gill's powerful and protective underworld associates bugged the jury room and determined who those brave fools were and picked them off, one by one.

Yeah, and the Gill's good friend, the Tweeze from Chicago, was one of the worst; he earned his nickname from the way he liked to pluck out all the hair on his victims' bodies, one at a time. And then there was the Douche from Sicily, a sick, depraved criminal who thrived on torturing enemies by forcing them to submit to enema after enema;

he'd torment victims with that plastic nipple until they had nothing left.

What? You've never had an enema before? You think that sounds silly. I can tell by your face, but there really are people out there who are obsessed with clean bowels. I'm from California, after all. LA is enema city. No, on second thought, jury intimidation would have only made things worse. It might have gotten the feds involved.

Then I thought: Therendipadoo! Why *not* get the federal government involved? Hanging people for crimes is barbaric. We've moved beyond the Wild, Wild West. Surely in this day and age, the federal government would never allow it. They'd step in and put an end to the tragedy of errors that was happening in Polite.

But how would I get the federal government involved? I could threaten the jury? I could contact the *Polite Whisper* with a made-up a story that had federal implications? Or I could simply ask Bobo to make an appeal to the federal courts.

"District judge here would thay out of it. He'th an old-fathioned conthervative. But you're mithing the point?"

Now he was sounding like a lawyer.

"Uh, Bobo? What point?"

"They got nuh-no body. You can't have a murder without a body."

It was simple and clear. That's why Bobo was a lawyer and I wasn't.

"Yeah, you're right. *I* was about to think of that. It makes sense. But if that's true, why is there going to be a murder trial in the first place?"

He smiled wryly.

"Becauth thome idiot led the preth to believe there wath thomething lurid and mytheriouth about Clyde'th dithappearance. Keep your mouth thut from now on. Juth let me do the talking from here on."

All right! I was an idiot and I had to keep my mouth shut and my geniuth lawyer was going to be my thpokesperson. So why wasn't I feeling especially assured that Bobo could prove my innocence.

Let me stop here for a second. I, I have a confession to make. No, it's not what you're thinking. I'm not confessing that I killed Clyde or anything like that, because I didn't. It doesn't even really have anything to do with my story. It's just that um, the whole idea of a murder trial was making me really nervous, and sometimes when I'm nervous I sorta want a drink. But as I told you before, the only alcohol Ben stocked in that penthouse jail of his was that um, was that horrible mmrnrp mrn ren da mrnriderer.

What? I said the only thing he had was that horrible White Zin in the refrigerator. There, is that better? Yeah, and one night I was feeling really anxious, so I went to the refrigerator, opened the door and looked in. I was utterly disgusted. There had to be 16 or 17 pink filled bottles in there. I slammed it shut. The next night, I lingered a little longer... four times. I was under so much pressure I thought I was losing my mind.

So on the third night, I reached in, grabbed one of those bottled carp by the neck, inserted a corkscrew and yanked out the rubber cork. Then pinching my nose so I wouldn't have to smell or taste the vile, vinifernal waste in a bottle, I poured a glass and gulped it down. My stomach threatened to return it whence it came, but I held it down through sheer will. It was always that first gulp that sickened me. After a glass or two, my mouth and bowels were usually numb enough to tolerate the rock gut brew.

Anyway, one night as Bobo and I sat there planning trial strategy, I offered him a glass. He seemed reluctant, but finally he shrugged and took a glass. Minutes later, I had stumbled upon the most fascinating discovery.

"What did you say, Bobo? Can you say that again?"

"I said, 'this case would have been thrown out in any other jurisdiction. It's a simple disappearance and nothing more.'"

I had to catch my breath.

"Bobo! It's a miracle! Do, do you realize you said all that and you didn't stutter once. You said 'ds' and 'ns" and you didn't stutter! And your lisp is gone!"

He didn't seem at all surprised.

"I know. I've been drinking. It happens when I drink."

I refilled his glass immediately.

"It's amazing! It's a miracle! So all we have to do is pour you a good stiff drink before the trial, and we're in great shape?"

He wagged his head in the negative.

"No, I never drink before a trial. It dulls the senses, and as a result, it goes against legal ethics. I have a duty to provide you with the best defense possible, and I can't do that if I'm drunk."

Maybe he *was* drunk, because he wasn't getting it.

"I didn't say *drunk*. I said 'have a good stiff drink.' You're a lawyer. You know there's a difference."

He pushed the glass away and sat back.

"Not for me. I know. One drink won't do it. In order for me to lose the lisp and the stutter, I have to be drunk."

I sipped again and contemplated for a moment. What would be better: a sober, rational lawyer with a stutter and a lisp or a drunk lawyer with impeccable though slightly slurred speech?

"I can live with that... with your being drunk, that is."

"You could if it were up to you, but it isn't. I never drink before a trial."

"How about just for opening and closing statements?'

The guy was intractable, even after I told him I would sign a waiver that would free him of any liability for "mild intoxication" during the trial. And yet I began to wonder if he was *really* a lawyer when he refused my $5,000 bribe.

Bobo fancied himself as counter-puncher who said he wouldn't even begin to develop his defense strategy until the prosecution rested its case. He conceded that it had happened before, but he said it was next to impossible to prove a murder in the absence of a body. He seemed confident in that.

I studied Bobo. After a few glasses of the WZ he wasn't half-bad looking.

"I don't get it. There's got to be some kind of weird process going on here: sober you stutter and lisp, but drunk no one would ever know. Maybe there's some kinda switch in your head that needs to be flipped."

"You're right. It's all psychological. I *did* lisp and I stuttered a little when I was a child, but I overcame the lisp in therapy and outgrew the stuttering. I was fine until I met Cressida. She's the woman I married. Less than a year after I married her, the lisp came back. Therapist said it was caused by profound anxiety, which was obviously coming from Cressida."

Grabbing the new bottle I opened, he poured himself a full glass.

"Anyway, she was vain. She wasn't having a husband with a lisp, so she started correcting my speech, constantly and in public, though she was polite about it. It was humiliating to me, and it's not surprising that with all the pressure I was feeling that I started stuttering again, as if the slight lisp wasn't bad enough in her mind."

I nodded consolingly.

"You know, I think alcohol serves the purpose of making you not give a crap about what other people think. It relieves the pressure. Technically, you should be able to speak just fine without it. You just need to know you can do it."

He suddenly seemed sober.

"You really think that's it?"

"What?"

"You really think I do it because I'm worried about what other people think?"

That's when it started coming together for me.

"Well, yes. I think that's what the problem is with this whole town. I mean, why is everybody in this town so damn 'nice'? And is it *really* nice? All my experience here has served to do is change my opinion about so-called 'nice' people."

Bobo shrugged before posing the question.

"So I take it you don't think Polite is the friendliest small town in the world?"

I thought a moment before responding.

"It's a place that *thinks* it's the friendliest small town in the world, that *wants* to be the friendliest small town in the world, but in reality, it's not so much how nice or friendly people are, it's their intentions that matter. They're all missing that."

Bobo nodded, continuing the thought.

"And it's not how much I stutter or lithp when I duh-defend you; it's what I'm thayin and not how it thounds."

I quickly grabbed the bottle and refilled his glass.

"Have another drink, Bobo, please."

He sipped and smiled, saluting me.

"You are not the first who, with best meaning, has incurred the worst."

I recognized the line. I was impressed he knew it. I patted his back and helped him toward the door. It was two a.m. and we were drunk. The trial was set to begin at nine, which was in seven hours. It wasn't until I opened the door and he was standing in the hallway that I thought of the response to his statement.

"The weight of these sad times we must obey;
Speak as you do, not as you ought to say."

Anyway, my head was pounding when Ben woke me up in the morning, and he seemed excited that the trial was so near at hand. He rushed me all through getting ready. I mean, he impatiently knocked on the door four different times when I was showering, he told me my hair looked great when I knew it didn't, he shined my shoes so that duty wouldn't slow me down and he turned off the bathroom light when I was checking my face in the mirror.

"It's only seven o'clock, Ben. We don't have to be at the courthouse until nine. What's the hurry?"

"Judge Knott told me and the jury pool: by the writ of the habeas corpus, we gotta rush ya ta judgment. Can't be late."

It wasn't until we were in the Polite Diner that I got a clear look at the thin wooden case he had been carrying. The writing on its side panels was Chinese. There were tiny bronze hinges along the top and its front was impaneled glass.

"So what's that?"

Ben smiled sheepishly and pushed the case toward me.

"It's a tradition started up by my daddy, Topeka Kissup, when he was sheriff. He said I'd probably have the privilege of doin it one day in my career."

I recoiled after I lifted the lid and sensed what I was looking at. I sought denial.

"What is it? A woven necktie?"

"In an ironic way. It's actually a silk noose, thirteen coils. Ol Topeka thought it up last time we had a hangin in this town."

My appetite had vanished. Was this barbarian actually considering putting that thing around my neck?

"You Polite people are crazy. So what is it with the silk noose?"

Ben yanked down his tie and unfastened the top button of his shirt.

"Ya know what happens to a person when they get hanged by a braided hemp rope?"

"They die?"

"Oh, that too, but that hemp is some kinda rough against the skin. It's a coarse fiber. It burns, it chafes, it even tears sometimes. Take the rope off, an ya got a nasty burn that runs 180º around the neck, dependin on where they position the knot."

I was completely flabbergasted. I didn't understand.

"You're *killing* a person. So why are you concerned with rope burn?"

"Obviously, you ain't seen what a braided hemp rope can do to a neck. When you're in the casket—even after all the make-up—friends and relatives would still be able ta see the burn, and it ain't pretty. It shows right through, especially in photographs an videos."

He reached into the case and grabbed the shiny, intricately crafted red noose.

"Now this silk noose here, on the other hand, is another story."

He stroked it, offering it to me.

"Virgin Chinese silk, hand-woven. *Feel* how soft it is against the skin."

I did not want to touch the disgusting thing.

"I don't believe you people. You want to choke me to death with a silk noose and *that* somehow makes it better? That somehow makes you nice people?"

Ben extended his open palm in a halting manner.

"Now hold on there now, Gill. No one's sayin we're gonna hang ya for sure. In this country a man's innocent until proven guilty."

"By a jury of peerless, White Zin chugging buffoons in a rush toward judgment. Oh I'm feeling really good about this whole situation now!"

So that's where I was the morning of the trial. As I sobered up, my newfound confidence in Bobo began to wane. But what bothered me more was Ben's seeming excitement about the prospect of hanging me with that thing.

Minutes after he pulled out the silk noose, other customers in the diner began staring at us with a phony, transparent "niceness" because they knew it was impolite to stare. Then an awestruck man came over and asked Ben if he could see the noose. He held it up, examining it with great fascination.

"Ya know, starin down from heaven, ol Topeka's probably real proud of you right about now. I know I am. We all knew ya was gonna do it one day. Followin in yo daddy's great footsteps."

He looked at me and smiled.

"Can I shake your hand, Sir?"

I don't know why I did it.

"Oh thank you! Thank you, Sir. I'll always remember this."

An older woman from the next booth took the man's approach and the fact that I shook his hand as a signal to rise and interrupt. Bumping the man out of the way, she snatched the bill from the table.

"I'm taking care of your breakfast, Mr. Gill."

She eyed the noose, turned to Ben and almost whispered the aside.

"So when are ya hangin him? Gotta mark it on my calendar."

Ben seemed disgusted as he nervously returned the noose to its case.

"Now let's not get ahead of ourselves here, Betty. We don't even know if we'll get to use this. First we gotta make it past the trial."

She was smiling at me, batting her eyes. If I hadn't known any better, I would have sworn she was flirting with me.

"Look at you. You're so cute! Why if I was ten years younger, I'd tell ol Ben he could send that slick little box back ta China where it come from. I'd tell im he could use a pair of my sexy red silk panniehose instead."

I almost lost my breakfast right there. Next, an old coot came up and complained he was out of town during the last hanging. At 93 years old, he had been afraid he wouldn't have another opportunity to watch one.

"Do it taday or tomorra. Trial would just drag the whole dang event out too long, an I ain't gettin any younger."

It may have been my imagination, but when I got to court, either that old guy, or some drooling old turtle who looked just like him, came in with the jury and took a seat in the front row of the box.

Bobo sat next to me, as sober as ever. He pulled out a blank notepad and just waited, tapping, annoying me.

The courtroom was full that Monday morning. In fact, it seemed the whole community was there. I learned later that the mayor had invoked a special town holiday called Hangin Day, though in his announcement he was quick to point out that no *actual* hanging would take place, "at least not today."

The one bright moment before the trial was 12-year-old Sonny, the kid I met on the day my arrest hit the papers. He was the kid who visited me at the condo and proclaimed to everyone that when he grew up he wanted to be a gangster, just like me. He was the same kid whose flattery caused me to name myself "The Gill."

Somehow, he had convinced his parents to allow him to sit directly behind the seat I was assigned to at the defense table. He winked at me as I sat and flashed some sort of gang sign I only pretended to understand. Later, he tapped my shoulder and whispered into my ear.

"Don't worry, Gill. I made a couple phone calls. The family's sendin two or three *goodfellas* on down."

It was almost cute, but I was on trial for murder in a capital case. Still, because he was trying so hard, I answered in my best put-on movie gangster accent.

"Thanks, ace. I owe ya. I knew the family would come through for me."

Anyway, the judge came in with a manila folder containing five 8x10 inch glossy photos of me. They were good pictures, so I surmised they had been retouched. The judge wanted me to autograph the pictures for his grandchildren, and he wanted me to sign them using "The Gill" as my name.

Then he announced the court would recess for what would probably be 30 minutes to do an impromptu photo session. I'm not sure why I agreed to it, but I was the star of that session. The townsfolk formed a neat little line that wound around the courtroom, each politely awaiting a turn for a snapshot with me. Two hours later, the judge tapped the gavel to call the court to order, but this was only to announce a one and a half-hour recess for a town picnic.

I couldn't believe my eyes when the court re-convened and I saw the prosecutor: the zip-up sweater, the generic tie-up sneakers, the tie, the neat little crew cut, the comforting demeanor and subtle, reassuring smile.

He looked like Mister Rogers. I swear I wanted to go up and hug him for the many times he had reassured me in my youth. But what else should I have expected after all I had been through in the friendliest small town in the world? Apparently, he knew all the jurors. He called a few by their names and inquired about kids and parents and pets even.

His opening statement seemed like story time from the Land of Make-Believe. He told everyone about Clyde's childhood and about how much Clyde loved cars as a little boy. In fact, the prosecutor *knew* Clyde as a little boy. They had gone fishing together at Throwback Lake and had never harmed a fish. He called Clyde a pillar of the community three times, and he asserted that Clyde Kissup embodied Polite, Kansas, that he loved Polite, that he was so attached to the place that he had never so much as ventured past the rock wall at the edge of town. He said Clyde loved community celebrations like Hangin Day and that only death could have prevented Clyde from being there that day.

Then he started on me. Naturally, he mentioned that I was the last person to be seen with Clyde, and that Clyde had, in the generous spirit of the small town, invited me out fishing. He invited the jury to do the math: "Two went out, one came back."

He put up displays showing photographs of blood on my shirt and face and blood in the boat. He promised witness after witness would come up and talk about how I had actually kept a bass from Throwback Lake and about how I wasted its life by throwing it in a hot, maggot-infested garbage can.

Others would talk about how I wandered about town later that night as I looked for a place to hide the murder weapon. And Fawn would come on to testify about my lack of character. Finally, while he asked the jurors to return a guilty verdict, he declared that he'd rather see me freed than have me hanged with a braided hemp rope. He insisted on a specific instruction that granted me the silk noose.

The jury and the audience applauded at the end of his statement. When I looked to my left, I was disappointed to see Bobo applauding too, though he stopped abruptly after sensing my displeasure.

"It'th tho thimple. Laidieth and Gentlemen of the jury. You have to athk yourthelf: where'th the body? It'th a bathic rule in jurithprudenthe. Nuh, nuh—no one can know what may have happened ta Clyde..."

It was a short and thimple thatement, but Bobo was on a roll.

"No one knowth if he'th duh-dead or alive. If the prothecuthion can't prove he'th dead, they thure ath heck can't prove murder."

He raised his hands in concession.

"Duh-don't get me wrong. I been waitin ta thee a hangin like the reth of ya, but unleth thomewhere along the line they find Clyde'th body and can provide the actual proof that the duh-defendant killed him, we can't hang thith, thith man."

The court audience groaned in disappointment. The judge actually had to pound the gavel to end the murmuring and complaining. Anyway, order was eventually restored and the judge asked the prosecutor to put on his case.

The prosecutor called Fawn, who appeared from the building's antechamber and slinked toward the witness stand. On the way up, she stopped and kissed a tall, ugly guy who was seated on the aisle behind the prosecution's table.

My mouth fell instantly open: the guy had the biggest hands and the biggest feet I had ever seen! I looked at my own hands and my own feet, self-consciously. In my years of religiously reading articles and opinions in women's magazines, women consistently said that size didn't matter, so I couldn't understand why I was experiencing feelings of inadequacy at that moment.

Maybe it was because Fawn was so gorgeous. She really did look good in that tight, silky bodysuit with the 4-

inch satin covered stilettos. It was exciting to think that I had
had sex with a woman that good looking.

The prosecutor began with her.

"Fawn? How do you feel right now?"

She wouldn't even look in my direction.

"Lied ta, betrayed, lucky ta be alive!"

Mister Rogers seemed genuinely concerned.

"Well, I'm very sorry to hear that. But would you
mind telling all of us why you feel so lied to and betrayed?"

She dabbed the corners of her big, doe-like eyes with
a red lace handkerchief.

"Oh I feel such a fool. I let him take advantage of my
natural generosity and my childlike naivety."

I started to object out loud. I mean the woman had
eaten steak out of my mouth! Bobo shook his head, his stern
eyes warning me to remain silent.

"And what do you mean by that, Fawn?"

"He *used* me to get the people here in Polite to accept
him, and then he up an kilt poor Clyde."

When I looked at Bobo, I realized that either he was
such a great lawyer that he could ignore defense rules and
conventions or I was completely on my own. I nudged him,
whispering loudly.

"Aren't you going to object? She just said I *killed*
Clyde!"

"Of courth thee did. Thith ith a murder trial.
Whadaya expect?"

She glanced over at me and quickly averted her eyes.

"And after I all I done for him, he made funna me."

I had no idea what she was talking about. I had
thought things were peachy between us, especially after the
way I had pleased her in bed. She said I was the best she ever
had.

"You said he made fun of you, Fawn? Will you tell us
how he did that?"

She was sobbing.

"He, he said that people who drink White Zinfandel wine have no class."

I didn't remember saying it to her, though I admit I was *capable* of saying it. It's just an axiom from the wine compendium: White Zin—no class. The words just go together.

Mister Rogers patted her shoulder.

"There, there, sweetheart. Now let's not feel bad. Sticks and stones, Fawn, sticks and stones. But you also said you felt lucky to be alive. What do you mean by that?"

"Well, he told me his real name... and I called him by it. Wanna know what it is? It's—"

The entire courtroom erupted in protest because no one wanted to know my name. It was obvious. The entire community was terrified of me. Many were standing timorously in the aisles while others were fleeing out the doors. I was "The Gill" to them, and they didn't want any part of my real name. Finally, the judge pounded the gavel and issued the warning.

"Young lady, if you say that man's name and put this whole town in jeopardy, by jingo I swear I'll have Ben lock you up with him until this trial's over!"

Fawn seemed genuinely disappointed by the crowd's reaction.

"Well all right, but I just don't see why I gotta be the only one in jeopardy."

The judge had to send Ben out the courtroom to find the prosecutor who had fled with many in the crowd. The prosecutor's hair had become frazzled in the stampede for the door and his shoulder had come completely out of his sweater. He adjusted and buttoned the sweater as he addressed the court.

"That will be all, your Honor."

When Fawn took the stand the next morning, Mister Rogers asked her about the blood on my hands, on my face and on my shirt. Then he produced an ugly photo of me that had been snapped while I was walking back to Fawn's house that afternoon.

Either the picture had been cropped or the moron photographer who took it left the camera on zoom, because the fish wasn't in the picture. It was just my bloody face with my gory left hand up in an effort to block the camera. I'll admit I looked a little deranged, but that was because I was so thirsty. Clyde wouldn't give me anything to drink on the boat!

The final area of questioning by the prosecutor centered on my whereabouts during the time I left Fawn's house shortly before Sheriff Ben Kissup came over. He asked what time I left and how long I was gone. He asked if I was carrying a bundle or package, something that might conceal "a knife, razor or other slashing weapon."

Fawn said I behaved suspiciously from the moment I returned from fishing. She said I drank two bottles of White Zin, ate three helpings of carp and passed out on her bed. Then she said I disappeared in the middle of the night for two or three hours. And yes, she said she thought I might have been concealing a weapon because I was walking funny when I left.

But she didn't tell the court about our late night extra-curricular activities. She didn't tell the jury about my remarkable sexual prowess and about how completely I had rocked her world that first night she came—I mean, that first night I came. She didn't tell them how she had fallen in love with me. And she didn't tell them about that second evening of ecstasy I provided. I wondered about that. Maybe she didn't want her basketball player to know.

Anyway, when Bobo declined to cross-examine her, I was nearly inclined to fire him. Yet he assured me that all was going well, that he had the other side right where he wanted them. He pointed out the jury: nice, decent people who basically liked me. The matronly woman in the second row had volunteered to provide a home cooked dinner for me when court adjourned that day, after all.

"We really got em nuh-now. We're kickin their atheth!"

I don't claim to know anything about law, but I do know enough about ath kicking to realize no lawyer does it sitting on his own ath with his mouth shut. That's why I left him hanging when he tried to high-five me.

As I sat there, I thought of Meursault from Camus' *L'Etranger*, about how fate or nature or life itself forces conflict, confrontation and resolution. Many times before, I had escaped and eluded the consequences that have naturally resulted from my easy and apathetic nature. But if life itself is a trial, then it's only a matter of time before we are forced to face the real issues of our individual characters. It was a murder trial in the most ostensible sense, but in reality the three daughters of Nyx had convened at the spinning wheel to adjudge my character.

Next, Mister Rogers brought on a series of witnesses who testified about a sinister, ominous figure that roamed the streets of town on the night of Clyde's disappearance. One old man said gold-toothed Annie, a hound with a complete set of shiny metal teeth and who was usually quite brave, was stricken with terror as "The Gill" walked by.

"She just up'n peed all on herself and me, but I didn't mind too much."

Another witness watched a man who looked like me linger at the rock wall at the edge of town before disappearing into the night. It was obvious from the questioning that the prosecutor was trying to suggest that I went past the rock wall in order to hide the murder weapon outside town.

Earlier in the week, the *Whisper* said that the sheriff and deputies had gone over the ground beyond the wall with blood hounds, metal detectors and infrared cameras, but no weapon or clues were found.

As I watched Bobo during the entire process of direct testimony, I got the distinct sense that he was more an observer than a defense attorney. It seemed he was being swayed by the prosecutor and the sworn testimony from the stand. I guess that's why he never cross-examined a single witness.

I think the judge was also being led down the primrose path toward my encounter with that silk noose in the glass case. He was nodding and cheering like the other mindless cretins in the courtroom. There was no help for me.

That's when I realized that the key to my survival was me, that it all boiled down to me finally coming to my senses. I was in the thunderstorm. I was in the tempest. *Blow, winds and crack your cheeks! Rage! Blow!*

Like Lear, I had come to the end of my life before becoming wise. And like Lear, my extreme vanity had kept me from understanding the essence of my existence.

Despite all the years I had lived, despite my inflated education, I had never come to the point of it: *Honesty is all.* I realized then that the most deceitful people in the world are sometimes the nicest people in the world; that life is for learning; that honesty requires courage and commitment.

I had no idea how the trial would end, but I determined that I would attempt to right at least one deficiency in my character. I leaned over and whispered into Bobo's ear.

"Start defending me or you're fired."

The response was immediate. Bobo stood.

"Objection, your Honor. Athoomth facth nuh, nuh, nuh, nuh—"

His eyes seemed desperate. He was drowning.

"Athoomth facth nuh, nuh, nuh, nuh, nuh—"

Of course, Mister Rogers had to be the voice of compassion in the courtroom.

"What he means to say, your Honor, is 'my question assumes facts not in evidence,' and I think he's right in this specific instance. I withdraw the question. Good *job* pointing that out, Bobo! May we have a sidebar, your Honor?"

I had no idea what cheap trick the prosecutor was up to until I saw him over in the corner taking Bobo through breathing exercises. Then he sat Bobo down and began with what seemed like a reassuring pep talk. I looked to the bench to object, but it was empty. Ol Judge Knott was leaning over the railing, encouraging Bobo, cheering him on.

In the meantime, a fly had somehow just decided to come in the courtroom and land in the middle of my forehead. Careful to maintain composure, I jerked my head to startle him off. He must have done a quick circle, because he came right back to the exact same spot.

Has that ever happened to you? By that I mean a fly deciding to just bug you by landing in the same spot over and over again. It happens to me all the time. That probably doesn't sound right.

Anyway, I jerked again the second time and swatted at it the third. Yet in the midst of it all, I thought of Socrates. I was being stirred to life by this fly, *always fastening upon me, arousing and persuading and reproaching me.* I had to choose.

When the sidebar was over ten minutes later, the judge called the court to order to announce adjournment for the day. I sighed, glad the day hadn't gone worse. And yet my heart sank suddenly when Bobo stood to make an inquiry, shooing the fly from his face.

"My client needeth a bath."

The judge, jury and audience seemed confused while I was deathly embarrassed. I realized I had been nervous and sweating, but I *had* showered and I used deodorant that morning. Bobo looked to Mister Rogers and took a deep breath.

"What I meant to say is 'my client needs a *bass*.' He'll need a living bass to demonstrate how he came to be covered with blood on the day in question."

The judge looked to the prosecutor's table.

"Do you have any objection to a living bass?"

The prosecutor seemed disgusted.

"Yes we *do*, your Honor. Living bass are unacceptable. May we offer a compromise?"

At that point, court was adjourned as the lawyers approached the bench. And then came the applause.

Minutes later, Sheriff Ben escorted Bobo and me past fans, autograph seekers and small town paparazzi to his car.

Along the way, reporters called questions to me and to Bobo. It was like a made for television movie and I was the star.

Ben's station wagon could barely inch forward as bodies were packed all around it. I don't know who it was, but some woman placed her bare breasts against the window directly next to me at one point. I had to close one of my eyes to keep from looking.

True to her word, juror Bea Biggie sent her marriage-minded daughter over with rabbit and dumplings, fried chicken, apple-stuffed pork chops, baked carp, barbecue beef brisket, potato salad, macaroni and cheese, cole slaw, baked beans, boiled cabbage, deep-fried brussel sprouts and Caesar salad just to name a few of the dishes. It was like a last meal—something that made me think of that silk noose. And suddenly, I wasn't so hungry.

Bea's daughter wasted no time launching into the feast, though. I had never seen anyone eat with such relish and appreciation. She ate like a bird, and by that I mean she ate *like a bird*—she didn't waste time chewing anything. She just swallowed things *whole*, like a pelican or egret. I swear I saw her gulp down a whole pork chop, bone and all. I watched the bulge travel down her thick neck to her distended craw. What? Was she fat? Well, I don't want to call her fat, but she *did* have to turn sideways to come in and go out the door. She really did.

Um, anyway, Ben nervously came in after dinner and told me I had a couple of visitors from New York or New Jersey. He was definitely anxious as he reminded me that he had always treated me well. He even brought up Dido.

"Heck, if I don't get ta hang ya, I still really *would* like ta have ya as a son-in-law. Make sure you let em know that I'm on your side."

Ben hurried out the door as the two big scary guys came in. One had to be over 6'7" and the other was about 6'3". They both wore black leather jackets and black glasses. The big one made sure the door was securely locked and then they came over to me.

"Yo Gill? Is that *really* you?"

I wasn't sure how I wanted to respond, but I *definitely* did not want to disappoint these guys.

"Yo, yeah, it's me."

The shorter guy stared at me in astonishment, studying me closely.

"We tought yas was dead. I mean, that's what they told us. But this is amazin! What they did with the plastic surgery an all, it's amazin. *Ain't* that amazin, Bruno?"

The tall guy was just as dumbfounded. He removed his glasses, squinting and answering in a low and lazy voice.

"Yeah Pauli, it's amazin. It's definitely amazin."

Pauli closed on me, peering into my eyes.

"I mean, it's really amazin. No one would recognize that that's you, Gill. Ya ain't fat no more! An ya what? Four inches shorter? An what theys did with the colorin an all! No one would know ya, I swear! Ain't that right, Bruno?"

Bruno approached and stared at my face.

"No one would know yas."

Pauli looked around the plush condo.

"Boss said ya was real smart. Said ya could get outa whatever problem ya was in without *our* help. We could bust ya right on outa here taday if ya needs us to. Ain't that right, Bruno?"

The big guy was breaking a walnut open with his teeth.

"Bust yas right out. Have yas back in Jersey tanite."

Pauli cracked his knuckles as he stared out the window.

"Ya want we should do anyting fa ya here, Gill?"

I wouldn't have minded them busting me out, but I wasn't ready to go to Jersey.

"No, I's alright. I's just be handlin thangs okay here."

"Yo, what was that?"

Oops! Wrong accent.

"Uh, I meant yutes can uh, yutes can head on back without me. I got unfinished bidness here."

I had never used "yutes" before, but I think I was in character. Then I hit my stride with the perfect gangster line. It was inspired.

"Fuhgeddaboutit."

I saw the gun when Pauli opened his jacket. When he reached inside, I was ready to scream like a woman, but he didn't go for the gun. He pulled out an envelope instead.

"Boss said in a million years he'll nevva figure out how yas got out from unda that cement unda all that wata an all, but bidness is bidness. Here ya go."

He handed me the envelope.

"Yo, what's this?"

"It's ya cutta da money. There's a key in there ta a security box at da Bank of New York, main branch."

He was still studying my face.

"And I used ta tink ya was good-lookin. It's amazin. If anyone earned two million dollas fa that job, ya sure as hell did. I mean, ya gotta walk around with that face fa the resta ya life. That's too bad."

He nodded to Bruno, indicating that he was ready to go. With Bruno outside, Pauli leaned back in the room to give me the skinny.

"My advice ta yas: go get yas two million from the bank and pay that plastic surgeon ta give ya anotha face. Anyting would be better'n that one."

As if his mook mug was any better.

"Yeah, tanks, Pauli. Tanks a lot."

Ben peeked into the room about five minutes after Fasolt and Fafner had left. His face seemed flushed, as white as a clean toilet.

"Ya know, we're just simple small town Polite folks out here, Gill. Why'd ya have ta call in the mob on us? Those were two scary guys! Got us all *nervous*."

Concerned very much about how poorly the trial was going for me, I sought to use the town's fear to my advantage.

"Of course you realize, Ben, those guys and the rest of the mob would never tolerate anyone trying to hang me.

They were pissed enough with you and the judge for letting this thing go to trial in the first place. They were um, they were cracking their knuckles and nuts and all."

Ben sat, crossed his arms and wagged his head.

"Funny, that ain't what they told me. The little big one, Mr. Pauli? He said hangin'd be all right as long as I saved yer personal affects. He said if ya was hanged he'd come back fer some kinda *key* he gave ya. Promised ta give me a thousand dollars for it."

And to think I thought gangsters were cool at one time. They all belong in jail, every last one of em! Believe me.

"Ben, I got a hypothetical for ya."

"No, I don't need one of those. I'm not constipated."

And for a moment, I had forgotten where I was.

"Okay, let's just say the jury finds me guilty and you all decide to hang me. How many appeals do I get?"

He just laughed.

"This is Kansas, not California. Ya don't get no *appeals* here if yer guilty."

"But it *is* America, and as far as I know, a person should have *federal* rights to appeal a, a serious decision like, like hanging."

Ben just shook his head.

"Not you, Gill. Now I know you're nervous an ya wanna save yer neck. But if ya remember, ya *waived* yer rights ta all appeals when ya was talkin ta the judge at the arraignment. I heard it. Ya said ya'd have nothin ta appeal."

"Yeah, but that's because I had no idea the arraignment was going on in the first place. I had no idea there was even going to be a trial!"

Ben patted my shoulder.

"Face it Gill, ya took a great big gamble and ya lost. Now if the jury finds ya guilty, you'll hang for sure. But I don't see why yer so worried bout it. It won't hurt much."

Maybe he knew something I didn't.

"How do you know?"

"I don't. What I really meant ta say is it won't hurt *long*. You'll be dead an it'll all be over in about five, six minutes max, and that ain't nothin when ya think bout it. Hell, I've had headaches that lasted days!"

That night I dreamed I was in a real jail, with real bars and with Lear's youngest, Cordelia, though she was actually Dido. Somehow I knew the jailer had been sent to hang us in our cell. And I remember. I wasn't worried about myself. I wanted desperately to save Cordelia, and through all the stress and struggle from within that confine I came upon a moment of clarity.

> *So we'll live, and pray, and sing, and tell old tales,*
> *And laugh at gilded butterflies,*
> *And hear poor rogues talk of court news;*
> *And we'll talk with them too,*
> *Who loses and who wins;*
> *Who's in and who's out;*
> *And take upon the mystery of things,*
> *As if we were God's spies.*

When the trial resumed the next morning, Mister Rogers, perhaps yielding to pressure from the community to "get it the hell over with," stood to announce that the prosecution would rest. The judge immediately called on Bobo to begin the defense case-in-chief.

"The defense calls Fawn Oliver, your Honor."

This was the moment I had waited for. Trial notwithstanding, she had gotten on the stand for the prosecution and somehow failed to make any mention of my unique gifts in the bedroom department. She had pretended there had never been anything between us, that I *hadn't* made the Earth move and quake beneath her feet. That made her a liar and I told Bobo she had impeachment written all over her White Zin drinking behind.

"Can you dethcribe for the court the nuh, nature of your relationthip with the defendant?"

"Well, when he come ta town, I was kind enough to offer him a place to stay. So he stayed with me for one night. Woulda stayed a second night, but he got arrested."

Bobo knew what she was doing. She was trying to pussyfoot around the subject! But how could she help not remembering earthquake after shaking earthquake that I probably delivered that night?

"And on the night he thayed, I mean *stayed* at your house, where did he sleep?"

"In my bed."

"And where did you thleep?"

That's when she lied. With the finger pointing, head wagging and passion of a former president, she perjured herself.

"I know what you're getting at. I did *not* have sex with that man!"

Oh yeah? Now she was either lying about not having sex with me, or she was lying when she said I was like the best she ever had. Or maybe she was lying when she said I had taken her to Heaven and Hell in the same moment. And when she said it was better with me than a lot of hot movies she had watched, maybe then she was lying?

Sitting there pondering, I just figured she *couldn't* have been lying about how *good* I was, or am, so she *had* to be lying about having sex with me in order to protect her reputation, which made me a little skeptical. That was good enough for me, but it wasn't for Bobo.

"And did you at any time *tell* him he was the best you ever had?"

I signaled to my lawyer, whispering.

"Uh, that'll be enough, Bobo."

In that instant, Fawn realized I had told Bobo everything.

"Well, I guess I *am* under oath, aren't I?"

"Yes, you are, and you better remember that."

She smiled politely.

"Then I'll tell you. I only *told* him we had sex. I, I didn't want to hurt his feelins. You men better be happy all women aren't under oath."

By that time, I was almost standing, giving Bobo the very ostensible "cut" sign. But Bobo, I guess he thought he was on a roll.

"Ah ha! And just *why* would a woman who *hadn't* had sex with a man tell him that she *did*? And beyond that, why would a woman tell a man he was the best she ever had?"

Fawn sighed, evincing discomfort. In fact, in that moment it seemed all the women in the courtroom were a little uneasy. Some looked nervously into their laps, fidgeting with their hands while others shuffled their feet.

"You mean you men *really* don't understand how it works?"

Bobo answered for all of us.

"How what works?"

"Well, most of ya are pretty *lousy* in bed, just plain pitiful. But ya all have it in yer heads that you're the best we've ever had, an there can only be one of those."

She kinda whispered, as if disclosing a trade secret.

"Now, if we like you at least a little bit, given your swollen egos, how could we *possibly* say anything else?"

Bobo looked accusingly toward his own wife whose head was bowed in embarrassed agreement, and then toward Fawn.

"Tho ya *lie* ta uth? I mean ya lied ta *him*?"

"What's a woman supposed ta say? You're the fifteenth best I've ever had? An the thirteenth biggest? I don't know why you men always get it in ya heads ta *ask* in the first place? If we told ya the truth it would only hurt your feelins."

It was a bust. But at least Fawn implicated all the other men in the courtroom. I saw em. They were all self-consciously sliding their hands into their pockets to comfort their wounded... egos.

So now, I figured she wasn't lying when she didn't mention that she had sex with me. Instead she was lying when she said she *did* and that I was the best ever. I don't think the jury got all that though.

It became obvious after Fawn's revelation that Bobo lost his grasp on why exactly he had called her to the stand.

"So how do we know if you really *mean* it?"

"Look inta her eyes. If they're crossed at that special moment, then ya know she's tellin the truth. But ya gotta make sure she *has* that special moment."

Ignoring protocol, the judge cut in.

"*What* special moment?"

Fawn sighed, her eyes beckoning validation from the other women in the courtroom.

"I rest ma case."

Bobo's next witness was a 19-year-old kid who worked at the A&P. I had never seen him before, but Bobo established that the kid had sold him a certain exhibit item from the store.

"And just what is Country Bass?"

"Well Sir, it ain't really a real bass. It just looks like a real one. It's got a rubber skin on it and it looks like a bass, but it's really just some kinda machine or fancy robot mounted on a piece of wood. It's got batteries an all."

Mister Rogers objected to the use of such a lifelike bass, but the judge overruled him, allowing Bobo to set up his final witness. And so at last Bobo called me to the stand.

The judge was uneasy.

"It is not necessary for you to state your name, Sir. We know who you are."

Although we hadn't actually rehearsed my testimony, Bobo and I did go *over* what he'd be asking. And just for the record, I thought the rubber bass was a bad idea.

"And does this imitation bass in any way resemble the bass you said you caught on the day in question?"

"Well, of course mine was bigger. Uhm, very big. A monster."

"But did it *resemble* this Country Bass? Was it a bass?"

Naturally, I conceded the point, but I didn't want Bobo to downplay my size to the public.

"Anyway, can you stand and demonstrate with this knife just what you did to the bass?"

"I didn't use a knife. I used cutting pliers."

The judge leaned over, warning me.

"You've already argued your point, and I've overruled you. There's a shortage of cutting pliers here in Polite. We couldn't find any. Just demonstrate with the knife."

I couldn't help thinking of the Christopher Darden fiasco with the glove, but the judge left me with no choice. So, just as I thought, when I grabbed the knife and faced the jury, a palatable fear gripped the courtroom.

Even the judge cringed, realizing the terror he had wrought. I mean, what if I was a *real* killer? What if I was the cold-blooded pro everybody thought I was? Here these Polite fools had put a *knife* in my hand.

The judge was standing behind his high back leather chair.

"Please pro, pro, proceed with uh, the uh, demonstration."

But the prejudicial impact of the jury seeing me with the knife in my hands was nothing compared to what happened next. You see, Bobo got nervous when he saw me approaching him and the bass with the knife, so nervous in fact that he accidentally pushed the red button on the wooden base. Suddenly alive, the bass arched its back and spoke.

"Please, please, good buddy! Cut me some slack!"

At first I thought it was my imagination, but I realized later that everyone else in the courtroom thought the voice sounded an awful lot like Clyde's too.

And if that wasn't bad enough, bumbling Bobo pushed the damn button again as he tried to rid himself of the "possessed" fish.

"Please don't kill me! Gatdammit, I'm too *young* ta die!"

At that point, I really did want to stab that fish with the knife. Or better yet, I wanted to stab Bobo. He should have taken the batteries out! Somberly, he stood to face the jury and judge.

"The duh, duh, duh, the dufenth rethth."

The prosecutor was awful in his closing arguments. He bordered on being unethical. He called Country Bass "a prophetic fish." Can you believe that? And he got worse.

"Ol Clyde was reaching back from the great beyond ta tell us an ta prove ta us beyond a shadow of a doubt that this man took a knife and murdered him, for *murder, though it have no tongue, will speak with a most miraculous organ.*"

Well, it was obvious his slander and sensationalism worked with the jury. It only took them 45 minutes to return a guilty verdict. Sentencing was immediate.

The judge smiled in triumph.

"Sir, you have been found guilty of murder by a jury of your peers, and for this crime you shall be hanged by the neck with a silk noose until you are dead. You will be hanged at noon tomorra."

It was the first standing ovation I had ever received. Then began the chant. They chanted, "Gill, Gill, Gill" until I left that courtroom.

So there you have it. I had just come from the courtroom when you showed up yesterday for the interview. Waitaminute! What time is it? Ten o'clock! I've only got two hours left!

Uh-oh! There's Ben. Wonder what he wants? No, no. Don't get up. I *want* you to stay. You have to stay here and be my witness.

Ahem. Excuse me Ben, but it's only ten o'clock. Why are you here so early? And why do you seem so nervous?

"Well, it seems we got a little problem here, Gill, somethin we're hopin ya can *help* us with."

This is almost funny, Ben. You wanna *hang* me, and you want me to *help* you with something. What do you want me to do? Put on a show? Read a speech? Make it a great hanging?

"Naw, I'm afraid it's more serious than that. I got bad news."

Well, what is it? What can be worse than me getting hanged in two hours?

"She's a comin. Yer gonna hafta wait a few minutes, but she's comin. An uh, Gill?"

Yes?

"This is uh, kinda like official court bidness here. Yer friend can't stay. Ya gatta ask yer friend there ta leave."

THE LOVE TRAGEDIES

STORY FIVE

LIBRETTO FOR AN OPERATIC PIECE

I

For once upon a time within a very ancient world there lived a poet of a man who, in his early years sang songs and psalms of life and love and lasting joy so beautifully that all the world would stop to hear. All while he sang was Nature still to listen in.

His was a splendid tenor voice that stilled the howling winds and raging seas and one that did subdue the savage beasts and men who did the world great harm. Grass would not grow while he did sing and nearly all the singing birds were silent for the haunting beauty of his voice. Only the nightingale was skilled enough to, in soprano voice, call a refrain to his poetic melodies.

So lovely were the poet's songs and psalms that once when scowling Death was passing by, he paused to speculate and smile and shed a salient tear, for never had he heard a sound so strangely full of harmony. The words and music made a strongly pleaded case for peace in all the Earth and heavens too.

The entity called Death thought then of what was truly joy and how he worked without respite to time indefinite. Death understood at last why menial man would fight so hard to struggle free from his compassionate embrace, and yet he grieved that life for man could be so full of joy that poets, like this man, could sing great songs that flew into the sky, while his was such an earthly lot, for never had he smiled for simple joy or laughed for foolish-hearted childishness.

His lot was rather one of trial and tragedie with those who also were like him accursed and in the world despised: for bloody Murder was his confidant, War was his wife, and Pestilence his cousin was while Massacre and Genocide were servants who did slave eternally in his employ. In every place that Death would go, his sister Sadness followed him... And O how he was hated for that which he could not help he was!

So as he stood alone and listened to the poet's brilliant singing voice, he came to bear a hate for man still greater than man's love of life, and since the poet glorified a life of joy, he came to hate the poet most of all. He thought to take the poet's life, and yet alack, this poet was no ordinary man, for he was favoured by the gods.

It was too true, for when a mortal man could do a thing that gods themselves took pleasure in, when man was able to amuse the gods who were not quick amused, he earned himself a favoured place within their eyes. For this is what the gods commanded Death: "Of all the living you may eat till full... But as for man the gods themselves do love you may not eat, for on the day you do 'tis known that you yourself will positively die."

And so as Death considered his revenge upon this man who sang, he knew that he would have to seek permission from the gods. Well now, unhappy Death, whose name was Thanatos, he knew he had no audience with him who was the one Almighty God in all the universe, and so Death sought out Lucifer, the god of Earth.

He knew this handsome angel well and often went to him to hear advice, but getting to his master was no easy task: he had to go past wicked demon heralds and the horrid wraithish scribes who made the task of speaking with their lord and master difficult. He called his brother, Hypnos, and the two, both being twins and sons of Night, did make their way into the audience of what was called "The Court of Lucifer."

Now this is much like what Death said in bass toned coarsely spoken syllables:

II

"Most honoured and respected Lucifer, the god of Earth: I come to you because I seek permission to destroy a man whose voice has pleased the gods enough to gain him recognition in your eyes. Why sure you know of him! He is that celebrated poet who, with titillating voice and palmy lyric skill, entrances all the Earth and Heavens too.

Now I have grown to hate this clever poet and I've come to you that I might gain permission to divide his fleshy body from its spirit part. More simply put: I want permission to destroy this man, his spirit and his flesh, which are inseparable and called his soul. Please grant my wish, for you full know till now I've served you well. What will you say or do for me, my Lord?"

Well now, the glorious Lucifer, he would not speak before he took the time and opportunity to think the earthly matter through. He sat a while, and then he stood.

He smiled at empty-headed Thanatos who was in truth his oldest friend. He kissed Death's bloodless cheek and then he welcomed sleepy Hypnos to his court. Thus finally he spoke to brutish Thanatos in words like these:

This poet I have heard and it is true
I have enjoyed the songs the mortal sings;
His voice is one unlike the sounds from throats
Of ordinary men who sing in vain,
And not like any I have heard before
Or any I shall ever hear again.
I love this poet well and so I ask:
Why have you chosen him to hate in all
The world of man? Why are you bent on him?
Just ask of me the lives of lesser men
And see how I will give you all you ask
Up to ten thousand dead in place of him.
Still must you be so bent on taking him?

In truth, Lord Lucifer, he knew Almighty God did love this poet with great godly love, so even Lucifer, for all his earthly pow'r, was powerless to grant permission to his servant, Thanatos.

But Death, his ever cold and dark and lifeless face contorted by great hate for man, he did not smile or even waiver as he stood before the wicked, crafty god of Earth. He spoke with raspy bass-enunciated words to this effect:

Not even for a thousand thousand would I e'er forget my burning hate for him. This poet sings of inward joy and lasting peace without, which bodes a peace within. Such is a joy and peace that I shall never have. I've chosen to destroy this goodly godly poet for the envy that he by his singing makes me feel. Why is it that the life of earthly man can be so full of joy if chosen carefully?—while mine is one of endless strife and tragedy in which I have no choice at all?! O cursed being that I am! And I, by universal law, cannot forsake the place I'm in. I'm doomed to endless wickedness!

Yet Lucifer, divine in wisdom, peered into the mind of brutish Thanatos and saw there was no trace of careful thinking in his head. Death was not wise and so the shining angel sought to use him as he had in times before.

He smiled again aloud to gain more trust of Thanatos and spoke to make Death speak, for this the angel knew: that those who spoke their hearts were easier to use. And so the scheming Lucifer, in baritone, did offer this:

My time to rule the wicked world is short,
And yet this poet makes me feel regret:
Reminds me that I once was not opposed,
That there was harmony in every work,
But I, cast as the wicked son of God,
Brought sin into the Earth and Universe;
Sin is my son and you his bastard son.
That man can choose in life, I've hated him;

That he is favoured in the heart of God;
That I was sent to minister to him;
That he is spirit and yet blessed with flesh;
That I, so wise, was cursed to challenge God;
For reasons such as these I've hated man,
And yet I love this poet for his songs
Which bring to mind the best in men and gods.
Tell, if you please, why you have hated man.

Then ancient Thanatos thought back a thousand years, and finding no offense, thought back five thousand more, and finally, while standing there, he learned why he had always hated man.

As I have said, my Lord, I hate him for the joy he lives, but more than that, I hate him for the place I'm in, for my predicament has much to do with man: When man did choose that fleshly form, rejecting the Almighty God who rules the universe, he cursed himself to Sin and to myself and cursed me to a bloody appetite. For I am cursed to do the work of God: that man should die for sinning in his spirit choosing flesh. Eventually, I'm given both of every man, but cursed am I. Almighty God has cast me with your lot. One day, into the 'lake of fire' we will go, which means a sort of second death, from which we'll not escape.

It's selfish Man who's cursed me to such cursed destiny, so why should any man have joy enough to sing these loving songs? The poet represents the best in man and all that is not subject to his selfish flesh and blood.

Still more, he represents man's inner harmony, a quality I would that I could end. By cutting short the poet's life and song, I'll make man's world a place of misery. Without the poet's songs, he will become a race of brutish beasts, respectful only of my coming-in and going-out. I'll not be hated as before, but worshiped as a god again. My reason being stated thus: I hate the poet for the love and light and joy and harmony he bears, and so I ask again for your permission to destroy all that he is, has been, will be, and represents. I want for man to worship me again.

Well now, Lord Lucifer, he did not want to grant permission, though symbolic, to his wasteful subject Thanatos, who seemed too arrogant and crude besides. He wanted rather that the princely poet be preserved for future use in opposition to Almighty God. If he could win the poet to his side, he'd have a powerful influence in his universally detested cause.

For Lucifer did see the poet's beauty as a crafty tool: to simple and unthinking Man, a thing of beauty must be good, while what seems foul is bad. The poet's handsome face was sure a fair disguise for impropriety, if only could he make him to oppose Almighty God. How perfect seemed his plan! But brutish Thanatos would think to waste the poet's life for vanity!

The errant angel smiled on shallow Death who stood there ign'rant to the workings in the angel's shining head. He'd not grant the request, and yet he'd fool conceited Thanatos to feel he offered something better still. And so did Lucifer appear sincere while singing words like these:

> *For this is what was written long ago:*
> *'There is no suff'ring in the grave of man.'*
> *Well now, it seems to me and should to you*
> *That if the poet dies, he'll serve no need*
> *Of yours or mine in our respective aims.*
> *Methinks you want for him to worship you,*
> *And yet you want to take his very soul.*
> *Both can't be had, unless you hear me out,*
> *That I might show you how to think on it.*

The angel's careful chosen words confused poor thoughtless Thanatos, who scratched his seeming hollow head and uttered in this way:

I'll humbly listen to your royal counseling, so tell me what it is that I should do.

And then the cunning Lucifer, convinced that he had once again deceived, he offered something much like this in song:

> *The handsome poet must not die;*
> *He must be used for subtler purposes.*
> *I'm loath to have denied your want and so*
> *I'll give to you a bloody war instead*
> *To satisfy your lusty appetite,*
> *Wherein you'll master forty thousand men,*
> *And yet the poet must be left to me*
> *And see: I'll make this poet worship you;*
> *I'll strike his flesh to cause a pain so great*
> *That he'll sing out in rueful agony.*
> *Eternal pain will stretch his days and nights*
> *So he can ever think of none but you.*
> *I'll cover him with rotting boils and*
> *With parasites that make him mad with pain,*
> *And when he reaches out for your embrace,*
> *You must, when nearly in his grasp, away!*
> *And finally, he'll seek to deal with you*
> *And you must say and with a royal voice:*
> *'Bow down and worship me, O earthly man!'*
> *And when he does, you must give him to me,*
> *But only for a little while, and then*
> *You may do to this poet all you wish.*

Well then, the beastly Thanatos did love the clever scheme for selfish reasons of his own, and yet the vanity of Thanatos is what the angel acted on, for vanity in man and beast is sure the adversary's greatest tool.

With Death agreed, the royal, princely angel slaughtered several former faithful men who had by their own vanity been made to sin with knowing sins gainst God.

Then Lucifer did pour their blood into three golden drinking vessels and he offered one to Thanatos, and then the second to his other guest and, taking up the third himself, he laughed aloud and offered up a song like this:

We drink the blood of holy ones turned bad
And to your feast of forty thousand men,
But let us go to hear the poet sing
A final song before I smite his flesh:
For never in the wicked world again
Will gods take pause to hear the songs of men.

III

The poet did not know his audience, nor did he know
that he would intonate his song of joy a seeming final time,
but he did sing with strength and clarity, with stirring
passages a composition e'er so sweet and full and rich with
harmony that glowing Venus paused to stare from northern
skies, and Jupiter at once aligned himself with Earth and all
the other deities did stand about to hear the poet sing.

The swirling singing stars themselves were silent
then and for a moment there was peace and harmony in all
the universe. The mighty hunter did lay down his heavy club
while his two dogs sat still, the larger shining brightly in the
night. And further, resting only months away, the Scorpion
thought none of doing harm but listened to the poet's
stirring song.

Then when at last the song was done, the universe
heaved out a pleasant sigh and marked its time again. And
Lucifer, his spirit moved yet most of all, felt much regret for
what he was and thought to reconcile himself to that
Almighty God above.

That he could change the past! Undo the things he'd
done! With knowledge that he'd learned through sin, he'd be
great help to God and man, but he had sinned a grievous
spirit sin, and he remembered that not even gods could
change the past: the die was cast, and he at last resolved
himself to smite the poet's guiltless flesh, but could not do it
lest he had permission from Almighty God above.

His head held high did Lucifer advance into the
radiant court of God, and thinking to deceive, he challenged

God before the other sons of gods yet standing there. He challenged God to test the poet's faith by granting that his flesh and bone be touched.

Almighty God could never be deceived, but he for love had faith in man, the poet being one that he was proud to love. For Lucifer believed no man would do the will of God without reward or safety to his flesh; and too he had no faith that any spirit person would serve God without reward; and so Almighty God agreed to let his adversary touch the poet's flesh and bone.

Permission being given him, Lord Lucifer went out at once and struck the poet's flesh to cause a painful boil reaching from atop the poet's tender head down to the bottom of his blistered feet.

At once the poet fell prostrate upon the Earth and prayed a desp'rate prayer to God to be relieved of fleshly life and misery. No answer came to poet sitting there who next began to stink and twitch for writhing worms within his flesh.

Before, when he could sing for joy, he was adored by man and beast alike. Now he was humbled by a loathsome, rotten, agonizing pestilence, this from a hand that was not man's. Why surely he had sinned a very wicked sin 'gainst God to be exacted punishment in such a horrid way.

The little children who had danced and laughed and lived to hear his voice now pelted him with stones and spat onto his balding lowered head. The starving dogs who once forgot their carnal appetites when he did sing now barked and nipped at him and ate his rancid flesh.

And on a spir'tual Earth he humbly sat for many years, low in the eyes of men and gods. While suffering for the pain that grew with ev'ry day, the poet did not sing or speak a word, but suffered silent knowing God was just.

Still as he sat, the sun and moon and stars grew dark, the clouds returned, the keepers of the house began to shake, the men of vital energy did bend themselves while ladies seeing at the windows found it dark. The grasshopper did drag itself along; the almond tree did flourish white, this while the caper berry bursted and the daughters of that glor'ous song fell low. It seemed his celebrated voice was gone.

In all the years that passed, the poet loved his god but did not understand his suffering, though never did he curse his god or seek or yet once worship Death.

IV

At last, begrudging Thanatos did grow impatient in the scheme, for being weak in heart and mind, he thought the plan had failed, and heated up with rage, he sought his master out to speak with flaming words.

You've lied to me, O villain there! to make me think the poet would e'er worship me. Yet all along you knew he'd still be faithful to his god! You are too wise to e'er be wrong, and knowing all before, you lied. You knew what he would do! And yet you made me think that he would worship me! Why have you used me so?

Well now, the disappointed angel truly had not known the poet would be faithful to Almighty God, but never would he say that he'd been wrong. Instead he sang the words, deceiving Thanatos again:

I was not wrong, for all is as I planned;
I knew he would be loyal to his god,
And that is why I fixed another scheme
To make him curse his god and bow to you.
Come let us speak to him with poisoned words,
But first we must become like friends who mourn.

Then Lucifer took on the guise of man and urged it so that Thanatos and Hypnos did the same, and finally the three approached the stinking poet where he sat, still scraping at his wounds with broken earthen plate.

The poet recognized the three as aged friends who also wrote but sang such simple songs that they were always lacking audience. They watched the poet for a year or more and did not speak a word to him.

The poet though, was ever humble, patient, and still loyal to Almighty God above, for often was he sweating blood while praying earnest pray'r with face bowed low to Earth.

Well Thanatos had never been the patient sort, and so while sitting there, he thought to draw the poet out, to make him see himself and how he suffered on the Earth without respite. Death started in his low-pitched voice while singing something much like this:

O poet there and friend! How have you lived to make yourself so utterly despised by God above? Why surely you must be a wicked, wicked man to yet exact a punishment so harsh from Him! Your heart, your soul, your flesh is evil to the bone. There is no help for you, and yet, for reasons unrevealed, he will not let you die. So you are doomed to torment in an earthly fleshly frame to time indefinite.

I am a poet too, and in your place I know what I would do: Curse your Almighty God and die! Debauch his holy name to strike at him. For generation after generation will examine what you've done (since you alone were favoured by the gods), and this will surely be your way to end the pain and suffering you've brought upon yourself. Curse God and Death will surely come.

While hearing this, the poet was still bowing low before his god. At last he raised himself to answer Thanatos.

I am not wicked as you say of me,
But loyal to Almighty God above;
Though good we men of flesh may never be,
He sees the good in us for his great love.
I'd rather suffer, never knowing why
Than O so vainly curse my God and die!

Then after saying this, the poet bowed again, when from the heavens came the angel, Azrael, who seemed much like the nightingale, and Azrael did sing a song to bring the poet peace, but when the song was through, the nightingale did seem more man than bird.

The angel listened as the softly-spoken Hypnos sang his song, that sounded in a low-pitched woman's voice:

> *Poets are wiser than all other men,*
> *Given the vision to see as gods would;*
> *Yet in the act and commission of sin,*
> *Poets and gods sometimes fail to do good.*
> *You say you're blameless; perhaps that is true;*
> *Men are all sinners and named so by He.*
> *If you are punished for some sin in you,*
> *You must confess it to make yourself free.*
> *If you are righteous and punished for naught,*
> *Then God is wicked for smiting your flesh,*
> *For a good god would e'er do what he ought:*
> *Wicked are cursed while the good he must bless.*
> *You seem to say you're more righteous than He;*
> *If that is true, a false god he would be;*
> *Tell who's more righteous so all may yet see.*

The poet once again sat up to face his seeming friends, while Azrael did stand apart from all to listen in.

The wretched poet thought a year before he spoke aloud and in such careful angry words he answered much like this:

> *Again I say I'm guilty of no wrong*
> *Deserving of the pains I now endure.*
> *I'm but a man who pleased my god with song*
> *That came from mine own heart with motives pure.*
> *Why must you seek to villainize my name?*
> *For I am righteous and yet free of blame!*

The poet did not sit this time, for he was angry that his seeming friends were searching for a grievous fault in him; they sought to say that he deserved such punishment.

The brilliant Lucifer saw opportunity in seeing how the poet's anger blazed against the other two. He smiled aloud, and with great care, he kissed the poet's heated cheek. The voice of Lucifer was softer, smoother than was Death's, so as he sang in baritone, he sought to win the poet's heart and soul.

> *My friend, you seem to me to be upright*
> *And one in whom our God should take delight;*
> *Though why he pains your flesh both day and night*
> *Leaves me to think your works escape his sight,*
> *Leaves me to doubt his sense of what is right,*
> *When works like yours should godly love incite...*

Yet Lucifer did pause to leave the poet thinking on those deeply spoken words, and then he sang again:

> *If I too deeply in your matters pry,*
> *It should my seeming wickedness belie,*
> *For looking on you no man can deny*
> *There's certain godly error in the sky.*
> *Our God is wrong to make you moan and sigh*
> *Your way of virtue does his guilt imply.*

The poet wavered then to wonder what was wrong in what this fellow said. At last he realized it was not possible for Almighty God to err, and still, he would not say that he himself had sinned.

> *Yet Yahweh is incapable of wrong;*
> *He's loving, just, yet powerful and wise;*
> *So still I'd glorify my God in song*
> *If that would grant me favour in his eyes.*
> *Though in my heart I know I have not erred,*
> *I know not why this pain I've not been spared.*

The poet sat again and in the silence that pursued, the angel Azrael stood up to sing another melody, that in a woman's highest singing voice. And brilliantly, as his great song began, the angel did approach the poet and his wicked friends.

V

His voice was high and clear, though sharp and full of anger as a violent storm began.

> Thus to the poet were these words:
> *You're right to say Jehovah God is good,*
> *For he is over all the Earth and sky,*
> *But you have loved yourself more than you should,*
> *To put your thoughts before your God on high.*
> *How small are you to think to judge your Lord!*
> *God need not answer any charge by you,*
> *For as Man acts so will his God reward,*
> *And give to earthly man all that is due.*
> *Consider now this storm that flies about!*
> *Stand still and show yourself his mighty acts!*
> *How they inspire fear and conquer doubt!*
> *His mightiness is proven in these facts!*
> *God loves the man who fears him for his part,*
> *Not he who would be good in his own heart.*

At once the four stood still and looked into the raging storm, then to the giant mountains standing further out, then to the sky so vast and so profoundly wide and full of stars about the Earth. As far as eyes could see the universe stretched on and on past any fleshly thought of man into infinity.

The thought was one on every mind: How small seemed man in all the boundless universe! How could he make himself more righteous than Almighty God?

The poet was there humbled by that thought and then Almighty God, from out within the storm did use a chorus of his glor'ous works to give an answer to the poet trembling there.

This was the voice of wind that whirled about the poet and his seeming friends:

> *How wilt thou answer me, O fleshly man?*
> *For where wast thou when I didst found the Earth?*
> *When I didst stretch it out with mine own hand?*
> *When I didst arbitrate its weight and girth?*
> *Canst thou tie fast or bind the Pleiades?*
> *Or use thy ropes to tame the unicorn?*
> *Behemoth I have made to humble thee,*
> *Leviathan to make thou fear and mourn.*
> *Gird up thy loins O man and answer me:*
> *Wilt thou condemn me so thou wouldst be right?*
> *Thou art not wise to listen to these three,*
> *For they have sought to bring to naught thy fight.*
> *Bow down, O man, and humble thine own heart*
> *To praise thy gracious God with all thou art!*

At once the humbled suff'ring poet fell before the chorus voice that whispered boldly in the raging storm that whirled about. His disposition changed, and he fell low before his skyward Lord to groan out words like these:

> *As man your godly ways I did not know,*
> *And yet I spoke though did not understand:*
> *I blamed my God for all my trial and woe...*
> *Pronounced my pain some slightness of his hand.*
> *I see, my God, that all your ways are just,*
> *So I repent in ashes and in dust.*

At once the storm did cease to rage awhile and here a glor'ous ray of sunlight fell upon the poet's humble upturned face, for God did urge the man to sing again. In all the time the poet suffered pain and woe and misery, he had not once called out a single melody.

He understood it only then that he, in all the time that passed, was feeling sorry for himself, was dwelling only on himself. And all along, if he had ceased to love himself so much, he could have known the cure for all his miseries! For man should be the best that he could be in spite of all—for self, for God, for all the world and universe. And doing so he ends his spir'tual miseries.

How good that man should learn humility! A simple song would heal the poet's pains, and as he stood to sing, the angel Azrael, again a nightingale, did perch on high to sing along. The man and angel at that moment sang a somber song so seeming sad and deeply meaningful and delicate in every way that all the universe was still to hear, for here was voiced a tragic song whose periodic poetry and simple truth and pointed practicality was more than merely music in the musing minds of men and beasts and gods.

On hearing such a song, how beastly Thanatos did mourn and try to sing along! And how his sleepy brother Hypnos tried the same! And falling to their knees they praised Almighty God above so that a change occurred within their hearts.

And then at last, e'en yet did Lucifer evince regret for all he'd done and sang along. He bowed his head and cried for shame and sadness deep within his spirit heart, a heart divine that truly hated pandemonium and one that tortured ev'ry day the separated spirit creature that he had become.

And yet while crying there, the angel Lucifer, he would not bow or kneel or even recognize the sovereignty of the Almighty God. It was unthinkable to him, for Lucifer was far more beautiful than every other son of God and thus he was afflicted by the greatest vanity of all.

Now when the song was through, the whirling raging storm began again and it was then that God (for how the shining Lucifer had stood opposed), he caused that storm to strike his son, to wound the perfect flawless face of Lucifer.

How vain was Lucifer! And how his seemly face was scarred to time indefinite! Now he could think of nothing but his ruined spirit face! The poet for his part, was healed and young again while Thanatos was satisfied at last for who and what he was, for Thanatos had made his peace with God and was a brute no more. His tired brother Hypnos also came to find a place with God. The poet, Thanatos and Hypnos left the storm in peace as friends and ventured back into the fleshly world of man.

Well then, the stricken angel in that place remained awhile, for he felt shame for being proven wrong, this by the poet who was just a fleshly man. For this he hated flesh and man still more than e'er he had before.

With vengeance he resolved to bring all flesh to ruin, especially that of those Almighty God does love. And as he did go down to find a place within the world of man, he cursed Almighty God and then began:

> *Stand warned! Beware!*
> *For I with vengeance come unto this place!*
> *My face! Is scarred!*
> *Both men and gods shall pay for my disgrace!*

And saying thus, the Devil, hot with rage, descended on the world of man.

THE SILK NOOSE
(FINALE)

Well, I don't know what to say. I guess I *am* a little late. First of all, I didn't realize there were so many people here in Polite. I, I recognize some of you from visiting hours at the condo. And then some of the other faces out there, I remember you from the courtroom. Uh, hi Pauli.

I guess we all know why I'm here. I'm standing on this platform with this, this gallows behind me, after all. And just up there, we can all see the red silk noose that you want to slip around my neck and hang me with. That is why *you're* here, right? Isn't that why you came out today? To see me hanged with that silk noose? I can see some of you even brought picnic baskets and little barbeque grills.

Anyway, it was nice of Ben to set me up with this microphone. Do you mind if I sit down? I might be talking awhile and I *am* understandably a little weak in the knees right now. Thanks. Ahh.

You know, I spent all last night thinking about that silk noose, about how I could be strangled to death with a secretion from a fat, ugly caterpillar. Not exactly a glorious way to go. But then I guess I wouldn't be the first person to go that way. You remember the Boston Strangler, that murderer, and those silk stockings? Maybe you people and DeSalvo have something in common.

Did you ever hear the story about the origin of silk? I realize you don't seem exactly interested, but I'll tell it anyway. About 5,000 years ago, the wife of some Chinese emperor was walking in a mulberry grove with a cup of tea in her hand. So for some odd reason this lady picks off a moth cocoon and it somehow slips out of her fingers and into the tea. And then when she starts to pull it out, it unravels in a single thread. Ah so, so she got an idea, and cha-ching! Next thing you know, we've got silk fabric, a silk road and that...

that silk noose up there. Of course they've had to boil or roast over a hundred billion poor caterpillars along the way.

I see you out there. Sighing, tapping your toes. You're not going to hurry me. I am not going to *let* you hurry me. For those of you, like the 93-year-old juror who just can't wait to get this action started, I'm *sorry*. You don't have a choice. I'm going to finish telling my story.

Well anyway, Ben Kissup seemed a little troubled this morning when he came to get me. I was talking with a nice writer when Ben told me he had some "highly sensitive bidness" to discuss with me. Turns out that bidness involved his daughter, Dido.

Just in case some of you don't know, Dido stayed with me at the condo for the first week after Ben arrested me. Over that week we became close... but not so close that Ben should be looking at me the way he's looking at me now. It wasn't like that. I think we had a lot in common. We really did. Why is that funny? You don't believe me?

So this morning Ben tells me Dido has something to tell me that might ruin his day for sure. For me, I guess I was just glad I'd get to see Dido one last time before I hung from that noose, whatever the reason. And then I thought maybe she was going to confess that *she* was the one who killed Clyde Kissup. But Clyde is her uncle. She wouldn't have killed her uncle.

So Ben takes me back to the condo and she's there, and she's even more beautiful than I remembered. Immediately, I could tell that she had been missing me as much as I had been missing her. What can I say? I was *excited* to see her.

There were so many things I wanted to say. I wanted to tell her there was nothing between Fawn Oliver and me, that there was no one else, that I just mistakenly *thought* there was.

"That's nice, but I didn't come here to try and start up a relationship with you. I came to save your life if I can."

Save my life? Maybe she *was* the one who killed Clyde and she was so in love with me that she had come to take my place at the gallows. Maybe that's why Ben said his day would be ruined.

I was touched, though reluctant to accept her self-immolation.

"I can't let you do it, Dido. Not without telling you I love you and that I really appreciate the great sacrifice you're making for me."

Confusion flooded her expression.

"You mean my daddy didn't tell you yet?"

"Tell me what?"

"Tell you the news about Clyde. He isn't dead. Friends of mine say he's been living just outside Plain over this past week. And the night before last, I think *I* saw him."

A cool river of relief coursed past me. For a first time since the verdict, I felt a new hope, though Ben didn't seem totally optimistic.

"As far as I can tell, them is just rumors, and you told me you weren't wearin your glasses night for last. The guy in them stories couldn't possibly be Clyde. I grew up with Clyde."

Dido pressed the matter to the predictable next issue.

"Daddy, you have to convince the judge uncle Clyde's alive so he can stay the execution."

Ben pressed outward with his palms in protest.

"Now I cain't do that. I cain't go to the judge with a cockamamie story like that about somethin this serious."

He yanked open the curtains.

"Besides. Look at that."

Outside the window, there were busy families going this way and that. They were smiling; they were laughing; they were spending quality time together. There were picnic baskets, coolers stocked with non-alcoholic beer, lemonade and White Zin; there were portable grills.

It was the perfect town populated by perfect people; it was a throwback to surreal 1950s television values—*Leave it to Beaver* and *Father Knows Best*; it was middle America at its finest.

"How am I gonna tell those people? How am I gonna tell those wonderful, hopeful, decent, God-fearin people down there that there ain't gonna be no hangin taday? You tell me that."

Dido yanked the curtains open still wider.

"That's not what I see down there, Daddy. I see the reason why I never liked Polite in the first place. Look at them! Nothing about Polite is real. Those people are whitewashed graves. Outside they look fine, but inside they're full of dried out, dusty bones and dark, dirty little secrets and desires. It's the problem that comes with havin to be nice all the time."

She rapped on the window to get the attention of one of the passers-by, but her knocking went ignored.

"Look at them and all their smiling faces. You would *think* they're going to a ballgame or a parade. They've got their kids, grandparents and *picnic baskets* for God's sake! And all they *really* want to do is watch a man get strangled to death. They're sick, all of em!"

Ben yanked the drapes shut and peeked out before turning.

"I knew I shouldn'ta let ya go ta California. They *ruined* ya out there... like they did this one. California's got the fruits an nuts an Hollyweird an earthquakes an gropin governors, but they ain't got decent people there, not like here."

He parted the curtains and peeked out again, this time nodding as he left the window.

"This is the friendliest small town in the world, and they're decent folks. They jus wanna *hang* the man. It's not like they wanna *hurt* im."

But Ben was really just stalling to delay the inevitable. You see, Dido had come out of her self-imposed exile for a very specific reason, and that was to tell everyone in Polite that she had recently seen her uncle, Clyde Kissup, the man whose murder all of you want to *hang* me for.

She said she told some Polite residents the same thing a day earlier, after she had spotted Clyde outside Plain, but no one wanted to listen. So this morning she came over with an offer of sworn testimony and proof in the form of a witness. She had called her father, Sheriff Ben, and she called Judge Knott, who really does look like Danny Glover, only older.

So as we waited in the condo for the judge to appear, Dido's witness came along, and whereas minutes before I had felt a sense of buoyant, jubilant vindication, my freshly ascending bubble of hope was pricked with new concerns.

I mean this guy had to be the most uninteresting and homely looking person I had ever seen. And he had an offensive body odor. Not that you have to be exciting, at least average-looking and smell good to tell the truth, but I looked at this guy and I kinda thought *he's an urchin, disgusting! Even I wouldn't believe this guy.* His "friends" called him Hobo Joe.

"I saw Clyde Kissup. I saw im. Why he was hangin out at the river with the hobos an he hadn't shaved or took a bath. He was stankin ta high heaven."

Ben unholstered his gun.

"You saw river trash. You saw another hobo like you. You ain't seen no Clyde. I grew up with Clyde, and I happen ta *know* Clyde has great hygiene—takes a bath every mornin!"

"It was Clyde alrite, Clyde Kissup. Showed me his fishin license. Said he was runnin from the law on accounta stealin a bottle a moonshine from Mahmood, the Arab that runs the big liquor store in town. Told me he hadn't brushed his teeth in a week, an ya know, I believed im."

It was obvious that Ben was in denial.

"No! Clyde always brushed. An he flossed—flossed at least three times a day. And I happen ta know Clyde don't steal."

The urchin shrugged as he disagreed, addressing the newly arrived judge.

"Stole a watermelon and a bag of apricots from Ol Miss Stinson's yard three days ago an trampled her spice garden while he was at it. Then he took a piss in her dog's water bowl. Dog drank it and got all *kinda* sick."

Grasping the filthy man's shoulder, Ben pulled him up from the chair.

"Lissen, if I wasn't sheriff of the friendliest town in the world, why I'd, why I'd really give you hell. My cousin Clyde is dead, and here you come tellin us all these lies about im."

Joe hiccupped, pointing toward Dido.

"She saw im."

Dido nodded solemnly.

"I did, Daddy."

"No. You, you were heartbroken, baby; you were depressed; you were hallucinatin."

Hobo Joe rudely slapped Ben on the shoulder.

"She wasn't hallucinatin and neither will you be. Neither will we *all* be when Clyde *gets* here."

Ben did not need to say a word; his horrified face asked the question for him. Joe answered.

"Yep. Soon as he fount out about the hangin y'all was havin, he said he had ta come back for that. He said he never saw a hangin before. He's probably out there right now."

Joe squinted at the clock on the opposite wall.

"Aren't y'all runnin behind schedule? Y'all should've already hanged this man by now. Yer late. An by the way, Judge, bein late ain't exactly polite or friendly."

Sheriff Ben cocked his head.

"Now let me get this straight Hobo, are ya tellin me ya *wanna* see this man get hanged like the rest of us do?"

"Course I do. I wouldn't wanna miss a hangin for anythang in the world."

Ben looked toward the judge for direction and got the nod he sought. He turned back to Joe, almost whispering.

"Lissen Joe, I ain't sure when ya had your last drink, but ya gotta put two and two tagether. Now ya *gotta* know that if you go out there an start tellin people Clyde's alive, there ain't gonna be no hangin taday."

Joe seemed confused.

"So what're ya sayin I should do?"

"I'm a sworn officer of the court. I cain't tell ya what ta do, cept put two and two tagether."

Angry and frustrated, Dido translated for her father.

"What this sworn officer of the court is telling you, Joe, is to go out there and *lie* by not telling people Clyde's alive. He wants you to lie so you can all get to the *hangin* you all want so bad."

Joe's eyes flashed with new understanding.

"Oh, I get it!"

He turned toward the judge.

"Clyde who? I ain't *seen* im."

Dido sighed aloud, glaring toward her father and the judge.

"So it's come to this? You two *so-called* officers of the court would ignore convincing evidence that no murder has occurred here. And you would do it just so you all can see a man, who happens to be innocent, hang from that red silk noose out there? All this in the friendliest little town in the world."

The judge muttered to himself. I'm not sure I, I don't know exactly what he said, but it sounded something like, *I'm getting too old for this shit*, and then he gruffly answered Dido.

"Ms. Kissup, the witness you brought before me is obviously a drunk, and by his own admission he's confused about what and who he saw. For me, that doesn't meet my threshold for stayin this execution. So unless you can come up with some other compelling extenuation or mitigating factor, I see no reason to delay this execution for one minute longer."

He nodded toward her father.

"So it's with great sadness and regret that I hafta tell ya, Ben, ta take this man out and get this action started. The crowd out there is gettin restless."

Dido stood between her father and me.

"What about the fact that people have seen Uncle Clyde? Hobo Joe said he saw him, and talked to him."

Judge Knott glowered, disapproving.

"I'm beginning to lose my patience with you, Dido, or whatever your name is now. This man just told us that he *hadn't* seen Clyde."

"Oh ma God! I saw im! I saw im!"

All eyes snapped toward Joe at the window, who flailed his arms in excitement. Ben, who had reacted to the seeming seizure by raising his nightstick, rolled his eyes.

"Oh beans an corn, Joe! What? Ya saw *what*?"

"Clyde Kissup. I saw Clyde Kissup."

Ben sighed.

"Ya just told the judge that ya *hadn't* seen im. Nah ya need ta make up your mind before your Honor here has ya arrested fa perjury. So what's it gonna be? Either ya seen Clyde or ya ain't seen im. What is it?"

"I seen im. I seen im just now!"

"Where?"

"He just walked by the window down there. I think he's comin *up* here."

There was a sudden bump on the door, and then it swung open. We all braced ourselves in shock, though none of us, save Joe, was prepared for the grunting, harking and spitting, grime-covered phantom that came in and clumsily locked the door behind him. He held a half-filled bottle of White Zin in his filthy hand. Taking a big swig of the vile liquid, he belched aloud and spoke in a boisterous tone.

"Howdy folks! Someone told me we was gonna have an ol-fashioned hangin right here in Polite. Serendipadoo! Did I make it here in time?"

Ben's face was contorted in horror and disgust. He cupped his hand over his nose as he approached the malodorous man.

"Clyde? Don't tell me that really *is* you, Clyde?"

"In the stinkin flesh! God it's great ta see ya, Ben!"

Ben squirmed in Clyde's brawny embrace, like a 4-year-old trying to avoid a kiss in the arms of an oversized though affectionate grandmother. He suddenly released Ben, who wiped the slobbery, dripping puddle from his cheek. Clyde was looking at me.

"You!"

"Me?"

"Yeah, you! I wondered what happened ta ya. Do ya realize you're the man who changed ma life! Ya made me what I am today. I been wantin ta thank ya."

This time it was me in his sweaty, yeasty embrace. He tried to kiss my cheek, but I turned at the last minute. I could feel the White Zin tainted saliva dripping from my violated ear. Eying Ben, I spoke.

"The important thing is that you're *alive*, Clyde. You had people thinking you were dead because you were missing for so long. Your being here changes everything, though. Right, Judge?"

Ben was removing his Clyde-soiled shirt, traumatized by his cousin's sudden reappearance. His daughter pressed for an explanation.

"Why'd you disappear like that, Uncle Clyde? And what's happened to you?"

Clyde made a fist with his right hand and symbolically tapped his heart.

"Freedom, baby. Freedom's what's happened. I got outa Polite an I saw a whole new world out there. I finally opened up my eyes thanks ta that fella rite there."

It was becoming a pattern: me being blamed for something I did not do.

"I cut the fish's gills. What's so big about that?"

"What's so big about that? What's so big about that? That wasn't a fish you caught. That was a message being sent ta me from the outside. I'd been a fool all ma life. Those messages had been comin at me for years, but I always threw em back. Well, the message finally *got* ta me when ya kept that fish!"

The judge looked askance at Clyde and sighed.

"Either someone hit ya in the head real hard or you're on some kinda mind-bendin drug. Which is it?"

Clyde pointed toward me.

"Him."

The judge glared at me.

"Did ya hit im in the head? Real hard?"

"No."

Ben cut in.

"That would be attempted murder, wouldn't it, Judge, dependin on how hard he hit im. Carries the death penalty in this state."

"Waitaminute! I didn't hit him in the head. Clyde, will you tell them I didn't hit you in the head."

Clyde was quick to respond.

"He ain't hit me in the head."

Ben rebutted.

"But Judge, can we really *believe* a man if he says he hasn't been hit in the head when he may have already *been* hit in the head. An because of it he don't have the good sense ta know or remember whether or not he was hit in the head in the first place?"

"Good point, Sheriff. When ya think about it. *I* say we can't believe Clyde. We can all see he's talkin crazy. Attempted murder it is then. Do your job, Ben. The crowd's a-waitin."

Dido stood between her father and me.

"I'm sorry, Daddy, but the only two people in here talking crazy are you and the judge. And uh, maybe Uncle Clyde a little bit. And definitely Joe—get your finger outa your nose, Joe. But Gill's the only sensible one here, and you all wanna *hang* him? So *who's* crazy?"

As her father edged toward me, Dido blocked him with her body, her hand extended. Ben looked from the judge's face to Clyde's, and then he heard the crowd chanting the words "Hang im!" outside. Becoming frustrated, he stuttered.

"Now I don't want it to come ta this, but if ya don't get outa my way, family or no family, I'm gonna hafta arrest ya for obstruction of justice."

Recalcitrant, Dido answered.

"You can't hang an innocent man for hanging's sake. It doesn't *matter* if you do it with a silk noose. Wrong is wrong, and so long as I can vent clamor from my throat I'll tell you it's wrong. I'm not moving."

By this time, Judge Knott was clearly annoyed.

"Listen Dido, or *whoever* you are! I *will* have you arrested for obstruction if you make me. Or should I call you David? Now I didn't want it ta come ta this, but I'm gonna go there if I have to."

Her expression was full of contempt.

"Go there, Judge. Say what you want ta say."

"You're gonna make me do it."

"I insist. Do it. *Say* what you were gonna say, cuz I'm not movin."

The judge shook his head in anger and sighed.

"Young man—Mr. Gill. You probably think you're in love with this young woman, and maybe she thinks she's in love with you, and that's all good, cept for one thing. I could not, the town of Polite could not, not in good conscience let you go on with this charade without tellin ya the truth."

Because I'm from California, I knew instantly where he was going. I looked at Dido, who crossed her arms and batted teary eyes.

"It's not what you think."

Judge Knott countered.

"It *is* what you think. That's right. I'm sorry to inform you, Mr. Gill, but the woman you know as Dido Kissup actually born David Kissup. And he was David all his life till he went to San Francisco after he grew up. Then he came back callin himself Dido all changed into a woman."

Because I'm from San Francisco, I thought I was quite good at recognizing cross-dressers and cross-overs, but as I looked at Dido, I just couldn't believe any designer or doctor could be so good. I mean, she looked more woman than any woman I had ever seen.

And still, I cringed with the heebie-jeebies as I tried to remember whether or not I had actually kissed her... or, or him. I don't think I did, but I couldn't help remembering all those penetrating hot oil massages. And the thought of what

I had done to Dido in my *sexual* imagination—the chocolate sauce raspberry fantasy, the mint julep warm buttermilk bath and all! I couldn't help feeling duped.

"So you, you're a man?"

She sighed and shooed me with her hand.

"I'll explain later. That's not important now. You *do* realize of course that my father wants to lay his hands on you so he can take you out there and *hang* you, don't you?"

"Yes."

"So what are you going to do about it?"

With every time Ben darted to his left, she shot to her right, blocking him, and each time he moved to his right, she spun over to her left. She, or he, was working hard to protect me. And still, I couldn't answer her question. I really didn't know *what* I was going to do about it. Vigilantly pivoting this way and that, she called back over her shoulder, out of breath.

"Uncle Clyde, can you help us out here? You said the message finally got to you when Gill kept the fish. So what was the *message*?"

Looking from me to the clearly irritated judge, Clyde walked up to Dido, taking a place between Ben and me. At six-foot-three, Clyde stood a full four inches taller than his cousin and outweighed him by no less than fifty pounds. But it wasn't his size that kept the sheriff at bay. It was his reeking, Sasquatch-like body odor and Ben's fear of possible contamination or infestation. Sheriff Ben backed, checking his watch.

"We're already fifty minutes behind schedule, Clyde. Will ya get outa ma way so I can do ma job?"

Clyde relaxed his defiant posture as a slow, acquiescent smile transformed his face.

"It's all right, Ben. I wanna see the hangin just as bad as the resta ya. But my nephew asked me a question an it's one I think I gotta answer. Will y'all give me a few minutes here?"

Sighing disgustedly, the judge undid the top button of his shirt.

"You have exactly five minutes, Clyde. So tell us,

what's this about that fish sendin you a message?"

Clyde turned toward me as he began.

"It's true. All ma life I'd thrown fish back, an I never stopped ta question why. It's just somethin ya do when ya fish in Throwback Lake, I guess. So the thoughta ever keepin a fish—ya gotta know how traumatized I was when ya clipped that bass's gills. But I was also awakened in that instant, in a twinklin of that fish's eye."

He shrugged.

"You're gonna think I'm a little looney, but that fish talked ta me all the way back inta the dock. Its blood cried out ta me. It told me again and again ta get off the boat an just keep walkin, so I did. I walked right outa Polite. I was a little nervous cuz it was the first time I had ever been outa this town."

He answered the expression on his cousin's skeptical face.

"It's something *you* oughta try, Ben. An you too, Judge. Cuz when I got out there, outside Polite, I began ta understan that everthang I believed before, everthang about my life an your lives an the lives of everbody in Polite. Well, somethin strange is goin on here. It's like that Matrix movie. It's a lie. Polite ain't really the friendliest small town in the world. It's just a town that wants ta be all that. An because it thinks it is, the people in Polite can never be what they truly are. I spent ma entire life aspirin ta be somethin I am not. So call Polite the lyin-est small town in the world an that would be more true. We shit here just like the rest of the world shits, only we pretend we don't. What? Are ya tellin me ya don't shit, Judge?"

Judge Knott nervously shifted in his seat.

"Let's, let's just leave me out of this."

"That's just ma point! Cuz what's worse? Ta be honest ta people an maybe hurt their feelins, or ta outright lie ta people ta spare em. What's more friendly? Tell me that."

Ben peered through the window down at the crowds.

"Why don't cha jus finish your story, Clyde?"

"Livin in Polite is like bein in church twenty-four-seven, an who wants ta do that? Soon as I walked outa this place, I felt a huge weight lift off me. I felt free. So I went ta Plain, thinking life would be better there, but they were just as bad as they are here, only the other way round. They fart out loud there, an sometimes they fart right on each other. Saw a man fart right on his girlfriend's head, right on her forehead, I think."

Looking at the judge, you'd think he simultaneously smelled the man's intestinal product.

"We get your point, Clyde. That'll be enough."

"An they burp out loud, an they pick an scratch their butts, an they curse, an they dig in their noses like Joe there, an they kiss in public, an they always tell each other the truth, an they shower only when they want to, an they take the last seat, or piece of pizza or chip or anythang else that's last, an they talk about sex an how they do it every night. Even women like an talk about sex over there. They do everthang in Plain that we don't do here in Polite."

Disgusted though intrigued by Clyde's descriptions, Ben had left the window.

"An that's why I ain't never been ta Plain. I'd be better off goin ta Hell."

Clyde smiled triumphantly.

"That's it! That's ma point, that's the message of the fish. If Plain is Hell an Polite is Heaven, then flesh an blood people don't belong in either. Neither is natural for people tryin ta go through life. If life is school, if it's all a big lesson, then none of us can afford ta stay in places where we cain't learn."

He threw an arm over Ben's shoulder.

"So that's why soon as the hangin is over, I'm gonna walk right outa this town an none of y'all will ever see me again."

He kissed Ben on the forehead.

"Need any help with the hangin?"

The judge interrupted, clearing his throat.

"Gentlemen, I regret to inform you. But Clyde, based on what I've heard you say this afternoon, I'm afraid I have to conclude that Mr. Gill there *didn't* attempt to murder you by hitting you in the head real hard. And because you're obviously still alive, I'm certain the murder conviction will be overturned. The sad truth is that at this point, we don't have a legal basis for hangin this man."

Ben's knees buckled. He panted, short of breath.

"Judge? Are ya sayin there ain't gonna be no hangin taday? What about the crowds?"

Clyde pleaded in his cousin's behalf.

"Was it somethin I said? I'll take it back! Can't we just forget I said it?"

"I'm afraid not, gentlemen."

He turned toward me.

"Mr. Gill or whoever you are—I just told Ben an Clyde there that we don't have a *legal* basis for hangin you, and that's true. But that don't mean we can't hang you if ya let us. You could still give us *permission* ta hang you."

"And why would I do that?"

He stood, approaching me.

"You've probably never thought about this, but my ancestors came to America in the hulls of slave ships, and what's worse, for the ones that didn't die along the way, they were auctioned as chattel and sold into forced servitude for the rest of their lives."

Joe, sitting in a chair by the door, was emotional.

"Why Judge, that's horrible!"

I couldn't help but agree.

"Yes it is, but what does that have to do with me giving you guys permission to hang me?"

"Even after slavery was ended, my family faced discrimination in every walk of life. And because of it, I was the first one in my family to finish high school. I was the first to finish college and law school. I was the first to become a lawyer and a judge."

He bowed his head.

"And today, I was all set to be the first in my family to have a man executed or hanged. And not only that, I was set to be the first African American judge to have a man executed in this state. Had my ninety-three-year-old mother fly all the way in from Charleston to witness my proud moment, but now it doesn't seem like it'll happen... unless you help us out here. What do you say?"

I felt guilty. I didn't want to disappoint the judge and his old mother, but I wasn't exactly keen about being hanged.

"I'm sorry, Judge. Maybe if I were a couple years older I could do it, but there are still a lot of things I haven't done yet."

"Are you a bigot, Mr. Gill?"

I had no idea where that had come from.

"Excuse me?"

"Are you a bigot, Sir? Do you have anything against African Americans?"

It was almost funny, but I had an answer.

"Barring the obvious, Judge, the way I figure: Africa's the birthplace of all humankind. So we're *all* African Americans. We all just got here at different times and under different circumstances."

"Then why would you want to keep me, an African American, from being the first African American judge to have a man executed in this state, and maybe in the whole country?"

In all fairness to people from Kansas, I think Polite had to be the exception. No other city in the state was quite like it.

"Once again, I'm sorry, Judge. I just came through here trying to do a favor for my ex-wife. I'm not the scapegoat for the sins of this town, and that has nothing to do with you being black."

"You, you called me black! I think you *are* a bigot, Mr. Gill. If I could, I'd hang ya for that.!"

In all my life I never imagined there was anything racially offensive about the term. Maybe I should have called it the "b" word.

"What's wrong with black?"

"How dare you call me black. I am not black. I'm, I'm an African American."

I was going to correct him. According to my logic, the judge was a *black* African American, as opposed to the reeking Clyde, who was a white African American. But before I could say anything, Ben began with his own appeal.

"Lissen Gill, if you won't do it for him, then maybe you'll think about doin it for the good people of Polite."

He guided me over to the window.

"Just look down there. Those really are wonderful folks, Gill, an all they wanna do is watch a little hangin, a hangin they've been lookin forward ta seein for weeks now. In fact, some of em camped out overnight ta get the good spots."

He yanked the curtains aside.

"An look at all the signs and banners they got down there. Look at that one. It says 'We love you, Gill,' an that one, 'Gill's a heckuvva guy!' They all *like* you. You're they hero. You can't let them down."

As I looked down, a pretty young woman in the crowd spotted me at the window. She pointed, screamed and fainted, causing waves of pandemonium in my boisterous sea of fans. My face was on posters sticking up in various places in an awestricken swarm that crawled anxiously toward the window. That's when I saw the buttons and the T-shirts with my picture on them, and the teenagers who dressed themselves and made up their faces to look just like me.

And some in the throng wore necklaces, and hanging from these necklaces were idols of me hanging from red silk nooses. Others embraced parts I recognized from the broken-down Reliant automobile that had stranded me in Polite. It was the closest I had ever come to being worshiped, the closest I had ever come to deification.

"I don't get it. Why are these people so obsessed with me?"

"You're a phenomenon, Gill. What you're doin means everthang ta them!"

A longhaired, overweight man at the front of the crowd struck the ground with his staff and shouted my name, though it wasn't really my name. After the first few calls, the crowd began to chant with him.

"Gill! Gill! Gill! Gill!"

You were all so fervent and hopeful, so intent and passionate, and your focus was solely on me. I could feel the spirit of your assembly directed at me. I felt what any human so idolized would feel. There was this sort of supernatural power coursing through my being, and I liked it.

It was... intoxicating in a very real way—so much so that as I looked over at the red silk noose at the gallows, I imagined the culmination of the event, with me hanging there and the crowd writhing before me in one intense orgasm. Though dead, I would be immortalized in that moment. Fortunately, I caught myself. I mean, what the hell was I thinking?

"What the hell are you thinking?"

Dido had come up behind me and had placed her right arm around my waist, hooking her thumb in the belt loop on my right side. I recoiled, naturally. More than that, I wanted to get away, but I didn't want to hurt her feelings, or his feelings.

I awkwardly glanced over at the judge and Clyde, who also seemed uncomfortable with the physical contact. Dido, who was taking it all in, didn't care. In fact, I got the distinct sense that she, or he, was getting some sadistic gratification from making them squirm. My hunch was confirmed when she/he unhooked her thumb, dropped her hand briefly and slapped my butt.

I smiled sheepishly, trying to back away, but Dido had grabbed flesh. And then, when she turned me and began pulling me toward her, I remember thinking that no woman could be that strong. It might not seem like it in these clothes, but I have muscles, big muscles, and she was just overpowering me. No woman was that strong. When it was all over, we were face to face, with her lips mere inches from mine. She whispered.

"Do you trust me?"

I could feel the other four sets of eyes in the room trained on me, on us. And I knew everyone heard what she had said. Did I trust her? I didn't understand what she was getting at. I placed my hands on the outside of her waist, trying subtly to push her/him away as I answered.

"Of course I trust you."

She wiggled her waist through my hands and pressed her body against mine.

"Then kiss me."

Looking in her eyes, she seemed so woman. Her cheeks seemed so soft, her eyes so alluring, those lips so inviting. She smelled luscious. Helplessly, I let myself move slowly closer. And then my imagination got the better of me: as her pelvis area rubbed the outside of my right thigh, I thought I felt something, something uh, fleshy. I immediately tried to pull away, but she had me; she held me tight.

"I *asked* you if you trusted me."

"I, I do!"

"Then prove it. Kiss me."

Suddenly that silk noose didn't seem like such a bad idea.

"You have to tell me. Are you a man?"

"Kiss me and find out."

In that instant, something deep within me told me to do it; something told me to take the chance. And so taking a deep breath to build resolve, I closed my eyes and kissed her. I could hear the other men in the room groan aloud in protest and aversion, but I continued kissing her. It felt good. It felt right. She had to be a woman! After nearly a minute, the kiss ended and I pulled back.

"I kissed you. So tell me."

She backed and smiled, her eyes falling to that erstwhile tight area in the front of my pants.

"Well, I already know what a *certain* point of your anatomy is telling you, but what does your heart tell you?"

"That you're a woman?"

She laughed.

"You mean you're not sure? You mean you can't tell a woman from a man?"

"I can. You're a woman."

"Yes, and you're going to have to take my word on it. We won't be going into any offers of proof, not here at least."

I wanted to believe her, but so far, it was her word against those of her father and uncle and probably the whole town of Polite.

"But the judge said—"

"Are you forgetting where you are? Polite? The friendliest small town in the world?"

Judge Knott obviously took umbrage with the remark.

"Now hold on here, David! And you're name *is* David, not Dido. I watched you grow up here as a boy. You spent the night at my house with my sons as a boy. You sat at my dinner table as a boy. Then you went out to California and changed yourself into somethin else. You might be able to get away with sayin people in Polite sometimes go a little overboard in the manners department or that we're maybe a bit too nice, but ta do a number an try ta pass yourself off as somethin you're not is a fraud. It's immoral, it's illegal and it's exactly what you're doin."

Dido looked toward me and shrugged.

"He's right. My real name *is* David. I was born David Aeneas Kissup, and I did grow up as a boy. I hung out with the judge's sons, I played little league and I even took a girl to the junior prom. I took Fawn Oliver. But I am not a fraud."

David's voice broke as tears swelled in her eyes.

"I'm not tryin to do a *number* on Polite or on anyone in this room. No, it's been the other way around. Polite and everything it represents has done a number on me. Polite is the fraud."

The remark had an immediate effect on Ben, who took a place next to the judge.

"What are ya talkin bout? How dare ya speak ill of this town. Polite is the perfect place."

"For *you* it was, Daddy. Maybe for everyone else it was, but not for me."

She looked toward me.

"It seems everyone else here has told their story. Well

now I'm going to tell mine. Come on over here, Uncle Clyde. You need to hear this too."

With everyone in the room settled before her, David began.

"Even from very early on, I realized I was different from the other boys. I wasn't as big or strong; I ran like a girl, I threw the ball like a girl, I sat down to pee and I preferred *dolls* to cap guns. I got called sissy a lot."

She nodded toward Clyde.

"Even by my uncles. For some reason when I watched TV, I identified with the female characters, and when I imagined myself all grown up, it was always as a woman. My first boyfriend was Judge Knott's son, Leroy."

Noting the abject horror on the judge's face, she held a hand up.

"But things were not the way they seemed. This is Polite, remember?"

Her father shrugged.

"What does Polite have ta do with any of this?"

"Well, it wasn't until I was thirteen that I realized it wasn't me. It was this town and the whole idea you have that it is a better thing to lie than to hurt someone's feelings."

Fearing the worst, the judge put the question.

"Why? What happened when you were thirteen?"

"My first menstrual cycle."

Ben's head snapped toward Dido.

"Your what?"

"My first menstrual cycle. I was *born* a girl, Daddy, but if you remember, you always wanted a boy. When Momma was pregnant, she had complications, and Doc Sanguine told her I'd be the only child she'd ever have. After I was born, she didn't want to disappoint you, so she got the doctor to go along with it and she told you and everybody else I was a boy. She dressed me like a boy, she cut my hair like a boy, she tried to make me into a boy, but I've always been a girl."

She smiled at me.

"And I'm a woman now. Anyway, that first menstrual cycle was a disaster. I mean with the cramps and all the bleeding, I thought I was dying. I had been climbing a tree when it happened and I figured I had ruptured something. So I went running home screaming hysterically, and Momma was there. She calmly explained it all to me for the first time then."

The judge reached out, offering his handkerchief to Dido, who blew her nose.

"Thank you. She said that after the first six months she wanted to tell you, Daddy, but by that time there was no telling you. She said you had bragged your little boy up from one end of Polite to the other. You told her all the time how glad you were that I wasn't a girl. And you had believed I was a boy for thirteen years."

"That's a sad story. That's *such* a sad story!"

Hobo Joe was sitting forward in his chair, wiping tears from his filthy face with a blackened shirtsleeve. Clearly annoyed by the interruption, the judge glared over at Joe, who immediately sat erect, like a scolded child in Sunday school.

"Please, go on."

David looked at her father.

"So after explaining all that to me, Momma begged me not to tell anyone, especially you. She made me promise. Then she promised me she would persuade you to move us out of Polite, and after we moved someplace else, we could all start a new life. It would save all the questions and the embarrassment. And that's when we'd tell you I was a girl."

She sighed sadly.

"But we all know Momma died when I was thirteen, just two months later. I'm convinced she died out of guilt. So there I was thirteen years old in a dilemma that could only be had in Polite. I remember thinking then that if Momma couldn't in thirteen years summon enough courage to tell you the truth, how was I gonna do it? I was just a little girl. And for me it was easier at that difficult time to let you go on believing the lie to spare your feelins, all at my expense."

She smiled triumphantly.

"I've always been a girl, Daddy. There, I said it. That's the big secret I've had to carry all these years."

She watched a tear stream down her approaching father's face as she continued.

"When I was sixteen, I realized I had to get out of Polite to be true to myself, so I ran away to San Francisco and started a new life... as a woman, as the daughter you never knew you had."

Ben reached for his daughter and the two hugged. It was a moving moment, though Clyde remained unconvinced.

"What's that you said you had? A menstrual cycle? I don't believe in that. Did ya have a sex *change* in San Francisco?"

"If that's what you want to call it, Uncle Clyde, but it wasn't an external thing."

The judge was still piecing past events together.

"So all those sleepovers and camping trips you and Leroy had when you were teenagers? You knew and he knew?"

"You don't want to know."

Ironically, it was Joe who brought us back to the original story line.

"That's all well an good, but what about the hangin? Is he gonna hang or not, cuz I'm gettin tired of all these distractin *segues*! Did I say that right?"

Clyde concurred, glancing toward me.

"He's got a point. Isn't that what we're all here for? So are ya gonna let us hang ya, or not?"

The judge continued.

"Aw, come on Mr., Mr. Gill. After all you put us and this town through, you kinda owe it to us, and Dido. Whatdaya say you just let us go through with it? We'll even rename Main Street that goes right through the middle of town after you, and we'll give you your own holiday. We'll change that Martin Luther King holiday to Gill Day. And it's a *silk noose*, for God's sake! It won't even hurt."

Yet before I could fashion a response, there was a

knock at the door. When Ben answered the door and let in a man and a little boy, I could hear the rumble of a large crowd out in the hallway. After whispering a few words to Ben, the man took his son's hand and approached me.

"Sir, you don't know me. I'm a nobody, but this is my son, Willie, and Willie has somethin ta say ta ya."

Looking at the boy's puffy eyes, I could tell he had been crying. He had to be about ten or eleven. In his shaking hands, he held a stack of papers, stapled in the top left corner.

"In, in my class we had to do a biography about the person we admire most, an I chose you. My report is called, *The World's Greatest Man*, an I want ya ta see it."

As I flipped through the pages, I was impressed by the boy's refreshing diction and great attention to detail. He had included my parents' names and the names of my brothers and sisters, he had included pictures of me (some clipped from newspaper articles and various polaroids) and he had drawn a picture of me hanging from the silk noose at the gallows.

The picture really struck me as odd, because as I hung from the gallows high above the huddled masses, my outstretched arms had formed the letter "T", but there were other familiar things. My feet were together, my shirt was off and I was wearing this diaper-like red silk swathe. The sun and moon shined above me with two angelic women attending me at each side. I swear this kid was all over that R. Santi guy.

"Mister, when everyone out there saw Mr. Clyde Kissup comin up here, we all knew ya hadn't killed anyone. Some folks said that meant there wasn't gonna be no hangin taday, but I told em they was wrong. I told em I always knew you hadn't done nothin wrong, but you'd let em go through with the hangin anyway. I told em ya'd do it for them. I told em ya'd do it for us."

As I looked down on the boy's gaze, unwavering and assured, I was overwhelmed by the power of his faith. His father stood humbly by, hat in hand and head piously bowed.

"I think what my boy is sayin, your, your Eminence, is

this town needs you. This town needs ya ta do what only you can do."

The throng in the hallway had forced itself to the door of the condo, where a sea of hopeful, faithful eyes washed over me. Never in my life had I felt such, such significance. I don't know why I said it.

"Give me a little time to think about it."

The judge's head snapped up.

"What? You're going to *think* about it, meaning you just might do this for us?"

I nodded.

"Yes."

"That's good enough for me. Ben, let's get all these people outa here! The man's gonna think about it! We don't want all these people confusing him."

As expected, Dido remained, disappointed. She approached, speaking in a soft voice.

"What are you doing? Why would you say you're going to think about it?"

I sighed.

"I don't know. I don't know why I do this to myself."

"Are you understanding any of this? These people want to *hang* you. It doesn't matter if they're the friendliest small town people in the world. It doesn't matter that they love you and attach all this significance to what you do. And it doesn't matter that the silk noose is so beautiful and soft and would be comfortable around your neck. The end result is what matters, and pleasing all these nice people only means you'll be dead in the end. Is that what you want?"

"No? No."

Ben interrupted.

"Dido? The man said he wanted ta think thangs out. Let's not start confusin im."

She ignored her father.

"The greatest vanity is self importance and the solution is a simple one. All you have to do is accept the truth and you can walk right out of this thing."

"What truth?"

"That you are not as important as you think you are; that what you do today won't matter in the grander scheme of things; that political and polite answers are usually lies. *Speak what you feel, not what you ought to say.*"

I could scarce respond to Dido's observation before Ben opened the door to a surprise. I didn't know what to think as Fawn Oliver stood there, smiling coyly at me.

"I missed you so much!"

I didn't get it. Wasn't this the woman who went before the whole town in court and told everyone she faked it with me? No, it was worse. She told everyone that she didn't have sex with me, and now she was pretending again.

"I want you."

It was a moment of truth. On the one hand, I had Dido: beauty, intelligence, loyalty, honesty and stability. On the other I had Fawn: totally hot, naive, promiscuous, polite and capricious. I could use lofty nouns to describe Dido's qualities—a good thing in a woman, while Fawn could only be described with shallow adjectives.

"Tell em you'll let em use that silk noose on you, an you can have me as many times as you can handle it, right now."

She licked and puckered her lips while pressing her firm, curvaceous, nubile, incredible body against me.

"Come on. It'll all be yours. I'll do anything you tell me to."

Her eyes must have had heat sensors in them, because they dropped, locking on that area of my lower body that was somehow warming up against my will. I took one step back and another toward Dido.

"Not interested."

By that time, it seemed everyone in the room had the heat sensors.

"That's not what your *body* is saying."

The woman had some nerve. I put an arm around Dido as I responded.

"What about your basketball player?"

"What basketball player?"

"You know what basketball player—the one with the really big hands and the really big—"

She interrupted.

"Oh, *that* basketball player! Stupid NBA! For some reason they're tellin all their guys to stay away from small, mid-western towns. He left two days ago."

Fawn, from the moment she came in the room, had been scrutinizing Dido. Edging close, she peered at Dido's face.

"Waitaminute! Those eyes. I'd recognize em anywhere. I *know* you, don't I?"

For the first time, the typically plainspoken Dido seemed apprehensive.

"I know who *you* are, but you don't know me."

"Yes I do. You're David Kissup! You ditched me at the junior prom. What are you doin all dressed up like a woman?"

Dido glanced furtively toward her father and the judge, answering.

"I *am* a woman, Fawn. I was born a girl. My mother tried to pass me off as a boy, but I was a girl all along. I ditched you at the prom after you told me you wanted to make out with me."

Fawn sighed, laughing aloud.

"Oh my god! An all this time I thought it was somethin wrong with *me*! You know, you're the only guy who's ever turned me down, and it bothered me my whole life. What a relief! All this time I thought it was me, but it wasn't me. It was somethin wrong with *you*!"

"You're right. It was me."

Fawn's eyes fixed on Dido's arm around my waist.

"So now I suppose *you* think ya got somethin goin on with him?"

"Well, I *suppose* you could say that."

Fawn was already unbuttoning her shirt as she grabbed my wrist.

"I'm sorry, because he's goin to the bedroom with me,

and then he's got a job to do out there."

I held my place.

"Fawn, I *said* I wasn't interested."

Dido grasped Fawn's forearm and took my wrist from her hand.

"I guess that makes him the only *other* guy who's ever turned you down."

By this time, the judge, who had sat listening the entire time with Ben and Clyde, broke in seeking clarification.

"I'm sorry, sir, but are we to understand that when you said you weren't interested, you were referring specifically to Ms. Oliver's offer? You still *do* have our other matter under consideration, don't you?"

I started to answer, but Joe nearly knocked me over as he rushed past me toward the quickly exiting Fawn. He was missing his two front teeth, but his brown, chipped-toothed smile and the twinkle in his eye had a certain hobo-ish charm to them. He stood before her, blocking the door.

"Ms. Oliver? I don't know *what's* wrong with all these guys, especially him! Hell, *I'm* not turnin ya down. I'll go in that bedroom with ya."

Tears swelling her doe-like eyes, she pushed past Joe, bowed her head and slipped out the door. I didn't know whether to feel vindicated or to feel sorry for her. And then I began to feel sorry for myself. Despite the seeming devastation in her demeanor, Fawn would soon forget me. All that would take is the next visitor to the Polite Hotel. She could, after all, go back to Polite society, back to a world of insincere compliments, false courtesy, White Zinfandel and the patented Polite smile, the grinning and macabre trademark of the world's friendliest small town. But where would I go?

Oh, I had options. I could have gone back to San Francisco and begged my former boss to rehire me at that dead-end job, and I know he'd have done it. I could have worn out the rest of my life writing copy for pantyhose lines and tampon brands, but the more I thought about it, the more the whole situation would have seemed like Polite. If it meant going back to that, I might as well have stayed here.

Or I could have moved to another city and started a brand new life. And when I got there, maybe I could have found a friendly young woman to take me in, intoxicate me and lie to me. And maybe I could have bumped into a man who would have befriended me and thirsted me to death and had me accused of something I never did. And maybe there I could have been rushed to judgment and fussed over on the way to the gallows where I could be comfortably hanged with a silk rope high above the crowds as a scapegoat for their sins, all of this in one way or another.

And I had other options. Until a few minutes ago, I was in possession of a certain key that opens a certain box with enough money in it to have retired me for the rest of my life. Right, Pauli? I could have been a millionaire, traveling all over the world, dating exotic young women, wearing gold and diamonds, buying a condo in Manhattan. I could have lived the good life, hanging out with that rap star/producer, Bo Diddy. But eventually that would have grown old.

Ultimately I'd have realized that the glitter and the smiles sparkling around me in that lifestyle would have been even more counterfeit than they are here in Polite. Besides that, wealth comes at a price; it depreciates character and attracts vultures in eld. I always thought I wanted to be rich, but there I was: I literally had the key to wealth, and I didn't want it. I would have given it to you, Pauli, but I didn't want to be responsible for the consequences it would have caused you.

But back to Ben and the judge and the rest of you. Ben wants to live up to the legacy of his dad, Topeka, who started the practice of hanging people with silk nooses in this town. And unless the NBA lets its players start coming back to small Midwestern towns, I might be Ben's last chance to make his daddy proud. So Ben wants me to volunteer to let him hang me.

Ben, I think what would make your daddy proudest is you accepting and acknowledging the daughter you never knew you had. The lovely woman standing over there—that's Dido Kissup, Ben's *daughter*.

And then there's the judge. He brought his ninety-three-year-old mother all the way out from Charleston to witness his proud moment of being the first African American judge to have a man executed in this state. Judge, African Americans have done many wonderful things for and in this country, but does being the *first* to do something necessarily have to be a good thing? What's wrong with being the first to *not* do something? And doesn't it matter that I'm innocent? In my mind, neither yours nor Ben's is a good enough reason for me to let you hang me.

So that brings us to you, the kind people of Polite. Why is it that you good people want to see me hang? You probably don't know and have never stopped once to think about it. I look out at you, and what do I see? I see the nicest people I've ever met, the friendliest small town in the world. You're like the calm, pacific surface of the sea. But anyone familiar with the ocean knows that beneath most calm surfaces lie deadly undercurrents.

Maybe you need to take the time to examine some of those thoughts, passions and motives you've been suppressing all these years. Maybe you should step out of all that politeness every once in a while and let yourselves be grouchy when you feel like it. Maybe you could refrain from complimenting a butt-ugly baby, show up late at church or speak your mind when it's important, maybe if you did those things every once in a while you wouldn't be standing around like a bunch of mindless characters from a Stephen King novel, just waiting to watch a man choke to death. It's sick, it really is! And the White Zin—get rid of it. The appearance of wine is not always wine.

Okay, I had finally decided to take Dido and get out of town. But what I *didn't* know—when the judge and Ben told me I had a choice, when they said it was up to me, they were just being polite. They were lying.

As it turned out, I had a choice, just so long as it was the right choice, the choice that hangs me from that silk noose. Our public servants have become public opinion servants. Not hanging me would incite a riot, so I'm hanging for the public good, with sheriff Clyde Kissup looking on, mind you. The appearance of a choice is not always a choice.

So there you have it. Now you can all rest assured that you didn't come out this morning and stake your territories in front of the gallows in vain. You weren't forced to sit through my speech only to have me ruin your glorious Hanging Day by not hanging. You'll get your sick little show.

I'm not the first who, with best meaning, has incurred the worst. Here's Ben, with the silk noose, the polite instrument of my demise. He'll get no fight from me. My fate is sealed. Now my wrists are behind my back and he's tying them together, but I won't struggle.

The fight against human nature is the most futile fight of all. No wicked deed against a man by cruelest enemy could wound more deeply than the well-intended, falsely sweet betrayal by a person called a friend.

As I stand here before you, the noose about my neck, is it betrayal I see? No, I see women weeping for me, I see children idolizing me, and I see men measuring themselves and each other by me. I see a crowd praying for me. And yet I never said you had betrayed me.

My own vanity is my undoing. I am hanged for being vain, which is the first and worst of all sins. This silk noose is a lie. It's wonderfully intricate. It's a work of art, and it feels soft, warm and gentle on my neck, but I'm not fooled. For all its beauty and worth, the silk noose kills with the same deadly violence as the braided hemp rope.

For those of you hearing my story, the point is fairly simple. In the end, appearances are false, flatterers tell lies and vanity is a snare, but plainness is the best of all. Unless you understand that, your ultimate fate is worse than mine. Your own silk noose will find you. And thus if you are wise, you will view my life as a cautionary tale: choose or forfeit choice.

The Essays

On Niggers and Squirrels

On Timothy McVeigh

On The Seven Year Hitch

The preceding stories were works of fiction. The essays that follow and the incidents described therein are based on the life, experiences and opinions of the author.

ON NIGGERS AND SQUIRRELS

During my college years, at a time I finally learned to appreciate the wisdom of older people, my grandfather Homer told me that the life of a "niggah don't amount to the life of a squirrel." Having lived the first seventy-five years of his life in and around Greenwood, Mississippi, he said that he'd seen white men go to jail for killing squirrels when it wasn't squirrel season, but he had never seen a white man go to jail for killing a black man.

From the early 1900s to 1975 when he moved to California, he had seen his share of lynching and other murders. He stood with the victim's grandfather as he watched lynched teenager Emmit Till's mutilated and bloated body being dragged out the river near Money, Mississippi. He had seen proscribed blacks who trusted the system enough to turn themselves in being dragged from the jail kicking and screaming only to have their mangled and burned bodies found hanging from one tree or another the next morning. He heard hushed whispers over the years that some of the worst murderers of black men and their families were friends and relatives of the judge. "That was just the way thangs was," he told me, "An ya couldn't go ta the sheriff cuz lotta times he was part of the lynch gang."

Notwithstanding, my grandfather was one of those black men who had faith in the criminal justice system here in America, though he didn't trust the guardians of that system. While he was never bitter, he always suggested that America is the only country where it's a crime to be a black man.

I grew up in Sacramento, the fourth of seven children in a middle-class family. I was a typical California teenager: I spent summers in and at swimming pools; I went to good schools where I played saxophone in the band, I ran track and I got involved in speech and debate and student government. My best friend was a white kid who lived on the next block. Yet when neighborhood kids swarmed to play football in the street in front of our house or basketball around the corner, we were black, white, Filipino, Mexican, you name it.

So It Begins...

I guess we were just too busy having too much fun to notice the racial differences between us. We knew who had an early curfew, we knew who got clothes from the second hand store, who had no outside shot, who had never kissed a girl. Those were the things that made us different then. It was an innocent time for all of us, yet by the time we were finishing high school, we were completely amazed at the way society had begun to force its distinctions and preferences on us.

There was a game the whole gang of us used to play at the mall. We'd go in and just walk through a department store. When we sent my best friend and his brother, they were able to move around unhindered. If they asked to look at the jewelry, the smiling, patient clerk would remove it from the case and let them examine it.

But when they came out and my brother and I went in, we were conspicuously followed by security guards who whispered into walkie-talkies. The clerks ignored us and balked at our requests to examine the jewelry. While we all laughed and were bewildered at the blatant absurdity of it all, it was then that I was forced to realize that throughout my adult life, I would be treated differently just because I was black.

The Death of Innocence

We were all involved in the typical teenage mischief during high school like the rest of our peers, but none of us ever got into any trouble with law enforcement. Nonetheless, my first conscious examination of the criminal justice system in America came in 1979, the year after I graduated high school. It centered on a significant incident in Sacramento.

A kid we went to high school with, a black kid, who was still a senior, had been stabbed to death by two white kids as he was walking home from school. His name was Milton Baker, and because his parents and mine were acquainted, I knew him well. He was a smart, quiet student who had played tuba behind me in band. I had the distinct impression he liked white people better than he liked blacks, evidenced by the fact he had few black friends and loved rock music. Anyway, after being stabbed numerous times, he tried to run home. Disoriented from blood loss, he collapsed next to a tree in a neighbor's front yard and died there.

His parents were understandably angry and outraged, my family was angry, many blacks in the community were up in arms, demanding justice. To our surprise, the two white teenagers who killed Milton Baker claimed they had acted in self-defense. They said that the quiet, mild-mannered kid I remembered had somehow attacked them. A witness claimed to see the boys still stabbing Milton as he was running away.

The boys were arrested initially, but they were released after a few days. Despite pressure by the family and the black community, they were never charged and made to stand trial. A few days in jail for viciously stabbing a human being to death! I'd known of people spending more time in jail for traffic violations. That's when I began to lose faith in the American justice system. The callous devaluation of Milton Baker's life devalued my own, devalued the life of every other black man, woman and child in America.

Notwithstanding, outside the criminal justice system, most notably in the fields of sports and entertainment, blacks prospered. Donna Summer was the disco queen and Earvin Johnson was bringing his unique brand of magic to basketball. O.J. Simpson was setting records and Oprah Winfrey was beginning her media career. Yet the wholesale devaluation of the lives of black people continued.

In Buffalo, two black taxi drivers had the hearts cut from their bodies. In Chicago, police investigated the sniper shootings of four black men in separate incidents. Elsewhere,

the FBI hunted James Vaughn for questioning in connection
with the rifle murders of blacks in five cities and the shooting
of National Urban League President Vernon Jordan. By mid-
November 1980 in Atlanta, eleven black children had been
kidnapped and murdered and another four were missing.
Most of these murders remain unsolved today.

Comedian Richard Pryor joked on an album about
special precautions blacks had to take when being confronted
by law enforcement, but in reality it was no laughing matter
to many like myself. I have been randomly stopped about
twice a year in every year of my adult life for no other reason
than being a black man on the road. The underlying injustice
is that while I am being stopped and questioned on a regular
basis, my white counterparts are not subject to the same
scrutiny or mistreatment.

Akin to Rape

One of the most significant events of my life
happened during one of these random stops by law
enforcement. I was twenty-two and I was staying with an
uncle in southern California, more specifically in Norwalk
between Buena Park and Whittier. My Uncle Bill, who was a
superintendent for the County Solid Wastes Department,
happened to live in one of the area's nicer neighborhoods.

Anyway, one rainy afternoon as I was driving back to
his house in my blue Ford Mustang, I noticed a police car
behind me flashing its headlights back and forth from left to
right. As I looked over my shoulder, he turned on the red and
blue lights atop the car and blared the high-pitched siren for
a couple of seconds. Already accustomed to being randomly
stopped, I pulled my driver's license from my wallet, placing
it on the dash next to the vehicle's registration taken from
the glove box. I then placed both my hands in full view on
the steering wheel and sat back in the seat.

Normally, such precautions were enough to insure
minimum harassment by law enforcement, but it became
apparent that this officer planned on taking the systematic
harassment I had been experiencing to a new level.

Responding to a tap on the window, I looked back almost directly into the long barrel of a .357 magnum revolver. I was certain he was going to shoot me, so I just held my breath and waited.

He tapped on the window again, insisting that I should lower it, which I did very dutifully and cautiously. He demanded to see my driver's license and the vehicle registration card which I, hands shaking, transferred from the dash to the window. During this time, in quick discreet sidelong glances, I couldn't help but see the gun pointed at the back of my head. He stood in the rain, carefully examining the documents for about a minute before lowering the gun.

"Stay in your vehicle. I'll be back."

The admonition was unnecessary. I hardly moved a muscle in the five to seven minutes he was gone. Nonetheless, through my car's rear view mirrors, I was able to determine that there was another officer in the police car. I'm not sure why, but the presence of another officer was a relief to me; I guess I felt that even the most rogue person on the force would have to exercise a little restraint in the presence of another officer. He tapped again on the window I had raised to keep the rain out. I lowered it, apologizing and explaining why I had raised it.

"Shut up! Just get out of the car, nigger!"

"Nigger," the notorious "N" word. It was a word that had never really bothered me. To me, it brought more disgrace to the person who used it than it did the person or persons being so labeled. Yet my subjective thoughts, however noble, were irrelevant in the situation.

The police officer had called me "nigger" for a very specific reason: to humble and humiliate me. I was apprehensive about getting out of the car. I knew I had no outstanding traffic-related warrants and absolutely no criminal record, so I couldn't understand why he was ordering me out into the street. For that matter, he had never told me why I was stopped in the first place. Politely, I put the question.

"Why did you stop me? What did I do wrong?"

His response was a series of threats, expletives and another demand that I step out into the rain, which I did.

"On the ground, nigger."

His cold eyes were full of arrogance and contempt for me. He held a large black flashlight in his right hand, tapping his thigh impatiently, ready for me to challenge him. Despite my generally pacifist nature, it was as close as I've ever come to physically assaulting anyone in my adult life.

I was prepared for the insults and intimidation from the beginning—those I could endure. It was just that I wearing a brand new 3-piece Armani wool suit. It was only the second time I had put it on. I looked from the muddy ground before me back up into the face of the man, who managed a sadistic grin as he neared, trying to appear more threatening.

"On the ground!"

I had little choice. I dropped to my knees, feeling at once the cold, wet, gritty asphalt through the fabric of my pants.

"All the way down!"

With his knee, he had forced me flat on my stomach and he remained there, his knee pressed firmly into the small of my back. After what seemed like a minute, he leaned his head down by mine whispering into my ear. I can still remember feeling his heated fetid-smelling breath as he whispered.

"You are a nigger, and that's all you'll ever be. I don't care where you live or how much money you make. You'll always be a nigger in my book, and I'm never gonna let you forget it. You got that, nigger?"

I just held my breath, saying nothing. He increased the pressure on my back.

"I didn't hear an answer. I said, 'you *got* that, nigger?'"

I nodded, laboring to breathe for the strain on my lungs.

"Yes."

His hand on the back of my head, he pressed my face into the muddy asphalt as he got up.

"You can go."

He tossed my license and registration onto the ground beside me. Slowly I rose, brushing the mud and tiny rocks from the front of my suit as I glanced around. The officers got back into the car and drove past me so close that I had to scramble away to avoid being hit.

Stumbling back to my car, as I fumbled to get the door open, I noticed that a woman had come out of the house next door and was standing on her lawn, watching me. She was an older white woman, probably in her fifties. Our eyes met briefly before I bowed my head, tears forming in mine. Beginning to shiver over the ordeal in the muddy, ruined, rain-drenched suit, I climbed back into my car and tried my best to move on.

It would take years before I was able to evaluate the event with any degree of analytical objectivity, let alone discuss it with anyone. The moral wrong committed against me that day was more akin to rape than any other crime, and from that day on I have felt a genuine empathy and sympathy for women who are victims of physical and emotional abuses.

Yet the feeling of helplessness I experienced during the event was augmented as I came to realize I was dealing with a system and society that refused to acknowledge the harassment of black males by law enforcement has become completely sanctioned, if not encouraged by the general public; that officers who do these deeds are shielded by a conspiracy of silence from within their respective agencies; that they are protected by a conspiracy of acquiescence and consent through default which extends to even of the blacks on the force; that the devaluation of the lives and rights of black males is considered a necessary and acceptable evil in society.

In silence I believe I experienced the same shame and humiliation and the same feelings of self-deprecation common to rape victims, and yet when I was finally comfortable enough to speak freely about the incident, the majority of my male colleagues who were white refused to believe that a police officer would commit such an offense.

In contrast, the majority of my male black associates understood me, and some shared stories describing themselves in similar situations, which were just as deplorable. It is a conundrum the media has devoted no more than a moment or paragraph to until recently.

In spite of the vastly divergent opinions between blacks and whites on the integrity and supposed impartiality of law enforcement agencies, few news editors have been perspicacious enough to truly tackle the issue in order to examine and determine its underlying causes. The polarized attitudes between blacks and whites are largely the result of our separate and consistently dissimilar experiences with the agencies we *all* pay to maintain.

The Rodney King Incident

Owing to my own experience, I was uncomfortable and almost became physically ill the first time I watched the tape of Los Angeles police officers beating Rodney King shamelessly, and yet I would have felt the same empathy for any person so abused by the police regardless of national origin, race, religion, sex or legal status. "Enforcement" is not synonymous with "punishment."

While it is the duty of the police to arrest and charge, it is solely the responsibility of the courts to punish. Because Rodney King had run afoul of the law, the officers who stopped him were within their right to subdue and arrest him. Yet despite the attempts by defense lawyers in both trials to trivialize such a brutal beating by saying that the four officers who abused him did so fearing for their lives, the tape revealed that Rodney King was punished as he lay in the street.

The most revealing aspect of the incident for me was not the beating itself, but the degree to which the police department defended itself and the actions of the officers.

Chief Gates of the Los Angeles Police Department ended up being the officers' most vocal advocate, manifesting that indecent treatment of black males was sanctioned in even the highest reaches of the department.

Blatantly, he called for general endorsement and support for the errant officers, but the public had seen the tape, and fortunately most people were too decent to offer ostensible affirmation. If not for the tape, Rodney King would have been just another "dumb nigger" who got taught a lesson, just another incident to brag about in the locker room, just another "gorilla in the mist."

O.J. Simpson

The O.J. Simpson conundrum divided blacks and whites in the country along racial lines for reasons that were superficially obvious, though a more careful and better-directed investigation reveals something more telling. Orenthal James Simpson, a black man, was accused of killing his ex-wife, Nicole, a white woman, as well as Ronald Goldman, another white person.

If such an incident had happened forty years ago, O.J. Simpson would have been lynched and Los Angeles County would have saved money on the trial. If Rodney King had been accused of murdering his wife in similar circumstances, he would have been tried and promptly deposited in prison.

O.J. Simpson however, was a rich and popular celebrity. In fact, he was the quintessential stereotype of a successful black man: *the athlete, the former inner-city delinquent, the nigger who wanted to be white, the sex-driven, lascivious lecher* and the *corrupter of young white women*. His celebrity status, the lurid nature of the murders and the obvious racial undertones of the case mesmerized America and dominated all aspects of the media, which I monitored during the trial.

I'm not ashamed to say that I have never been a fan of O.J. Simpson. I saw him as a man of questionable character, and it didn't matter to me whether or not he got convicted or acquitted. What *did* matter however, were the methods used by police in order to produce evidence or facts, methods and results, which were relied on by prosecutors in their attempt to get a conviction.

Those methods had a special relevance to me and many other black males in this country as a result of our fatalistically consistent experiences with less-than-professional individuals in law enforcement. When the glove and evidence-planting theories were advanced, when the conspiracy theory was advanced, I did not and *could* not automatically reject it. I knew better. My own life experience made me at least *consider* the possibility of corruption before forming an opinion.

The Black and White Divide

I have a very good friend, a lawyer, with whom I loved discussing and debating details of the trial. He's a white guy, a former California Highway Patrol officer who worked in southern California during his time on the force. He is also one of the most honest and principled people I have ever met.

He rejected the conspiracy theories as impractical, suggesting that in his experience with the agency, the number of people who would have to be involved in such a conspiracy and the degree of collusion required made the idea of anyone manipulating evidence next to impossible.

As I told him about my traumatic experience with the Los Angeles area police, he listened carefully, denouncing the officer's behavior as "despicable." He insisted he had no idea that such gross misconduct ever occurred down there, claiming he hadn't remembered hearing anything like it in his years with the Highway Patrol.

Yet it happened to me, and it happened to many others like me in cities across America. It happened to people who are forthcoming about being harassed, devalued and humiliated by law enforcement.

Conspiracy of Silence

So why was my friend, a former law enforcement officer, in the dark about it? The answer lies in the nature of conspiracy itself. As Dr. Martin Luther King Jr. so insightfully reasoned, "He who passively accepts evil is as much involved in it as he who helps to perpetrate it. He who accepts evil without protesting against it is really cooperating with it."

Thus a "conspiracy of silence" is not a conspiracy of action. Rather, it is accomplished by a lack of action, willful or unconscious, when action *should* be taken. It involves no scrupulous planning, no whispering, no plotting and no collusion.

A "conspiracy of silence" is by its very nature a "conspiracy of consent," meaning that a person who has knowledge of impropriety and does not oppose it in effect sanctions it. During my own experience, as I lay on the muddy asphalt, bracing myself as that harsh officer assaulted my very soul, I looked over to see his partner standing there, doing nothing. Was that man involved in a conspiracy? Absolutely.

The various other law enforcement officers who stood by and did nothing as they watched Rodney King being beaten—where they involved in a conspiracy? Imagine there hadn't been a videotape and consider that question again.

Thus a "conspiracy of silence" can involve the actions of even *one* person, protected by the silence, inaction and ignorance of many. Persons who have been abused by law enforcement know it only too well. "Some men wish evil and accomplish it," penned discerning American writer Steven Benet, "But most men, when they work in the machine, just let it happen somewhere in the wheels."

The Real O.J. Debate

Within the context of the O.J. Simpson trial, *that* is where the line was drawn. The so-called media experts missed the point. It wasn't that blacks, blindly siding with the defendant, were willing to buy into a far-fetched conspiracy theory. It was rather that persons of all races who have been harassed by law enforcement, the actual victims of this "conspiracy of silence," were more inclined to consider the possibility of corruption.

Certainly there were many blacks who blindly believed in O.J. Simpson's innocence and would have embraced any suggestion which supported their intractable position. There were no doubt hordes of whites who wholesale believed him guilty, rejecting any suggestion to the contrary. But in the middle, where the actual line was drawn, were the thinking people, were the people who were willing to listen to arguments and consider opinions other than their own.

On the question of police evidence integrity, what separated black from white and indeed black from black related to a subjective view of the police. For those persons, black or white, who have been victims of invariable harassment and misconduct by law enforcement, because they didn't trust the police, it was easier to consider a theory that involved improprieties by the Los Angeles Police Department. At the bottom line, it was not a racial issue.

When considering the O.J. Simpson case, many black males like myself didn't mistrust police methods and motives because the police were white and the defendant was black. Race had nothing to do with it. For that matter, for some of us O.J. Simpson had nothing to do with it. Rather, after years of systematic profiling and persecution by law enforcement, it was just difficult to believe the pristine, virtuous and ethical image of police that prosecutors and police were trying to sell.

A "conspiracy of silence," after all, could have involved the actions of *one* corrupt and unethical person, protected by the silence, inaction or inattention of others. As the primary victims of injustices and deliberate persecution by police, blacks were acutely aware of the Rampart corruption, other criminal behavior and cover-ups in various divisions of the LAPD literally years before the scandal broke.

All Too Common An Occurrence

In September 1997 I heard a story that for its very implications should have disturbed the whole state and indeed the entire country. Here it was: a man in Sacramento had allegedly been savagely beaten by the police after leading them on a high-speed chase; the man had died in police custody; the police were claiming the beating had nothing to do with his death; there were witnesses to the beating— people who requested that their faces be obscured because they feared retaliation by the police.

I quickly snatched up a week's worth of newspapers, pouring over stories, day-by-day, section by section, but I could find nothing on the event. I found it odd that the *Sacramento Bee*, an established paper with an ethical duty to investigate and report on such matters, had for some reason shirked its responsibility and ignored the event. To fully understand the magnitude of the story, a person need only remember that Rodney King was beaten in a like manner and he *lived*!

In this case there was no videotape, though there were witnesses, but this man had *died* in police custody after being beaten! He was dead! So why wasn't the story airing on every channel? Why wasn't it on the front page? Why wasn't the city in an uproar? The insidious answer to those questions illustrates how law enforcement, political officials and the media can participate in a cooperative "conspiracy of silence" much to the detriment of our society and the very security of American citizens.

My Investigation

I called the *Sacramento Bee* immediately and was referred to the reporter who had investigated the account. Apparently, the paper had run a terse, inconspicuous story on the event in its Metropolitan section shortly after the man's death. When I asked if there would be a follow up, the reporter said that until he got the coroner's report, he didn't want to "fan the flames."

I asked him if there was a more involved investigation underway by the *Bee* to which he replied in the negative; I asked him if there was any action taken against the officers, such as administrative leave pending the results of an internal investigation, but he said there had been none.

I told him that I was amazed by the conspicuous degree of non-coverage relating to the story. His reply was that he would make some calls and look further into things. When he countered that the man who had been killed was driving a stolen car and that he had been combative, I asked if he thought that driving a stolen car and a combative nature (whatever that means) was meritorious of the death penalty, which indeed was enforced, if the story as I understood it was true.

He finally admitted that the death of a detainee while in police custody should have been a bigger story. But it wasn't, and apparently the *Bee* would maintain silence until the coroner's office released its report.

My next call was to Fox 40 News, the one television station in town with the integrity to initially run the story. The person I spoke with told me something that almost frightened me from pursuing the matter further. This reporter said that the police had visited the station shortly after the account aired and that they "came down on the station," threatening non-cooperation in the future if the station continued to pursue the story.

Careful not to falsely impute impropriety or sinister motives to the police, I called later and confirmed their visit and the perceived threats with an official at the station. There was also the suggestion that the police were actively working to keep the story from the public, possibly attempting sanctions against the coroner in order to delay a public statement. Needless to say, the story didn't run again on Fox 40 News, and it ran on no other station.

I also learned from the person I spoke with at Fox 40 that the decedent's body was being buried that day, October

9, and yet there was still no coroner's report, so I called the coroner's office and asked when I'd be able to obtain a report on the man who had died in police custody. The woman on the phone told me an autopsy had already been performed and a final report with toxicology findings might take weeks or more than a month. When I asked if he died of natural causes, she would only say the cause of death was still under investigation.

While I am no expert at forensic science and medicine, I thought it odd that, after the autopsy, it would still take such a long time to determine the *cause* of death. I'm not necessarily suggesting that the coroner was purposely delaying making the report public, but one thing was certain: the absence of a prompt statement by the coroner would no doubt perpetuate the silence surrounding the event and the public would remain largely uninformed.

The woman I spoke with, however, was completely forthcoming about the name of the victim, Albert Thiel, and she said I could obtain the report for $20 once it was issued.

Somewhat frustrated, I called the other television news stations and asked why Fox 40 was the only station in town with the courage and temerity to run the story, but one news director promptly pointed out that Fox 40 had abruptly *stopped* airing it, adding that, according to his understanding, no station would air the story until the coroner's report became public.

Off the record, another news director said he was "dumbfounded" about the way the police chief and the city were handling the matter and that "the public had a right to know what happened." Nonetheless, he said he was more concerned about the death of the detainee than he was with police methods at attempting to control the media and the message. He volunteered that the victim's race probably played a part in non-coverage since race relations were already "somewhat strained" in California.

It Strikes Close to Home

It wasn't until after I obtained the coroner's report that I learned I knew the victim. He was one of the neighborhood kids who played football in the street with us, and when we played basketball, we all called him "Lame-O Thiel," owing to a funny-looking, ineffective jump shot. No one knew him as Albert because we called him by his middle name, Glenn. He wasn't in the neighborhood long, though I remembered him as a genuinely nice and sensitive kid who respected older people.

I hadn't seen him in twenty years, but my brother saw him a few years earlier at a track meet in Vacaville. Glenn had followed my brother all the way back to Sacramento just to say hi to my parents and to see how they were doing. Notwithstanding, I am not attempting to canonize Glenn. I have discovered that he had his share of problems over the years. In fact, he was driving a stolen car on the night he led law enforcement on that high-speed chase which ended in his beating and homicide by four police officers.

The police initially said that because he was under the influence of drugs and alcohol, he ignored the pain and was irrational and combative, justifying the use of the extreme force administered in a potentially mortal choke-hold restricting the life-sustaining carotid artery. The coroner's report later indicated that he had 4/10 of 1/1000 of a gram of cocaine in his body—barely a trace—and that his alcohol level was .06, which was under the legal limit. The coroner's cause of death: homicide. Because the dead are incapable of speech or replies, no one will ever be able to hear the victim's side of the story.

The one indisputable fact however, was that Glenn was dead, and the mortician who prepared him for the funeral told Glenn's mother that she had never seen anyone so brutally beaten in her decades of experience.

Properly, the police should be held accountable. It might be stressful and uncomfortable, but they have to answer the tough questions that *must* be asked, and if the news media in Sacramento is too beholden to them, too indifferent or too inattentive to ask the questions, then *someone* has to ask them. There are some who might think that a "conspiracy of silence" and the passage of time might lessen the interest and the pain, but for others of us, the incident just strikes too close to home.

You see, we have to go out into those streets and will inevitably be pulled over by one law enforcement agency or another. Our brothers have to go out into those streets. Our sons will one day go out into those streets. Our fathers go out there.

If *someone* doesn't make the police accountable in the homicide of this black man, if someone doesn't ask the questions that make law enforcement agencies consider the behavior, policies and procedures of their officers, if someone doesn't rip the shroud from the collective conspiracy of silence practiced by law enforcement, local officials and the media in cities across the country, then it becomes just a little too easy to brutalize, kill and devalue the life of a black man and to pretend that nothing significant has happened.

Due Diligence

In the case of Glenn Thiel, what perhaps should have happened from the beginning is some manner of a forum between the police and the concerned community. Because the incident ended in death, there should have been either a full explanation or the promise of a full explanation of the event within a reasonable time frame.

There should have been a full investigation into the background of the officers involved and of the actual incident itself. There should also have been a full explanation of police policy relating to the carotid choke-hold used and the manner of training officers receive relating to its application. There should have been an explanation of what behavior, short of an actual exchange of blows, is considered "combative."

In my own incident with police, would the officer have been justified in administering a mortal choke-hold if I had resisted lying in the street? And finally, there should have been a review on overall police public policy. Ideally, the police, city officials and the media should have had demonstrated more consideration for not only the black community in Sacramento, but also for the community at large.

Rather than evading the issue with the hope that it would somehow disappear, there should have been a more ostensible effort at investigation, reporting and some manner of explanation that might have allayed well-placed concerns in the community. In that sense, the police, city and county officials and the local media have been derelict in their duty to the community.

The question that looms largest for many of us is "why?" Why would the police seek to suppress the story? Of many possible explanations, two come to mind: 1) they truly do have something to hide; and 2) they are uncomfortable with public scrutiny and accountability. In terms of suppression to hide impropriety, there may be unflattering facts related to the event that they want to keep from the public, and yet while non-disclosure may go a long way toward decreasing public hysteria and racial tension, the community has a right to know what happened.

Such an explanation may seem unlikely to many, but concerned persons are forced to wonder why, even years after the incident, the police have issued no official public report. On the issue of scrutiny and accountability, it's perhaps natural for the officers involved to want their names and individual histories withheld. The Rodney King incident and the O.J. Simpson trial has given them examples of police officers under scrutiny, being branded "corrupt" and "racist," their families and careers in upheaval.

Most people can understand how they wouldn't want that. I wouldn't want that, but then again, I am not a police officer involved in the homicide of an unarmed civilian, and I am not a police officer whose future actions, proper or improper, intentional or unintentional, could cause further loss of life.

Accountability

While accountability isn't often pleasant, it is a responsibility that should rightly accompany the immense power and discretion law enforcement is given by the people and it is the only way to earn and maintain the trust and respect of people in a given community. A very wise man observed that *God shall bring every work into judgment, with every secret thing, whether it be good, or whether it be evil.*

If the police in this incident were guilty of nothing and the suspicion of some in the community was misplaced, then an open, fair and objective investigation of what happened would have led both sides closer to a relationship based on effective communication, mutual respect and goodwill.

Although the majority of this essay has related to blacks and law enforcement, its most salient points are underscored by a much broader issue that involves the civil rights and constitutional issues for all Americans regardless of background.

We are unconditionally bound by the shared belief that we are *all created equal,* that we are *all endowed with certain unalienable rights; that among these are life, liberty and the pursuit of happiness.* "Injustice anywhere," spoke Dr. King, "is a threat to justice everywhere."

Never should any American accept a lesser or devalued status among his or her countrymen and countrywomen regardless of the trouble caused for addressing perceived wrongs. Never should any American put up with the murder or mistreatment of fellow patriots regardless of the expense and difficulty at reaching a real and equitable solution. Finally, never should any American remain silent or do nothing when justice and goodwill call for speech and action, for in the words of Edmund Burke, "It is necessary only for the good man to do nothing for evil to triumph," and "When bad men combine, the good must associate; else they will fall one by one, an unpitied sacrifice in a contemptible struggle."

An Obligation to Speak Out

As I began to conclude this essay, I shared it with my father, and he advised against ever publishing it, claiming that it would create unnecessary difficulties for me. A few friends who read it suggested publishing it under a pseudonym to avoid making enemies. I almost begged off, but one night even as I was considering the implications of how, when or if I would send it out, I was pulled over by the California Highway Patrol.

Now, I wasn't speeding or swerving and I hadn't run a traffic sign or light. My offense: I was a black male driving home from work at night. I was taken to the station where I tested under the legal limit. Nevertheless, I was held at the jail for fourteen hours before finally being released.

While the DA rejected the single charge of "driving under the influence" as "groundless," I was inconvenienced in a major way nonetheless. It was simply not fair. I should have never been pulled over in the first place. A distinguished American jurist probably put it best when he opined, "The greatest dangers to liberty lurk in the insidious encroachment by men of zeal, well-meaning but without understanding."

Unless I articulate the frustrations I share with many black men all across America, no one will ever understand the institutionalized persecution we put up with on a daily basis.

In the past thirty years, we've all somehow allowed our shared public consciousness to slumber on matters relating to civil rights and constitutional issues. Perhaps the state and nation, as Socrates suggested, are "like a great and noble steed, who is tardy in his motions owing to his very size, and requires to be stirred to life." In that sense, I seek to serve the purpose of the tiny gadfly in "arousing, persuading and reproaching you, irritating and awakening you when you or the state are caught napping."

The behavior of law enforcement in California and elsewhere, in stopping motorists merely for being black, is reproachable. The devaluation of the lives of black people by law enforcement throughout our country is reprehensible. Police agencies must stop murdering black people. It's equally condemnable that the media, once a symbol of freedom and democracy, has lost its courage, conscience and sense of purpose. Sadly, the media in America has lost its very soul.

It's easy for many to believe that because the previous fervor for which blacks sought equality in America has waned, we somehow live in a society in which persons are *judged not by the color of their skin, but by the content of their character.* While such a thought is a noble ideal, it is merely a dream, and dreams are dreamt in slumber. In my personal American journey, nothing could be further from the truth. I can only hope I've stung some thinking Americans awake to that stark reality.

Call to Action

So where do we go from here? What do we do about our deeply rooted, entrenched problems, which manifest themselves as a festered boil in the flank of our great and noble steed? In order to examine the boil, a critical and candid discussion about the devaluation of the rights and lives of black males becomes necessary.

This is why I am petitioning others like myself to come forward with their stories; this is why I am entreating others to share like frustration and discuss similar experiences in something of a public forum.

More than merely abhorrent, it's frightening, in light of our literal persecution and devaluation by law enforcement, to read about an unarmed man in New York being shot 19 times by a New York City Police death squad who fired a total of 41 rounds, about another man whose rectum and intestines were permanently damaged after being ruptured by a broomstick in the hands of the New York City Police, about a handcuffed gang member being shot/murdered by a rogue faction of the LAPD, about a possibly unconscious woman in Los Angeles being shot more than 12 times by law enforcement.

Such incidents send an unmistakable message to the nation: that the lives of black people are somehow less valuable than the lives of other Americans. The sheer regularity of like incidents makes the killing of blacks with little accountability mundane and commonplace. They tend to desensitize the public to these outrages, making it easier for any officer to squeeze the trigger when the person on the other side of the barrel is black or brown. They make it easier for hateful, misguided demoniacs to think they can chain up a black man, drag him to pieces behind a pickup truck and think they can somehow get away with it.

Only by combining our voices on the atrocities committed against us will we be able to lance, open and expose the wound to the public forum that we have brought to light. Only by engaging the American people in a solution-oriented, comprehensive and spirited debate with institutions and agencies about questionable practices and policies will we be able to examine, with the hope of discovering a cure for, the complex and difficult societal-disease germs which are its underlying cause. Only by working diligently to create legislation that limits, regulates and holds accountable the very institutions and agencies that have traditionally humiliated, devalued, persecuted us and taken our lives will we be able to allow the wound to heal in "the light of human conscience and the air of national opinion."

DWBB – Driving While Black or Brown

In 1999, California State Senator Kevin Murray introduced legislation that would require the Highway Patrol to report to the Commissioner, "in the manner prescribed by the commissioner, as to the number of motor vehicle drivers stopped by law enforcement, whether or not a citation or warning was issued, for each stop, certain specified information (race, ethnicity, reason), and other information."

The bill would have gradually required city and county law enforcement agencies in California to report to the Highway Patrol Commissioner in the same manner. Senator Murray began introducing the legislation after he himself was summarily stopped and questioned by law enforcement in southern California for the crime of "driving while black."

According to the bill's sponsors, "Although anecdotal evidence across the country suggests that police stop members of minority groups for traffic enforcement purposes in numbers greatly disproportionate to their presence in the driving population, the research on the issue is limited.

Limited research and studies confirm what many know to be a common occurrence. *Although African-Americans comprise 14% of the overall population; some studies indicate that African-Americans account for upwards of 73% of all routine stops* (Source: U.S. Justice Department and U.S. House Judiciary Committee)."

Although Mr. Murray's bill passed in both the Senate and Assembly with bi-partisan support, California Governor Gray Davis vetoed it, stating, "There is no evidence that this practice is taking place statewide." Ironically, the very purpose of the bill was to *substantiate* whether or not the practice is taking place in the state.

Until our lawmakers and our governors direct objective studies that examine whether or not racial profiling is indeed taking place on statewide levels, the only evidence available *will be* anecdotal and therefore cannot be substantiated.

Thus Mr. Davis and other insensitive governors that follow will always be able to evade the issue by claiming "there is no evidence." I wondered if the governor feared that taking a stand by addressing the concerns of black and brown males would somehow make him less popular with voters in the center. The governor's callous veto of such a munificent message from the legislature is a direct, unmistakable insult to every one of us who have been pulled over without cause and harassed by law enforcement.

In lieu of endorsing the bill, the governor asked the Highway Patrol to coordinate a *voluntary* data collection system, an option that caused me to recall an observation Dr. King made during his unjust imprisonment in a Birmingham jail.

He commented, that "we have not made a single gain in civil rights without determined legal and non-violent pressure. Lamentably, it is an historical fact that privileged groups seldom give up their privileges voluntarily. Individuals may see the moral light and voluntarily give up their unjust posture, but as Reinhold Neibuhr has reminded us, groups tend to be more immoral than individuals. We know through painful experience that freedom is never *voluntarily* given by the oppressor; it must be demanded by the oppressed."

That demand, a mandate that we *all* take a closer look at racial profiling in California, as endorsed by both houses of the legislature, showed up on the governor's desk in the form of Senate Bill 78 in 1999. As impossible as it seemed to many of us, Governor Davis placed himself *squarely in the center of the road*, in effect blocking the way of our path toward justice.

Notwithstanding, the struggle will continue. In 2000, Senator Murray reintroduced the legislation as Senate Bill 1389. It passed in both houses, though Capitol Democrats allowed the governor to render any effective provisions of the bill effete through backroom deals and compromise.

In 2001, Assembly Member Marco Firebaugh brought the issue again, and so racial profiling will come before this governor and future governors again. Only in the future, if anecdotal evidence is all we have, let us build a mountain of anecdotal evidence and "bring the mountain" to the governor's doorstep.

Collecting the Empirical and Anecdotal Evidence

Let us all take the time to write our stories down. Let us recall every memorable detail from every improper traffic stop. Let us compile these stories in such quantity that it will be literally impossible for any good and responsible governor to answer, "there is no evidence."

Beyond California, Congressman John Conyers, Jr. (D-MI) introduced legislation that would require the Justice Department to conduct a study of racial profiling on a *national* level. The efforts of Mr. Conyers and like-minded leaders would be greatly benefited by a victory in California and the mountain of evidence we must work diligently to amass.

Yet a victory on the racial profiling issue must not be an end, but a beginning. We must renew the fight not only for justice, but also for the value of our lives. We must make anyone who takes or devalues a black life as well as any other life answerable not only to the courts, but to the families of the victims, to the national community and to history.

Talking to Our Children

When my son was younger, I occasionally took him to Capitol Park where we'd walk in the shade of stately trees and feed the squirrels. Early one morning as we were strolling along, we came upon a dead squirrel whose stiff body had been squashed and smashed into the soft earth.

Becoming agitated, he demanded to know what had happened to the poor squirrel. I told him I did not know, that the animal could have gotten too old and just tired out, that maybe he had an accident and slipped, dropped and died after the fall, that maybe the policeman on the horse in the distance had accidentally stepped on him. It was impossible to tell. He asked me what was going to happen to the squirrel, but again I had no answer. When he asked if we could take it home to bury it, I told him that people don't bury dead squirrels.

What I did not tell him is that some people look at dead squirrels and feel sad for a moment, but then they walk away and quickly forget about what they saw and how bad they felt. He prayed for the squirrel that night before he went to bed and he never mentioned it again. I'll probably take him to the park again soon, to talk about father and son things. I have not looked forward to it, as I have always worried the day will come when I will have to admit to him that many of the things I told him were lies.

I told him the things my father told me, though I could no longer believe them. I always stressed to him that it does not make a difference what race or color people are, that we are all the same. I told him that if he worked really hard, he could earn himself an illustrious and secure life. I told him the police put bad people in jail and serve the interests of honest citizens. I told him that America was the greatest country in the world, and like most children, he believed everything I said without doubting for a moment.

So how do I tell him I deceived him and why? When do I admit I lied to protect his young heart, his precious sense of morality even as it developed; his innocence and all his potential for accomplishing good? How can I tell him that when he grows up, he'll be targeted and persecuted for the rest of his life, that no matter how well he does professionally, he will be stopped and devalued by law enforcement who will never let him forget that he is a "nigger?"

My Responsibility as a Father

Do I tell him he will probably one day go to jail, regardless of whether he's committed a crime? Must I warn him that if he does something that might subjectively be considered "combative," he might be murdered by the police? Should I prepare him to witness the anguish of his closest relatives, their very sanity tested, suffocating under the crushing force of continual and unrelenting harassment? Do I tell him that, in my own experience, "the life of a niggah don't amount to the life of a squirrel?"

No, I refuse to let that be his future. I will not tell him any of those things. I will just keep on telling him the things my father told me when I was a boy. Only from this point on, I will not be lying.

Rather, I'll be working within myself and with others to help bring about lasting change. I'll be willing to sacrifice my very life so that his experience and the experiences of other precious little black and brown boys and girls are richer and happier than mine. I'll hope and exercise faith in God and in the goodness and goodwill of others. I'll speak out frankly even when stinging words must be spoken and ask the difficult questions when those questions must be posed.

My duty is clear. Thus in the words of a truly great man, *With malice toward none, with charity for all, with firmness in the right, as God gives us to see the right, let us strive on to finish the work we are in, to bind up the nation's wounds, to care for him who shall have borne the battle, and for his widow and orphan, to do all which may achieve and cherish a just and lasting peace among ourselves and with all nations.*

Dedicated to the memory of Homer Jefferson, 1900-1988

ON THE EXECUTION OF TIMOTHY McVEIGH

I know I was sadly disappointed, and no doubt millions of Americans like me were extremely disappointed about the pathetic way the federal government dealt with mass murderer Timothy McVeigh. Frankly, the government let a singular opportunity for entertainment just slip away.

The timing could not have been more fortuitous—right in the middle of the summer blockbuster movie season. *Pearl Harbor* had opened just weeks before. *Shrek* was wooing young audiences all over while Nicole Kidman's sexy performance in *Moulin Rouge* baffled us all about Tom Cruise's sexuality. It was June after all. Could the execution have been timed any better? *Tomb Raider* and *Atlantis* were set to open on Friday, with *Jurassic Park III* waiting in the wings.

I was certain that the execution had been moved from its original date of May 16th to June 11th in order to take advantage of the public's appetite for summer entertainment. I don't think any of us really bought the story about the FBI mysteriously forgetting to turn in 4,000 pages of important investigation related documents anyhow. No, the real intent behind the government's sheepish admission was to place the execution right in the middle of America's picnic table, an entrée in America's summer entertainment feast.

A Missed Opportunity

The federal government killed Timothy McVeigh all right, but they were outright wimpy about it. I mean the truth is, if you're going to ignore all those left wing, pinko-commie, tree-hugging, pro-abortion, pro-gay, marijuana smoking, free-love activists and kill a man, you might as well do it right.

Lethal injection? Please! Where's the entertainment value there? I didn't see the execution, but if the boring newspaper and television accounts of that moment shortly after 7 a.m. were accurate, I didn't miss anything. All that hype, and the show was a dud. The American media, as typical, did its best to milk the event for all they could, but there was nothing there. It had to be the most boring execution in history. Who was the director anyway?

I don't have a whole lot of experience at it, but I could have directed that show better. I could have made that execution *the bomb*. No lethal injection. I wouldn't have even considered it.

My Production

First of all, I'd have to cast the show. I would have hired one of those secret government doctors. We all know they exist, those scary amoral doctors trained by the CIA to extract information from traitors and spies. I would have made that doctor, whom I'll affectionately call Dr. Botha (after one of my favorite torturers), the star. During the weeks leading up to the execution, Botha would make an appearance on Larry King Live to talk about his expertise at torment and persecution. America would salivate at the possibilities and the prospect of watching this fiend work on McVeigh. Then Botha would have to go on Oprah to discuss his painful childhood, endearing him to liberal women all over the country. Just for kicks, ol Botha could make a surprise guest appearance on *Fraiser* as Daphne's loveable Uncle Buck, and he could be gay. And finally, CNN could bring Bernard Shaw back to interview three of Botha's victims before arranging a traumatic face-to-face encounter.

Death, torture, execution—all heavy subjects. So I, like every good director, would realize the need for comic relief. It would probably take some big money negotiations with federal prison officials in Terra Haute, but I think they'd do it. Just for the duration of the execution, I would replace the regular warden with a plucky, jive-talking stand-in. I'd probably get Eddie Murphy, that wonderful Negro comic who was the jackass in *Shrek*. America could take bets on whether or not, one-on-one, in an enclosed cell, Eddie could make

Timothy McVeigh smile or crack up laughing. I'd put my money on the colored guy. And when McVeigh asked for two pints of mint chocolate chip ice cream as his last meal, a snickering Eddie could direct marshals at the prison to secretly replace the chocolate with ex-lax.

Everyone in America except McVeigh could be in on the joke as he squirmed in the chair while trying to face execution stoically. He could claim to be captain of his soul, but that ex-lax would be the master of his fate. I'd direct the cameraman to get a close-up of the sudden alarm on his trademark stony face, his darting eyes making for raucous laughter for audiences across the country. He'd be funnier than Jim Carey as he writhed about, strapped in that chair.

Only then would I bring Dr. Botha in to begin his brilliant performance. If I still had money left in my budget, I'd cast a scantily clad, gun-toting Angelina Jolie/Lara Croft as his trusty assistant. Beside the doctor as he sat, would be a rack containing hundreds of instruments of torture. There would be drills of varying sizes, ball-pein hammers, long-nose pliers, cattle prods, bamboo razors, nail guns, hot pepper oil-filled douche bags, you name it.

Smiling pleasantly, Angelina would spin a large wheel that displayed many of the instruments on the racks and all America would wait breathlessly until it stopped. A ball-pein hammer! At that point, the good doctor would take a small hammer, walk over to McVeigh and slam the pein savagely onto his kneecap, completely obliterating it, giving a whole new meaning to "collateral damage." Naturally, McVeigh would groan aloud in pain as tears ran down his face and the seat area of the orange prison jumpsuit became suddenly darker.

Next spin? Icepick! Thus demonstrating his versatility as an artist, Botha would place the pick in McVeigh's ear and gently pierce his eardrum. A trickle of blood would drip onto his neck. The pain would be horrendous, causing the prisoner to scream aloud, much to the delight of victims' families who would be allowed to watch and cheer from an observation area.

When the cheering stopped, Angelina, in fishnets and high heels, would be peddling a cycle/generator as Botha placed the arcing prods at McVeigh's crotch. When McVeigh screamed aloud, the doctor, in a clever, sophisticated move, would slip a pair of long-nosed pliers into McVeigh's mouth and could clamp on the third molar on the bottom right jaw. Putting his foot against his victim's throat, Botha would yank as hard as he could.

Despite his athleticism, the doctor would fall sprawling to the floor as the tooth, root and dangling nerves left McVeigh's mouth, a surge of blood spilling over the prisoner's quivering lip. According to my script, only after the doctor began drilling a $3/8^{th}$ inch hole in McVeigh's right elbow would McVeigh move the action toward a conclusion.

"Okay! Okay! I'll say it!"

"You'll zay vhat?" Botha would answer as he squeezed with all his might, the pliers clamping on McVeigh's big toe.

"I'll say I'm sorry! I'll say it!"

Gripping McVeigh's hand, the doctor, prepared to insert a bamboo razor under the thumbnail, would warn.

"Then zay it, and it better be goot or else."

At this point, all the networks would be notified that a McVeigh apology was forthcoming. Cameras would close to a head-and-shoulders-shot of McVeigh as he panted there, fearful of the bamboo razor off-camera. Seemingly heartfelt tears would be streaming down his face as he turned toward America.

"I'm sorry I did it! I'm so, so sorry I did it! I'll never do it again!"

And that would be enough. There might be a few skeptics out there who might think he wouldn't mean it, but that undue cynicism wouldn't matter to many of the friends and relatives of victims looking on. They wouldn't care if he meant it. Just *hearing* it would feel good. And over time, we have to consider the awesome power of television. Played over and over again on TV, anything, even the most blatant lie, becomes the truth. A television news editor told me that.

Anyway, revenues for the rights I could sell to the taped confession, the books, the "making-of" documentary and un-edited, un-cut movie would more than pay my expenses. After I paid for the prison privileges, for Murphy, for Jolie, for the doctor and for the production crew, I'd probably still have enough money to launch a Hollywood company that produced execution entertainment on a regular basis. I'd at last be the media mogul I've always dreamed of being.

The Show We Got

But leave it to the federal government to ruin it for me. How did they punish a horrible man who on April 19th, 1995, consciously set out to kill and maim people? How did they punish this man who bombed a federal building, killing 168 persons, including 19 children, wounded more than 500 and caused pain and suffering in thousands more who lost loved ones? They gave him what he asked for. They gave him the easy way out. They let him retain his hate, his anger and arrogance to the end, completely assured that he would die a calm, peaceful, painless and remorseless death. Now where's the equity in that? Where's the justice?

When I realized the execution date had been moved to June 11th, in the middle of the summer blockbuster movie season, I made several attempts to contact government officials in Washington in order to make a pitch for me directing the show. They were no better than the folks in Hollywood. All I got was hang-up after hang-up. That's when I got really pissed off. If they weren't going to let me do my treatment, they could have at least done something better than a lethal injection!

You think families watching that painless, remorseless lethal injection got any satisfaction from it. Hell no they didn't! Just ask them. Ask persons who lost children to the action of that sick asshole if they consider lethal injection collateral damage. Ask a woman who lost a husband if she feels justice was served. Ask a boy who'll never grow up with a father if he feels a sense of equity has been achieved.

Ask a grandmother who's lost two grandbabies if giving McVeigh exactly what he wanted somehow makes everything better. Take a poll, and you'll find many of those people are left feeling unsatisfied. You'll find that they would prefer *my* show to the one the government put on.

But I don't completely blame the federal government. They're a government of all the people—so try as they may, they can't ignore the protests and antics of all those left wing, pinko-commie, tree-hugging, pro-abortion, pro-gay, marijuana smoking, free love activists out there who no doubt believe that no one should be cruel to even Timothy McVeigh. Yet I have to fault the federal government for not availing itself to another alternative, perhaps the most reasonable and equitable alternative of all.

The federal government could have given Timothy McVeigh *life in prison without the possibility of parole.* Initially, I scoffed at such an idea. I mean, I just imagined him sitting in some country club prison, sipping mint juleps, working out in the weight room, doing occasional media interviews and watching television with a huge, hip, buffed, dark-skinned soul-mate named Bubba. To me it sounded more like the life of a Hollywood actor.

Yet in the days after the execution, I began to reconsider the whole notion of putting a man in a prison and never letting him out. And after thinking more, I realized that forcing Timothy McVeigh to life without liberty for the next 40 or so years would have been the most equitable and most effective sentence of all for many reasons.

Punishment

First of all, you have to consider the notion of Hell—not Hell itself, because many people don't believe in it, but the notion of it. The very idea of a nether realm where the damned are sentenced to suffer everlasting punishment appeals to our innate sense of justice. The notion of justice and retribution transcends religion and philosophy because it is uniquely bound and ingrained in our humanity.

Despite the diversity of our cultures, we as humans believe it is proper for the wicked to suffer for their wicked deeds. Perhaps the most central concept in the whole notion involves suffering, namely that the wicked should *suffer*. Whether it has been a witch burned alive at the stake in Europe, a murderer chained for the rest of his life to his victim in Africa, the entire household of a traitor put to death in Asia or an assassin skinned alive and boiled in hot oil in Persia, human society has approved of suffering as punishment for the wicked.

Yet here in modern America, during the national debate on the appropriateness of putting condemned criminals to death, death penalty advocates made a strategic landmark concession. In answer to critics who believed it was unusually cruel to kill criminals in electric chairs and gas chambers, they devised a technique that involved *killing without suffering*. Lethal injection—veterinarians had been doing it for years.

Thus employing lethal injections, death penalty advocates and prisons have overcome cruelty and suffering objections and have been able to put men and women to death regularly in bushy states like Florida and Texas. Simply put, lethal injections took the pain and suffering out of the death penalty.

So you're a mass murderer like McVeigh and you have two punishment prospects before you: On one hand, you could be taken into a quiet peaceful room after eating whatever you wanted; a compassionate marshal would strap you to a chair; someone else would hook up an IV; and then, with friends, family, fans and a comforting priest nearby, you would simply and painlessly go to sleep and never wake up.

On the other hand, you could be taken to a prison and be assured that you would live the next 40 or so years that remain in your life in a cell; you would be assured that you would never be free again; you would be assured to live out that dreadful existence in isolation because the rest of the prison population would represent a danger to you; you would have zero choice; you would not be the captain of your destiny or the master of your fate; you would be assured to waste your life away in dull routine; you would suffer in your own private Hell on Earth; you would grow old and feeble... alone there, past the time you might represent a danger to society; and finally, you would die there.

Which punishment prospect would you choose? Ask Charles Manson if he's enjoying the country club life he's maintained for over the past 30 years. Ask Sirhan Sirhan if he's enjoying a life of ease the next time he's up begging the parole board to please understand *just how very sorry* he is. Murderer Gary Gilmore insisted on the death penalty, claiming *life in prison without the possibility of parole* was a fate *worse* than death.

And the Winner Is...

Although a jury, and not McVeigh, decided his fate, he ultimately got what he wanted. Maybe it was that *remorseless* gag he played. Maybe he was acting. Maybe he played the hard, unrepentant role in order to goad the jury, the federal government and the American people into giving him what he wanted. Did anyone ever think of that? Now wouldn't that be the ultimate mockery?

Maybe he played us all. That, we'll never know. But we should certainly all realize by now that we gave him many of the things he wanted. All of us did. We gave him celebrity. We gave him headlines and television coverage right up to the end. We gave him a bestseller in an off-hand way. We gave him a secure place in our history. We gave him a voice. We gave him an easy, painless way out. And worst of all, we gave this wicked, twisted and demonic man—we gave all his hate, malice and illogic a surrogate form of legitimacy. In the end, he went out like a movie star.

Is this what anyone in this country besides McVeigh wanted? No. He played us all. It was interesting to read the comments from family members of victims, some of the 232 family members who watched the execution. One woman said she wished the electric chair had been used "because it would have been more painful." A man who lost his mother as a result of McVeigh's callous attack wanted McVeigh to feel the terror she felt. Disappointed about the painlessness of lethal injection, he offered, "I thought I would feel something more satisfying, but I don't. So many people suffered, and for him to have gone asleep seems unfair."

The problem that family members and many Americans had with the execution of Timothy McVeigh has its roots in our innate sense of justice, equity and retribution. We would all have a problem if the government executed an eighteen-year-old before a firing squad for failing to stop at a red light. The punishment would not be appropriate to the crime.

Yet by the same token, the federal government took this cold-hearted killer, the worst mass murderer in American history, a man who spent months planning and scheming destruction, a wicked man who was directly responsible for the deaths of 168 people and lifetimes of suffering for thousands more—they put this monster in a peaceful little cell and let him just drift painlessly off to sleep. It was not equitable. Justice was *not* served.

A Lesson Learned?

How much better a thing it would have been to have had ol Timmy around for a few years, suffering a dull life of endless routine in a prison cell. *Life in prison without the possibility of parole* is the only punishment sentence in which justice would have been served on McVeigh. He would have probably complained about it, but who'd care? Just as innate as its need for justice, the human soul also craves liberty.

Take away a man's liberty and his spirit begins to die. The eyes dull a little each day as the life force is extinguished. It is a process that sometimes takes years, and occasionally during that process, remarkable things occur.

Who knows, maybe thirty years down the line, McVeigh might have had a change of heart. Maybe he might have overcome his hate, his wickedness and his arrogance. Maybe he might have realized the error of his ways. Maybe he might have apologized and might have truly meant it. Maybe that scintilla of good in him *might* have triumphed over all his evil. But now we'll never know. They let him sneak out on us, his arrogance and hate intact.

Three days after the execution, I called Washington again to give my review of the show they put on. I told them that the lethal injection gimmick just doesn't work, that critics all over were panning them for it. I told them that if they truly wanted to punish wicked, evil killers, they should let those souls stew in the bleak and dreary realization that they will never enjoy liberty again.

And finally, I pitched that if the federal government is going to kill people, they should do it with a little more style, with a little more flair, with a little more pizzazz. I told them I'd be happy to direct the show. I'm still waiting for their production people to call me back.

DEDICATED TO THE FAMILIES OF THE VICTIMS OF TIMOTHY MCVEIGH'S ATTACK ON THE ALFRED P. MURRAH FEDERAL BUILDING IN OKLAHOMA CITY ON APRIL 19TH, 1995

ON THE SEVEN-YEAR-HITCH

I certainly remember that movie moment. We all remember her standing there that sultry summer night, her knees together, her hands pressing the front of the garment to her legs as the sudden breeze from a subway car passing below animated the bottom of her white skirt, exposing those trademark Hollywood gams. The story goes that her husband got pretty pissed off about the scene and divorced her soon thereafter, something I found a little ironic, ironic because the movie was about marriage in a way.

The plot centered on a professional manuscript reader, a middle-aged, kind of dweeby guy à la Walter Mitty, who struggled with a theory proposed in a psychology book: *after being married or otherwise institutionalized for seven years, the human male experiences an irrepressible urge to cheat.* Now I know from personal experience that just isn't true. No, the phenomenon is not limited to males. Women are at least as bad, if not worse.

The Problem

Let me cut to the chase: the institution of marriage is in trouble. It is in dire need of an update. The world is moving forward at breakneck speed, but marriage simply hasn't kept pace. The truth is that we live in a disposable, throw-away society, the metaphoric mountains at our landfills symbolizing the impermanence of the improved modern and fast-forward lifestyle of twenty-first century America.

When our babies are born, we swaddle them in disposable diapers, clean their little butts with throw-away wipes and strap them in plastic car seats that we replace every other year as the children grow. The fast foods kids eat are so full of steroids and growth hormones that childhood has been shortened by at least two or three years, and the hybrid adults that result have become America's prime consumer market, accelerating the pace of life still faster.

Every other month, new products are updated and mass produced, rendering the previous generation of goods outdated and useless. No one keeps a cell phone for more than a couple of years, computers are crippled and effete at age three and a brand new car is out-of-date and ready for replacement by the time it's paid for.

And manufacturers aren't dumb. They gamble putting inferior products on the market at cut-rates to drive prices down, thus encouraging the trend of impermanence. No product, whether it be a software program, the DVD player in your home or your coveted telephone long distance service is impervious to the trend of constant replacement and renewal.

So is it any wonder that marriage, an institution once considered the bedrock of permanence in society, is it any wonder that marriage has lost its clout as a stabilizer? Marriage vows, like words of the latest MTV song, sound good but have no real meaning:

> To have and to hold from this day forward; for better, for worse, for richer, for poorer, in sickness and in health, to love and to cherish...

till death us do part.

Those words still fresh on the lips of the new bride or groom, both hope for a long and prosperous marriage, and yet both realize such hope is quixotic at best. By the time they've made avowals, many of today's newlyweds have already considered exit strategies in case the marriage doesn't work. The prenuptial agreement has become fashionable, even outside California. The Census Bureau projects that half of all marriages in America will end in divorce.

The Idea

I don't know how it all came to me, but I got this great idea about how to save the institution of marriage. It was just a light that went off in my head, a stroke of genius, really. And it was doable, but I would need help.

So the first thing I did was catch a flight to Washington DC to pitch my idea to the people who could make a difference: the president, Congress and the Supreme Court. I figured that if anyone had a stake in the welfare of marriage in America, it would be the men and women from the three great pillars of government. All I got was polite excuses and closed doors. It turns out that half the people in Washington were divorced or had opted out of their marriages in one clever way or another.

I came home dejected, though not defeated. I still had my idea after all. So I figured that if I could make my proposal work in California, it would probably catch on in the rest of the country. And though San Francisco's gay marriage crusade wasn't exactly the beginning of a national movement, it gave me an idea about how to put my proposal before the people.

In order to modernize marriage, I figured I would have to begin on the state government level. Marriage licenses are issued by cities and counties, subject to the state's definition of marriage, which is why so many states are passing legislation to limit that definition and to ban same-sex unions.

But my proposal has nothing to do with the definition of marriage. Rather, it proposes a change in the term of the license. Unlike most other licenses in California, a marriage license is open ended. It basically remains in effect for the life of the licensee, something that just doesn't fly with the need for efficiency in our constantly changing world.

I spent three days walking the streets of downtown Sacramento, researching various agencies, boards and state departments with reference to licensing requirements, license terms and related rationales. When I finished, I was just beginning to understand why the institute of marriage had fallen to such a state of dysfunction.

I started at the Department of Fish and Game, where an employee said she couldn't tell me why fishing licenses are issued for one year at a time, and that basically the only requirement is cash. There is no exam, but the department does issue a pamphlet explaining rules and restrictions. At the Pest Control Board, I found that the term for a pest control operator's license is about average for renewal times. After three years, an additional fee is paid and the license is renewed.

It was obvious the people at the Dental Board took certification seriously. They only issue a license after the applicant passes grueling written and demonstrative exams. The license has to be renewed every two years and proof of continuing education must be provided.

Real estate agents—five years; milk handlers and architects must renew licenses every other year, but if you're a court reporter or bail bonds agent, it's one year. If you sell machine guns, your one year license is issued by the Alcohol, Tobacco, and Firearms Division of the U.S. Treasury Department. I could go on, but I think I've made my point.

All you need to get a marriage license in California is a driver's license or other valid identification. No exam is required, not even a blood test. There's no waiting period and no requirement for continuing education, though the license costs about $45 cash. But the key factor in the inefficacy of marriage licenses in the state is the lack of any renewal obligation.

The Proposal

And thus I propose to the people of California a sensible provision in the language of marriage licensing to require renewal every seven years. If a couple were to allow the license to expire, then all the legal and tax benefits that marriage entitles them to would be null and void. There would be no penalties or late fees to renew the license. However, until the license was renewed, both parties would be legally considered as *unmarried*.

In order to administer the new and improved licenses, the state would have to establish a Department of Marriage, paid for by renewal fees, complete with a Marriage Commissioner. This statewide office holder would have the power and discretion to suspend or revoke marriage licenses, based on the deeds and misbehavior of licensees. Suspension or revocation would be the most extreme measures, reserved only for chronic spousal abusers and de facto bigamists. Attitudes must change. More than a mere right, *marriage is a privilege.*

The Debate

I realized early on that there would be opposition to my plan from various segments of society, but my proposal is to save marriage, not to trivialize it. Before I answer my critics, we all have to admit that marriage, as it exists today, just isn't working. Sure some people get married and remain married, but half the people who get married get divorced plain and simple, which brings me to my first group of detractors.

Divorce lawyers now euphemistically call themselves family law attorneys, but they are lawyers nonetheless, and thus the State Bar would naturally oppose the renewal requirement. Just imagine the money lawyers would lose because some people would choose *not to renew* rather than divorce.

Not re-upping after all isn't as hostile as divorce. There isn't as much a rejection factor, so the dissolution of a marriage would be less fractious. No doubt "family law attorneys" and the courts would still be necessary for the equitable division of community property and for child custody issues, but divorce lawyers would significantly lose position as players, instigators and money makers.

If marriage licensees were required to renew every seven years, divorce rates would fall off precipitously, cutting into the overweight profit margins of many of the state's most prestigious law firms. So when the lawyers launch their campaign against my proposal for marriage license renewal, just remember what's at stake for them and why they would oppose saving the institution of marriage.

I imagine some of the churches might also dispute a provision that would require married persons to renew marriage licenses, but I also expect at least part of their initial resistance would be something of a knee-jerk reaction. They'd see it as a radical step, and yet I believe if they took a step back and gave themselves a little time with the idea, they'd eventually see the merits of renewing the commitment. We're natural allies, duly concerned and committed to protecting the institution of marriage.

The times we live in oblige us to make a distinction between the institution of marriage and legal marriages, or civil unions. Many Americans believe that the institution was created by and ordained by God, *that a threefold cord is not easily broken*. Others believe marriage is fundamentally a bond between two people and that God and government have no business in it. And still others see marriage as a tax consideration. But I think we can all agree that the legalities of marriage have very little to do with the marriage itself. Marriage is a personal and sometimes public commitment, but it is not essentially a legal commitment, though legal implications exist.

With all due respect, the Catechism of the Catholic Church actually supports the distinction, wherein marriage is described as indissoluble. According to the church, *[Divorce] claims to break the contract, to which the spouses freely consented, to live with each other till death... Contracting a new union, even if it is recognized by civil law, adds to the gravity of the rupture: the remarried spouse is then in a situation of public and permanent adultery.* Here there is a clear difference between real marriage and unions recognized by civil law.

Nonetheless, the proliferation of divorce in America has presented the clergy with a dilemma. Many churches have members and parishioners who are divorcing at rates commensurate with the rest of society. Thus our religious institutions are under enormous pressure to make concessions on divorce and remarriage in order to keep up with the times. And with the concessions comes the realization that marriage will never be the rock solid foundation it once was.

For couples who believe marriage is a sacred covenant ordained by God, my proposal presents the opportunity for regular confirmation of a profound commitment. The covenant is reaffirmed in the symbolic Sabbatic year of the marriage license so that the fiftieth year truly would be a Jubilee.

And for those who counter that *what God has joined together let no man put asunder*, the truth is that no external person or persons put marriages apart. The individuals within the marriage do. Moreover, many couples today do not choose to invite God into their civil unions.

The decision to have a God ordained marriage is a personal one, and those who choose such marriages willingly subject themselves to God and/or the rules and guidelines set forth by the clergy of their respective religions. The marriage renewal requirement takes nothing away from God ordained marriage.

The Detractors

The third group to oppose the renewal requirement would be a motley crew, made up of moralists, abusive and controlling spouses, underachievers and insecure persons. The moralists would argue the requirement would make it easier to dissolve the marriage bond, and the latter groups would naturally fear their victims would be unwilling to renew the license at the end of its term.

Of the moralists I ask: is it truly ethical to bolster marriage by using the difficulty, stress and financial loss associated with divorce as a deterrent? Is it *more* moral to coerce couples to stay trapped in unwanted or unhealthy marriages? Is marriage honorable when millions of spouses secretly seek outside sources to meet physical and emotional needs? The absence of a divorce does not necessarily indicate the existence of a marriage.

For obvious reasons, abusive or controlling spouses would not support a change that empowers the objects of their domination. But abusers and controllers are often in dysfunctional though *symbiotic* relationships. As hard is it might be for many rational persons to believe, some poor victims have convinced themselves that being in an abusive or controlled relationship is preferable to being alone and/or responsible.

Despite the changes in the term of the license, many of these persons would feel compelled to renew, though some would be saved by the provision. And perhaps in a few rare cases the abuser might change or get help as a condition precedent to the renewal.

The underachiever is the man who gets married and like a tick, his rectum promptly attaches him to the couch, the TV remote in his hand. He goes to work, he comes home and he reattaches to the couch. He doesn't bathe every day, he lets his nose hairs grow and his stomach and butt start to get doughy. He won't take his wife out to dinner like he did when they were dating, he doesn't compliment her and seldom even talks to her unless he needs something. He ogles other women, he gasses out loud and he's spent his wad long before his wife begins to get aroused. If she doesn't re-up the marriage license, there's no surprise there.

The underachiever is the woman who once married, really lets herself go. She puts on 30-40 pounds, she becomes obsessed with Oprah and she discontinues spontaneous sex. She doesn't get around to cleaning the house though she won't work outside the home, she secretly maxes out the credit cards and she belittles her husband in public. She refuses ever to cook, she berates the kids, she disrespects her mother-in-law and she hates every member of his family. If he doesn't want to continue in that vein after seven years, can anyone blame him?

Low self-esteem is a significant cause of insecurity, but so is a person's realization that he or she has not invested heart and soul in the marriage. A person who gets married and simply goes through the motions can't expect recommitment from a disaffected spouse after seven years of lukewarm devotion. A good marriage requires the four Cs: commitment, consideration, creativity and communication. Insecure persons are often astute enough to recognize problems exist, but they are too self-absorbed to commit to making the marriage better.

Of course my proposal, like all proposals, contains one or two inherent disadvantages. Under my plan, established marriages certainly would be easier to escape and leave behind, so the marriage renewal requirement would apply only to present marriages that have not exceeded seven years and to all future marriages. Couples married longer than seven years would be grandfathered in and would not have to ever renew.

The Legal and Financial Concerns

Other concerns involve legal status and financial consideration. If a couple's license has been expired for more than eighteen months, the simple renewal would not be available. The couple would then be required to reapply and to actually remarry. After a seventh renewal (forty-nine years), no further renewals would be required.

If a woman or man in an expired marriage wishes to pursue spousal or child support, that person would have to file a *Notice of Intent Not to Renew* with the family court. The court then would determine whether or not to grant support and if granted, the court would fix the amount of the award.

It is obvious though, that the advantages far outweigh any inconvenience the renewal requirement would bring. Many marriages would falter initially, and many of the unions without solid foundations would fail. But in the disposable mentality of America, marriage would benefit from regular renewal, recommitment and redirection.

The Ideal Marriage

Over the years, marriage has been likened to fishing. You bait up your hook and throw it out there, dangling that lure in front of your potential spouse. When it's taken, you set the hook, and struggle as it may, you reel the quarry in. When it's over, if you're lucky you've landed yourself a great catch. Wrong analogy. In the end, you're going to either fry that fish or let it go.

Marriage is much better compared to daily training to stay in shape or in good health, training that a team of two accomplish together. Marriage should not be an end, not the goal or the finish line. It is rather a starting point, an ongoing journey, a lifelong adventure. The needs of a marriage at seven years are different from the needs of a twenty-eight year old marriage or a new marriage for that matter.

In the course of daily training it is helpful to stop at strategic intervals or junctures and check progress. Sometimes small adjustments are required and at others major changes are necessary, but regular reevaluation, recommitment and redirection serve to strengthen a marriage. For common sense reasons, it is a far better thing to renew marriages rather than to discard them, which is what we do wholesale in America. Though we live in a disposable, throw-away society, we must all appreciate that the institution of marriage is *worth* preserving.

The Truth

I thought about asking a local legislator to carry my proposal before the statewide Assembly or Senate, but I get the sense that term-limited local politicians are even less motivated to accomplish good than their securely seated counterparts in Washington. And though I have been disinclined toward the initiative process as has been exploited in California, I think mine is truly a grassroots proposal.

Why? Because for millions of Californians, the prospect of marriage license renewal strikes close to home. How many wives get discouraged in a marriage after three or four years? How many husbands secretly envy the lifestyle of their unmarried counterparts? How many spouses wonder if the marriage was a mistake? How many couples in second or third unions quietly worry that they'll never find happiness in marriage?

Whether we're jaded, bitter, cynical, idealistic, naïve, hopeful or pragmatic, most of us have distinct opinions about marriage. According to the last census, there are more than 5,500,000 married couples in California, which translates to 11,000,000 individuals who are directly affected by the present decline of the marriage institution. If we include the children whose lives are indirectly influenced, we're talking about 24,000,000 people in California alone. Some of these will frown on and disparage my proposal, while others will eagerly promote it. Love it or hate it, it is necessary to address the problems with marriage. Those who truly want to save it are obliged to offer solutions.

The Plea

Thus I put my proposal before the people of California and before America. Saving marriage does not require changing the essence of such an honorable institution, only the terms of its licensing. Let us seriously consider a provision in the language of marriage licensing to require renewal every seven years. Let us engage in months of impassioned debate on the subject. Let us look into our own lives, into our own marriages and share among ourselves. Let us recommend what is working and warn against what is not. The requirements for a good marriage are the same requirements for preserving the institution: commitment, consideration, creativity and communication.

In the movie I mentioned at the onset, the neurotic human male manuscript reader was coming up on seven years of marriage. With his wife and son away on summer vacation, he worried that he would yield to the seven year itch, that irrepressible urge to cheat. There was after all a gorgeous young woman who had unexpectedly invaded his living room and his life.

How did the story conclude? The beleaguered husband, if even in his own mind, was beset by a trial that required him to reevaluate himself, his wife and their union of six plus years. In the end we were as certain he did the right thing: he eagerly recommitted himself to the marriage.

And was anyone surprised? That marriage didn't suddenly fall apart because circumstance required the man to reconsider it after almost seven years. His marriage, like any good marriage, only grew stronger as a result of the recommitment and renewal.

Although the movie was made over forty years ago, it speaks to our times, hinting at a solution. Marriage is in trouble in America, and saving it requires commitment from all of us in considering proposed remedies. In order to save marriage, we must update its licensing requirements so that the union must be renewed every seven years. Agree or disagree, but by all means, let the debate begin.

HANGIN

After this my third short story collection, I think I'm just beginning to loosen up a little. I'm not as worried about what you might think of me. I know what I am. I've looked up to writers I've admired over the years, though recently I've learned to look within. I don't always like what I see, and I'm certain some of you might prefer my lighter stories, but I have a dark, twisted, cynical side that I'm slowly learning to accept.

This collection is certainly more eclectic than the previous two. I started with one of my favorites of the collection, *Denouément*, a cautionary tale about the fate of living the selfish life. *Dork* explores how a rose by some other name might never get smelled to make the comparison.

And then begins *The Silk Noose*, or *Le Lacet de Soie*, written in three distinct parts, or three acts. It's a yarn I've enjoyed reading or performing for audiences because the narrator is somewhat neurotic, like me. Between the acts are the two parables, *Bad Advice* and *The Singing Poet*, or *Thanatos*. The latter is an operatic libretto based on the Bible book of *Job*. I dreamed I watched a performance of this opera, and I sketched the story line when I awoke.

After The Silk Noose trilogy come the essays. I wrote *On Niggers and Squirrels* in the late 1990s, and it is clearly the most personally felt of the three. It was originally published in pamphlet form and sold out quickly. It has been used by school districts for teacher diversity training and as required reading in college classrooms. *On Timothy McVeigh* is a cynical look at true punishment and *On the Seven Year Hitch* contains a modest proposal to save modern marriage.

At last and because I am a poet at heart I included *Goddess*, in which I've cast myself as Pygmalion, though instead of cold stone, I used heated words to sculpt the perfect woman.

And so we are at the end of another book. You are now literally reading the last page. In keeping with the pattern of alternating novels and short story collections, my next works will be *Murder From the Grave*, a serial murder thriller set in San Francisco, then *Sanity Slipping*, another short story collection, and finally *Viral Vector*, a sequel to *Legal Thriller*. The story turns on an emerging pattern of murder of California Death Row inmates.

I hope you have enjoyed *The Silk Noose*, other stories and essays. I'm already working on stories for the next collection. In the meantime, if you have any comments or suggestions, please feel free to share them through my email or website. Until the next time—I'll see you between the covers.

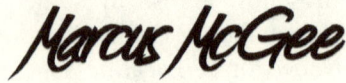

GODDESS

In me Pygmalion is returned to life,
For I have wrought a woman with these words,
A graceful figure in the likeness of
That goddess born of foam and sea.

At first I form her foot,
With careful artistry I sculpt each tender toe,
And then I shape the feet—
The graceful arches and the gentle heels.
Her ankles give me pleasure as I trace
Their subtle outlines with my eyes.
I hold an ankle up before my face
And marvel at its elegance.
I work for hours on the contour of her legs;
I fashion with my hands their pliant lines
And cast their curvature in silky flesh.
I carve her knee for added sensitivity.
I linger on her thighs to shape them properly;
I make them firm and soft against my face.
I let my fingers test the smoothness
Of her bottom and her hips.
In near delirium I watch her belly quiver
As my fingers trace its curves,
While right before my face a fragrant flower blooms.
I hold her waist in my two hands
As I begin to mold the subtle muscles of her back,
And then I form her shoulders and her arms—
I make them strong that she might hold me tightly in
The throes of making love.
Her hands I labor with, for these are hands
That I will want to hold and gently kiss,
And hands that ult'mately will comfort me.
I shape each finger so her hand might

Compliment my own,
So that each hand is truly half a hand,
Complete at last when linked with mine.
And then I kneel and reaching up,
I form her breasts.
I make them full and round and firm.
I shape one with each hand,
I marvel that they are so soft and warm,
Imagine they are pressed against my chest.
With heated breath I gently blow on one
And watch arousal signaled all at once.
I lay my head between those breasts
And want to sleep,
But she is not complete.
I slowly sculpt her neck,
I make it soft and lithe and sensitive,
In need of constant kissing and caress.
And last of all, I form her face
In ev'ry way resembling
The progeny of Leda and of Zeus,
I set her brilliant eyes like Helen's eyes,
Her jaw, her nose and mouth are Helen's too.
Her lips are shaped to meld with mine
For kisses far more sensual
Than any I have known.
Her skin is smooth and taut,
Her natural scent arouses me.
I frame her face with tresses fleecy soft
And wonderful to drag my fingers through.
Her glory is her hair.

Now she is done, but yet she is inanimate.
So I look longingly upon her consummated form,
I study her and call out loud,

O Aphrodite! Goddess of erotic love!
Beloved Aphrodite, hear my earnest prayer!
You know I've hated women all my life,
And yet I am in love with what I've wrought.
Please, if it pleases you—
Bestow upon her life and fleshly form.
Let ichor surge within her mortal veins,
Give her a soft and soothing voice,
A gentle caring heart,
A soul more faithful than your own.
Grant her compassion for the widow and
The child who longs for love.
Endow her with a shrewd and active mind,
Assign her wisdom that she can
Discern where she is truly loved
And then the strength to act on what she knows.
Dear Aphrodite! Goddess who
Inspir'd this overwhelming love
That torments me in wake and sleep.
Bring her to life for me,
And you will have my everlasting dedication then.

I heard the goddess whisper, "She is yours!"
So boldly did I venture my own heart
To share my soul and kiss her tender lips
And all at once, in doing so,
The veil of human memory was snatched away
And you awoke.

OTHER TITLES
AVAILABLE BY MARCUS MCGEE

FOUR STORIES
(Short Stories, 210 pages paperback)
Humorous collection of short stories

SYNCHRONICITY
(Short Stories, 245 pages paperback)
"The Club," "Anthropophagi" and other stories

SHADOW IN THE SKY
(Suspense thriller, 265 pages paperback)
Asteroid threatens Earth, Last year of life

LEGAL THRILLER
(Suspense thriller, 439 pages paperback,)
Murder mystery set in San Francisco

MURDER FROM THE GRAVE
(Suspense thriller, 425 pages paperback)
Berkeley professor-turned-SF police detective
matches wits with a killer who wants to commit
seven murders after he is already dead

Coming Soon:

SANITY SLIPPING
(Short Stories, @ 275 pages)
VIRAL VECTOR
(Suspense @ 375 pages)
Sequel to Legal Thriller

Order at www.pegasusbooks.net